"Hal Brognola is going to die."

"You've got that wrong. Whatever else happens, my friend is going to live." There was icy determination in Mack Bolan's voice, a steely resolve that masked a cold fury held tightly in check.

He raised his binoculars and focused on the scene at the bridge: the cab of a truck parked near a clump of bushes; the roof of a sedan shining in the rain; people gesticulating and rushing about. The macabre stage for Brognola's murder was being set.

The rain gusting across the valley plastered Bolan's hair to his face, weighing down his clothing and making the polished stones treacherous as he made his way up the sheer cliff. Every inch of progress became a test of willpower, coaxing agonized muscles and overtaxed sinews to hang in for just that extra second until he found a firm foothold. Every fiber of his being was fixed on his task—the life of his friend rested squarely on his shoulders.

Suddenly the crevice supporting his left foot crumbled, and the Executioner plunged into space....

MACK BOLAN®

The Executioner

DON PENDLETON's EXECUTIONER
MACK BOLAN.®

Vendetta in Venice

A GOLD EAGLE BOOK FROM
WORLDWIDE.®

TORONTO • NEW YORK • LONDON • PARIS
AMSTERDAM • STOCKHOLM • HAMBURG
ATHENS • MILAN • TOKYO • SYDNEY

First edition September 1988

ISBN 0-373-61117-X

Special thanks and acknowledgment to
Peter Leslie for his contribution to this work.

In Venice . . . their best conscience
Is not to leave 't undone, but keep 't unknown.
—William Shakespeare

Ruffians, pitiless as proud,
    Heaven awards the vengeance due;
Empire is on us bestowed,
    Shame and ruin wait for you.
                        —William Cowper

Sometimes the awards and the repayment are a little
slow in coming. I'm always ready to help accelerate
the payoff.
                        —Mack Bolan

THE
MACK BOLAN®
LEGEND

Nothing less than a war could have fashioned the destiny of the man called Mack Bolan. Bolan earned the Executioner title in the jungle hell of Vietnam.

But this soldier also wore another name—Sergeant Mercy. He was so tagged because of the compassion he showed to wounded comrades-in-arms and Vietnamese civilians.

Mack Bolan's second tour of duty ended prematurely when he was given emergency leave to return home and bury his family, victims of the Mob. Then he declared a one-man war against the Mafia.

He confronted the Families head-on from coast to coast, and soon a hope of victory began to appear. But Bolan had broken society's every rule. That same society started gunning for this elusive warrior—to no avail.

So Bolan was offered amnesty to work within the system against terrorism. This time, as an employee of Uncle Sam, Bolan became Colonel John Phoenix. With a command center at Stony Man Farm in Virginia, he and his new allies—Able Team and Phoenix Force—waged relentless war on a new adversary: the KGB.

But when his one true love, April Rose, died at the hands of the Soviet terror machine, Bolan severed all ties with Establishment authority.

Now, after a lengthy lone-wolf struggle and much soul-searching, the Executioner has agreed to enter an "arm's-length" alliance with his government once more, reserving the right to pursue personal missions in his Everlasting War.

1

An early fall afternoon with the lowering sky east of Amsterdam full of rain—maybe it was a crazy time to take a long walk. But the American with the bulky body and the tired face wanted to get away from the other members of the conference.

Why did he want to walk? Because he had a problem.

He had to make an official speech the next day. Because Uncle Sam's voice was the strongest it was also expected to be the wisest, the most positive. The speech had to be damn good, plus it had to be as convincing as hell. He would be speaking to fifty law-enforcement chiefs from all over the world. The question before them: the spread of terrorism and how best to combat it.

The speechmaker's name was Hal Brognola, and his problem was that he had no answer to the question. It was tough, finding a tactic that would discourage religious fanatics brainwashed to believe it was an honor to die for some madman's cause; useless to threaten punishment when the assassins were happy to transform themselves into human bombs; pointless appealing to the finer feelings of the scum prepared to gun down innocent women and children in the hope of media coverage quoting the name of a manic revolutionary cell.

The terrorists, whatever their political or religious color, didn't play by society's rules; for them there were no innocents; for them the whole world was guilty. Faced with a dangerous increase in terrorist activity, Brognola's briefing, effectively, was to stall.

"We got think tanks working on this in every state in the Union," the man in the Oval office had told him. "Military men, shrinks, infiltration experts, guerrillas, you name it. Every day I hope someone will come up with a foolproof system to smash these bastards, to outsmart them. Until then you've got to play it close to the vest. So you cozy these guys along, Hal. But make it sound like we're close to a solution."

Oh, sure, Brognola had thought. Keep everyone happy. Hell, that kind of talk was for diplomats. So what the hell was *he* supposed to do?

Whatever it was, it cried out for thought—and space to think, away from the hearty backslaps of the other lawmen. Brognola had already made the tour of the Amsterdam canals. He had been to Delft, to Leiden, to Arnhem. He had visited the radio station at Hilversum and the Philips electronic empire in Nijmegen. Today, he figured, it was time to give the countryside a whirl.

The huge area of reclaimed land filling in the lower half of what had once been the Zuider Zee seemed made to order for a man who wanted to let his thoughts wander. Between the flat earth and the sullen sky there wasn't a damned thing to distract a man's attention.

Brognola took a bus to Harderwijk, then crossed the Nuldernauw to the island of East Flevoland. Won back from the sea just before World War II, the place lay featureless beneath the hurrying clouds. He walked along a road perched on top of a dike. On one side there were inundated fields; on the other, the cold gray waters of the Ijsselmeer stretched away to the cranes, smokestacks and mellowed brick facades of the Amsterdam waterfront.

The Fed walked for five or six miles, turning over in his mind the different options open to a man who had to make a speech full of evasions that nevertheless appeared to say something. The sun broke through the cloud cover, momentarily silvering the waters of the inland sea. Minutes later it withdrew behind a darker, more menacing cloud bank blowing up from the west.

Brognola hesitated. He scanned the sky, and his bloodhound face creased into an expression of irritation. He had intended to continue another seven or eight miles to the new village of Lelystad, hoping to find a cab there that would take him to Kampen, back on the mainland, and then Zwolle—from where he could take a bus back to the city. But it was getting more and more overcast, and it was cold. He hadn't brought a raincoat, and it sure as hell looked as if it were going to rain. Also, a sudden ache in his belly told him he needed food.

Abruptly he turned around and retraced his steps. Hell, he would go back the way he had come; it would be quicker in the long run, he would eat sooner and, if he was lucky, maybe he would find a shortcut and avoid following the curve of the coast the way he had come.

The island was crisscrossed by dikes. Soon he found one leading inland in the direction he wanted and left the road.

He had been striding along the waterlogged pathway surmounting the dike for less than fifteen minutes when there was a low murmur of wind, stirring the grasses at his feet. A squall of fine rain blew past him like a cloud of smoke. Soon a persistent drizzle was falling from the leaden sky. It rolled up behind him from the west, dewing the shoulders of his jacket, soaking his pants behind the knees and trickling down his neck. Amsterdam had vanished in the mist, and the ripples flowing across the Ijsselmeer were breaking into tumbles of gray foam.

Below the dike, the green of the drenched polder was almost indecently bright beneath the dull sky. Farther away, plowed fields were awash, the ridges only just surfacing above the water in the furrows. A long way to the south the domed tower of a church rose above the flatlands, but otherwise there was no sign of life. Not even a windmill, Brognola reflected bitterly, forgetting it was the emptiness of the island that had attracted him in the first place.

When he came at last to the strip of water that separated East Flevoland from the mainland, he found to his disgust that he had screwed up: he was nowhere near the bridge, and there wasn't a causeway or a ferry slip to be seen. Fuming, Brognola hunched deeper down inside the wet collar of his jacket and squelched along the waterlogged grass at the canal edge.

Before long he rounded a stand of willow and found himself a few yards away from a boatman sitting inside a crude wooden shelter. At his feet, a flat-bottomed dory rode the rain-pitted swell lapping at the sandy bank. The Fed looked over the channel. It was maybe three hundred yards across. Beyond a belt of trees on the far side he could see the roofs of a village and the wet gleam of passing traffic on a road. From over there, surely, he could get a cab to take him back to Amsterdam.

Brognola knew no Dutch. "Hello, there," he called in German as he approached the boatman. "I'm afraid I've lost my way. Could you take me across?"

"Took your time, didn't you," the boatman grunted, rising to his feet. He was a tall man, rawboned and craggy.

Brognola was distracted; he was thinking of food. "There's not a single sign pointing the way to the bridge," he said absently. "What . . . ? What's that?"

"Right, then," the man cut in, ignoring the question. "In you get, and we'll be on our way. I been sitting around long enough in this damned rain." He stretched out one foot and drew the dory to the bank. Brognola stepped in and sat down on a sodden thwart as the man poled them out into midstream with long, powerful strokes. For a while he watched the two identical lines of low-lying land, one receding, the other approaching. Then, feeling a little guilty, because after all the boatman didn't have to help him out, he tried to make conversation.

"It's very kind of you," he began. "But I guess you don't get too many people asking for a ride at this time of year."

The boatman grunted again.

"Lucky for me you happened to be there," Brognola pursued. "You're a fisherman by trade, I guess?" He looked expectantly at his pilot.

"Best not to talk," the boatman replied. "The less anyone knows about anyone else the better, eh?"

Brognola shrugged. He stared for a while at the gray water sliding past the stern. Judging from the wet mark on the pole, it couldn't be more than four or five feet deep.

When they were three-quarters of the way across, the boatman stopped poling and let the craft drift to a standstill. "Maybe we better settle up now," he suggested dourly. "No point hanging in there by the bank, is there? That's all very well for Jaap, on the other side of the island, where there's nobody to see, but we have to be more careful. Anyway, I guess you'll want to be off quick as you can. Your kind always does."

"Why...why sure," Brognola said, reaching for his wallet. "How much do I owe you?"

He wasn't really paying attention. He was cold, he was wet and he was miserable. The ache in his belly clamored for attention. All he could think of was making it back to his hotel—and a large, hot meal.

The boatman had moved forward, rocking the dory. "One hundred fifty guilders," he said curtly, balancing the pole across the width of the boat and holding out one hand.

Maybe, the Fed thought, as he counted out bills into the callused palm, he would be able to locate one of the city's Indonesian restaurants that opened early for dinner. A selection from the famous *rijstafel* would just about score ten out of ten. Twenty and twenty made forty, and five was forty-five, and another ten made fifty-five— *"One hundred fifty guilders!"* he shouted suddenly, his hand in midair. "But that's almost fifty dollars!"

The boatman stared at him impassively. He said nothing.

"Fifty dollars? For crossing less than a quarter mile of calm water? You must be out of your mind!"

"One hundred fifty guilders. That's the price."

"But that's outrageous! I absolutely refuse. I—"

"Look, the *fare* is paid," the man said strangely. "This is extra for me. For waiting. For the weather. For whatever you like. But you either hand me the money or I tip you into the water." He rocked the frail craft from side to side threateningly. "You pay your money or *I* make the choice," he added with a crooked grin.

Brognola was speechless with rage. "Blackmail!" he managed to choke out at last. "An outrage! I never—"

"Keep quiet. If the cash is so important to you, you should have made sure Jaap got you here earlier. You had the whole day, for God's sake. You think I enjoyed sitting around here for eight hours? Come on now—decide."

The Fed was so angry he could hardly think straight. God knew what all this meant. What the hell had this extortion to do with Jaap, whoever he was? Just the same, the boatman was a very big guy, and he had already parted with one-third of the money. Also, even if he demanded to be taken back to the island, he would literally be back where he started . . . and fifty-five florins poorer. And with no means of crossing the water.

He glanced at the oily surface—the water looked extremely cold—and shuddered. Scowling, he counted out the rest of the money.

"There! That's better!" The boatman was suddenly almost affable. He stuffed the notes into his hip pocket, took up the pole and began punting the craft rapidly toward the bank.

"Will I be able to get a car?" Brognola growled a few minutes later. "I'm in a hurry, otherwise I wouldn't have paid your goddamn price. And I want to go back—"

"Relax," the big man interrupted. "Of course you'll get a car. It's all taken care of. Just stop beefing, okay?"

The Fed shrugged and fell silent. A final thrust of the pole sent them gliding toward a narrow creek that penetrated a clump of alders at the water's edge. Soundlessly they slid in beneath the branches.

"You'll have to lend a hand," Brognola snapped. "There's a bank here, and it's too steep and too wet and slippery to climb unaided."

"I told you not to worry," the boatman said. As he spoke, arms reached down through the screen of leaves and hauled Brognola up and out of the dory. A few scrambling steps later, he was panting on top of the bank, staring at two men in soft hats and heavy, belted overcoats.

"Come on if you want the car," the taller man murmured. "It has already attracted enough attention as it is." He took the Fed's arm and drew him through the bushes toward a footpath that skirted a field.

"Yeah, but I didn't . . ." Brognola looked over his shoulder. The dory was already back in the open water, the figure of the boatman blurred by the clouds of drizzle gusting in from the island.

"Best not to talk," the shorter man said.

Ten minutes later they emerged from a stand of trees to find themselves at the edge of a country road. At the far side, a huge Minerva taxi stood in a parking bay half hidden by a pile of stones. Brognola's eyebrows rose. Minerva's Brussels factory had ceased production before World War II.

The short man looked each way and then beckoned them across the blacktop. He leaned in the driver's window and spoke to a chauffeur in a peaked cap while his companion jerked open a rear door and ushered the Fed inside. He sank onto the stained Bedford cord upholstery with a sigh of relief.

Before he could say anything, the door was slammed, the engine grumbled to life and the car surged forward onto the road.

Brognola twisted around to look out the small oval rear window. The two men, dwindling now in the approaching dusk, were standing by the roadside, each with a hand raised to the brim of his hat. He shrugged his shoulders again and settled himself well back on the seat. Perhaps the exorbitant ferry fee included conducting him to a cab. Yet nobody could have known he was coming; it was clearly no regular ferry. In which case—why *was* there a cab and guides to take him to it?

Brognola was toying with the obvious explanation—mistaken identity—when he realized he had given the driver no instructions. Would the guy go automatically to Amsterdam, because there was no civilized place in the other direction? Or had he himself told the ferryman where he wanted to go? He couldn't remember.

Unable to picture the map details mentally, he stared through the raindrops pockmarking the windows. They were rattling along a narrow cobbled road that ran beside a canal. On either side yellowing leaves drooped from the branches of dripping trees. Soon they passed a wooden bridge spanning the canal. There was a signpost on one side of the timber superstructure: Harderwijk, Amsterdam, Ermelo, Elburg, Oldebroek…and, on the post pointing across the canal, Nunspeet.

He exclaimed in annoyance. The Amsterdam indicator was pointing back the way they had come. What the hell was going on? He leaned forward to slide aside the glass partition separating him from the driver. It refused to move. Cursing, he tried again, harder. Zero. He rapped on the glass, but the solid set of the chauffeur's head remained unchanged: the peaked cap didn't turn by as much as a hairbreadth.

Brognola began to feel alarmed. Maybe the setup *was* for him. Could it be some kind of trap? A terrorist kidnap plot to prevent him from making his speech tomorrow? No way: he hadn't decided yet just what he was going to say.

A ransom demand, then? He recalled stories of doors that wouldn't open from the inside, of toxic gas pumped into the back seat through a speaking tube. He stared around the huge, shabby limo. There *was* a speaking tube, hooked to the armrest on the left-hand side.…

Panicking, he grabbed the tarnished door handle and jerked. There was an icy blast of wind as the heavy door flew open, letting in the rumble of the Minerva's suspension, the oily hiss of tires on the wet road. Feeling rather foolish, Brognola leaned out into the spray thrown up by the wheels and dragged the door shut.

Maybe the driver was just deaf.

A few minutes later the taxi slowed down by a long red-brick wall, finally turning into a rutted lane that led to a junkyard. The driver braked to a halt, jumped out and opened the Fed's door. "Very well, *mynheer*," he said. "The other party is waiting."

He jerked his thumb at three men in long green leather overcoats who were leaning against a wrecked truck in the shelter of the wall. One of them pitched the cigarette he'd been smoking into a puddle and slowly straightened.

"You took your time," he said. "We'd almost given up."

"Wim was late with the boat," the driver replied. "According to Hendrik he never explained why. Just pushed off again to the island."

"Forget it. As long as the client's here. Okay then, Herr Bird of Passage, let's have your passport."

Bewildered, Brognola clambered out of the car. He looked at the outstretched hand of the man in the leather coat. "Are you talking to me?"

"Look, don't fool around," the man said coldly. "I'm not likely to be asking for one from the cabbie here, am I?"

"Yeah, move it, man," another member of the reception committee called from the truck. "We're damn near frozen, waiting in this dump."

"You want my passport? My *passport*? Are you some kind of plainclothes police patrol?"

"Police patrol he says! That's a good one." The man in the leather coat guffawed. "Of course we want your passport. You don't think we'd fix you up with a new one until we have the old, do you?"

"I don't know what the hell you're talking about," Brognola growled.

There was a sudden silence. It was quite dark in the lane now. A gust of wind shook heavy raindrops from bare branches overhead. Squelching in the mud, the two other men moved slowly to Brognola and their companion. "*What* did you say?" one of them asked softly.

"I said I had no idea what you were talking about," the Fed snapped. "And I don't care. All I want is to get back to my hotel in Amsterdam. So if you'll kindly permit my driver to turn—"

"Amsterdam? Hotel? What the hell are *you* talking about?" the first man asked angrily. Then, struck by a thought, he added, "What's your name?"

"If it's any of your business, the name is Brognola. And—"

"*Brognola!* You're not Helmut Wünsche?" the chauffeur exclaimed blankly.

"Wünsche? I never heard of him. I insist—"

Brognola broke off with a gasp as he was seized abruptly from behind. Rough hands dragged his jacket down over his arms, effectively pinioning them. At the same time the man who had first spoken snatched his passport from the exposed inner pocket. Scowling, he flicked over the pages. "By God, he's telling the truth!" he said hoarsely.

"Of course I'm telling the truth," Brognola shouted, scarlet in the face and struggling. "Whatever this setup is, I'm telling you you'll be sorry—"

"Shut up!" the third man rapped out. "You mean it's definitely not Wünsche, Conrad?"

"Apparently not. Come to think of it, he doesn't look like him."

"Then who the hell is it?"

"That, my friend, we shall have to find out."

"Release me, right now," Brognola yelled. "You can't go around roughing people up—"

Suddenly he choked on his words. The lane spun up and slashed him across the face as an enormous weight descended on his skull, and the inside of his head exploded into a crimson night.

2

"And I don't remember anything else," Brognola concluded three days later to the tall man in black, "until I woke up in a damned shop doorway at four o'clock this morning. There was the mark of a hypodermic on my forearm."

"Okay. They had to keep you quiet while they confirmed that you were who you said you were and not some Fed out to blow their setup."

"So I was dumped here in the city, outside a liquor store in the Kalverstraat. I was still groggy, of course, and the two policemen who found me . . . well, they jumped to the obvious conclusion and they called up the wagon and slung me inside for the rest of the night."

Bolan grinned sympathetically. "I can just see the headlines, Hal. 'Missing U.S. Spokesman Was Alcoholic. Found Smashed Out of His Skull Outside Liquor Store.'"

"That was the way it looked," the Fed admitted. "Until they let me contact my colleagues at Interpol. The chief of police was apologetic. But of course it gave them a head start after they had gotten rid of me. By the time they let me out the trail was cold. Don't even mention the conference ending without a peep from the U.S. rep. No firm course of action was decided upon. And the Man is as sore as a nest of hornets."

"You went straight back there with a team?"

"Sure. But there was nothing to see." Brognola shook his head again. He winced. He still had one hell of a headache. "Nobody had ever seen or heard of a boatman called Wim. Nobody had ever seen a Minerva cab, which is crazy because you'd think a mid-thirties monster like that would attract attention. Nobody could be found, naturally, who knew anything about three men in leather overcoats."

"End of story?"

"Just about. We did locate the junkyard, but there were so many tracks and it was so muddy that the cops couldn't identify any one set." Brognola stared at the raindrops sliding down the window of his hotel room. "What do you make of it, Striker? Cook me up a theory to fit these facts."

"A straightforward case of mistaken identity," Bolan offered. "Here's this organization all set up and waiting to go. Ferryman ready to make the crossing…two linkmen on hand to liaise with the cab, the chauffeur, the men in the truck ready to supply fake ID. All they need is the client."

"Okay, but why pick on me?"

"They were expecting someone from the island, someone they didn't know very well by sight, and you showed at the right time. Maybe you inadvertently gave the right password, or unknowingly came across with the right answer to a coded question."

"That's what I think," the Fed agreed. "I spoke in German, something along the lines of 'Hello, I'm lost.' Then I asked if the guy could take me across. He didn't reply directly. He said something about it being late. Then I said there wasn't a sign pointing the way to the bridge."

"Well, that's it. The approach in German—and then, by some coincidence, the right sequence of words to complete the coded exchange."

"It figures," Brognola said, "because, come to think of it, I spoke in German, but he replied in Dutch. And that's

the way it went on—German from my side, Dutch from his.
I don't speak Dutch, you see, but I can make out what it
means. That was probably part of the routine, the twin-
language deal. How do you read this thing? In its broader
aspects?''

"As a continuing organization, I guess," Bolan replied
after a moment's consideration. "Not a one-shot deal."

"Why do you say that?"

"Several reasons. The boatman figures you'd want to be
out of there as quick as possible, and added 'Your lot *always* does.' Secondly, the insistence on not talking. A hastily improvised, one-shot plan would risk nothing by talk.
But if there was going to be more of the same, well, obviously the less known and said the better. Then there was
the fact that nobody knew that taxi, although it was easily
identifiable. On a one-shot deal they could have used a local car and bluffed it out, but a mystery vehicle spells organization to me."

"Yeah," Brognola said. "But why the hell choose such a
standout vehicle, tell me that?"

Bolan shrugged. "As to what the organization *is*, my
guess would be that it exists to smuggle undesirables—drug
dealers, guys on the run, maybe terrorists—into Holland.
From what you say, this guy Jaap lands clients on the north
coast of your island, and they hoof it across to the south and
meet up with the boatman. Then he passes them on to the
cab and the hoods in the junkyard."

"Going where?" Brognola asked quietly. "If they're already in the country, why would they need to be escorted
farther?"

Bolan was silent for a moment, then said, "Long green
leather overcoats? Kind of a dark bottle-green? That sug-
gests northern Germany to me. You see coats like that all
winter in Hamburg, Bremen, Oldenburg."

"So you think Holland's only an interim stage? That would explain why the client was to pick up his false papers *after* he entered the country: he'd need them to cross the *German* frontier."

"Could also solve the taxi mystery," Bolan said. "Suppose it's a German vehicle, only showing up in Holland when there's a job to be done, when they fit it out with phony Dutch plates? That would take care of the fact that the locals aren't familiar with it. Then, once the client has been fed his new ID, the boys simply change back to the genuine plates and drive across the border."

"There are two dozen small frontier posts between Emmen and Enschede," Brognola agreed. "We could have been targeted on any one of them when they tumbled, realized they'd picked the wrong guy. Maybe they use a different one for each job, to cut down on the risk."

"It adds up," the Executioner said. "Even the client's name—Wünsche—is German. I'd figure it for a big-time organization, too. Your boatman said the 'fare' was paid. You hand over the money in advance and every little thing's taken care of from then on, like in a travel agency package. In my book that means an efficient, large-scale operation. The ferryman shook you down for the extra because Jaap's man was delayed and he thought, taking you for the fugitive, you wouldn't dare refuse."

"Where would you say Jaap's man, the real one, was from?"

"Looking at the map, I'd say they undertake to bring in illegal immigrants from anywhere outside Europe. I'd think the clients are stowed away on ships docking in Amsterdam. Then, once they get there, instead of walking down the gangway they drop over the blind side, make their way to the neck of land separating the canal from the Ijsselmeer and pick up Jaap there."

"Unless he's so well-known, so much a part of the landscape, that he can sail right in among the docks and pick them up."

"That's always possible," Bolan agreed.

"But why the hell should they take the trouble to cross an inland sea, traverse an island and get themselves ferried back to the mainland again when it would be easier to make the same location simply following the shoreline all the way around?"

"Because of the relative danger. A guy on the run is a natural target in a seaport, on the streets of a capital city, along the highways, all of them covered by cops. But take him to a desolate, underpopulated stretch of country and put him in touch with people who can supply papers *there*, and you minimize the risk of detection right away."

"I thought strangers were supposed to be more noticeable in a country area than anyplace else," the Fed objected.

"They are. If they stick around, if they're going to make camp there. Not if they're just passing through. They hit it lucky, nobody sees them at all."

"You could be right, Striker. In any case," he added, "you're going to find out for sure when you check this whole thing over and run these guys to earth."

"Me? Wouldn't the police...?" Bolan paused, unwilling to voice the thought that the mystery wasn't high enough on his list of priorities to occupy his energy and time. "Hell, this isn't in my ballpark," he finished.

"I've got to have answers for the White House. I want you to handle it—as a personal favor to me. Please. I have a hunch it could turn out to be big, and you're the best man for the job. Plus it'll look good if we hand the West Germans something on a plate for once. If we can wrap this one up, it could cancel some of the operations the Company screwed up."

"Okay, Hal," the Executioner murmured.

Ten minutes later someone tried to kill Mack Bolan.

3

"Bolan? You're sure that's the guy, Conrad?"

"Sure I'm sure." Conrad hunched deeper into his overcoat, his pale eyes fixed on the glass-canopied side entrance to the hotel across the street. The imposing main entrance was on Damrak, around the corner, but the American wearing the black sweater and jeans had gone in this way. It was a reasonable guess he'd exit by the same door.

"Muscular dude, few inches over six feet? Dark hair, blue eyes?" the gunner man with the MAC-10 insisted.

"Look, Willi, I *know* the son of a bitch. His mug's on file. I saw the picture in a spook dossier I saw last year. It's not a face you forget."

The third man was at the wheel of the Mercedes off-roader. He twisted around in his seat, scowling. "Will you two knock it off?" he snarled. "We're double-parked on this damn corner, and if the law shows, my ass is in a sling. I gotta watch out for them, watch out for the mark, check for holes in traffic, keep the engine idling so I'm ready for the getaway, and that's just for starters. You think it helps my concentration to hear you bums arguing the toss whether it's the right guy or not? If it turns out to be the wrong guy after you hit him, then we'll get the right guy another time."

"All right, Nils, all right," Conrad smoothed. "There'll be no mistake."

"Just the same," the gunner said, "I'd be happier if Bart knew we were handling it this way. We don't know if he—"

Conrad exploded. "Will you for Pete's sake stop bellyaching! You know there's no way we can contact Bart. We were hired by him to handle Wünsche. The asshole never showed, and then we screwed up—or the Dutch half of the team did—latching on to this Brognola. Now that we know who he is, and that he's involved this Bolan creep, the least we can do is wrap the whole thing up before he picks up the trail."

"Yeah," Nils growled. "For our own sakes as well as Bart's." He stiffened, dropping his right hand to the vehicle's gearshift. "I think we're in business."

The uniformed doorman beneath the hotel canopy spun the revolving doors, and Mack Bolan strode through from the lobby. The gunner raised the stubby Ingram, but an instant before he squeezed the trigger, a youth with both his feet up on the bar of a moped zigzagged from between two parked cars and spluttered away toward the Damrak, spraying a fan of mud from the rain-wet street.

Mud splatted against the panels of the Mercedes and arched toward the hotel entrance. The gunner started back involuntarily as he fired. The hail of subsonic .45-caliber slugs jetting from the silenced SMG climbed slightly as they hosed the street, missing the Executioner by inches and thwacking across the doorman's chest like a leaden whip.

The subdued crack carried by the bullets was drowned by the exhaust note of the receding moped, but Bolan's warrior nerves, honed to the finest edge by a lifetime of combat, signaled the danger before the initial burst had streaked from the Ingram's muzzle.

Flung back against the wall by the impact of the death-stream, the doorman slid to the steps with a line of crimson additions to the row of medals studding his pale gray uniform. Before the dead man hit the ground, Bolan dived for a panel truck parked at the foot of the steps. A compact automatic pistol, snatched from a holster on his right hip, was nestled in his hand.

A second burst from the Ingram chipped fragments from the hotel stonework as it followed the Executioner down, but Bolan was already below the line of the truck's hood. Glass shattered and metal sang. The truck shuddered on its springs with each burst of heavy rounds. Bolan maneuvered himself until he had a perfect line, then kept on firing until he scored.

The automatic was a Beretta 93-R, his favorite handgun, modified to take a suppressor and equipped with specially machined springs to cycle subsonic rounds. Prone between the truck's offside front and rear wheels, he squinted up from under the chassis and lined up on the man with the Ingram. His left hand steadied his right wrist; his elbows splayed on the wet asphalt.

Yet another burst from the SMG thudded into the truck's cab, and somewhere to Bolan's right, gasoline from a broken fuel pipe splashed onto the roadway. He had to get off a shot before enough vapor gathered for the flash to ignite.

Bolan held his breath and triggered a 3-round burst from the automatic. Angled up toward the window of the Mercedes, the 9 mm parabellum skullbusters tore away the top of the gunner's head to spread a relief map of blood and brain tissue across the inside of the vehicle.

Nils cursed and slammed the lever into first, stamping on the throttle as he released the clutch. The Mercedes jerked forward, wheels spinning on the greasy road surface.

Conrad thrust away the corpse and smashed the rear window with the barrel of a 6-shot Colt revolver. Knocking aside shards of toughened glass, he fanned the hair trigger half a dozen times to send the whole cylinder of .38-caliber slugs blazing toward the Executioner.

Bolan had rolled out from under the rear of the truck, dodging unexpectedly into the center of the road to choke out three fast shots toward the Mercedes driver.

After the near-silent exchange of Ingram and Beretta, the roar of the Colt was deafening. Pedestrians, hurrying through the rain, stopped at the end of the street to stare. A cab turning in from the Damrak braked to a halt.

Bolan's move took Conrad by surprise, and the off-roader's tail was already slewing sideways under Nil's brutal acceleration. The Colt's stingers flew wide.

The Beretta's trio didn't.

In the instant that the driver's window of the Mercedes slid into his sights, Bolan chalked up two hits, one drilling the hood's left shoulder, the other gouging a strip of flesh from his cheek. Nils slumped against the door with blood pouring from his face. The door burst open, and he plunged to the ground. At the same time the Mercedes clipped the front of the panel truck. Bolan didn't know whether it was one of his shots or the rending of metal against pavement that generated a spark. All he saw was the sudden spurt of flame as the gasoline vapors ignited... and the giant fireball that bellowed up between truck and off-roader a quarter of a second later with a flat, thudding explosion that cracked his ears.

Blazing debris scythed through the rain. Nils rolled, screaming, from the inferno, his leather coat set alight by burning liquid flooding across the road from the ruptured fuel tank. Black smoke veined with scarlet boiled up into the sky between the buildings on both sides of the street.

Conrad leaped from the far side of the Mercedes and ran.

Bolan emptied the remainder of the Beretta's magazine in his direction, but the heat was too intense, the wall of fire blocking the road too fierce, for him to see if he scored.

Reception clerks ran out from the hotel to drag the murdered doorman away from the scorching heat. Passersby cowered as a gust of wind stirred the flames their way. The cabdriver, wielding a rug, was trying to beat out the tongues of fire licking at the wounded Nils.

There was nothing more the Executioner could do. Pushing through the smashed revolving doors, he crossed the lobby and ran swiftly up the hotel's emergency stairway to Brognola's room.

4

"Did one of the guys who took you have sandy hair and pale eyes?" the warrior asked Brognola later that evening.

"The leather coats? Yeah, I think so," Brognola replied. "He was mean-looking—looked like a slum-bred street fighter, if you know what I mean. The others called him Conrad."

Bolan nodded. "Clearly the same team was out to hit me. It must be a big deal if they're prepared to kill to block a possible investigation. One blown away, one wounded, and a Mercedes off-roader lost in the attempt. It's significant, too, that they were onto me so quick. They must've been tipped off that I'd been to see you, guessed I'd be checking. Like I say, it's organized."

"Good to be proved right."

"Look, Hal. I'll say it again. I understand you're angry about being shoved around by these guys. It's natural to want to hit back. And our conversation earlier today was an interesting exercise in deduction. That's one thing. Mounting an undercover operation in a friendly NATO country without being invited is another. Sure, there's bad vibes here, but isn't it up to the Dutch and West German police, working in tandem to wrap the thing up?"

"You're thinking too much about me, the man who was taken by mistake," Brognola said, "and not enough about the guy who should have been there."

"Wünsche?"

"Right. I put out a few feelers, and I think I know who he is. If I'm right, then you're wrong, thinking our friend Jaap picks up his clients east of the city docks. Wünsche would have come from the north, from Denmark. Outside the North Frisian Islands, then inside the East and West Frisians and through one of the giant sluice bridges beneath that sixteen-mile causeway that cuts off the mouth of the old Zuider Zee. From there you'd have a clear run, and a couple hours' sailing in a medium-size powerboat would bring you to East Flevoland."

"What makes you so sure?"

"Intel that's been channeled in since I saw you," the Fed replied. He took an envelope from an inside pocket and read out the notes scrawled on the back. "Wünsche, Helmut. German national sentenced to six years in the cooler for his part in a big-time company swindle in Copenhagen. He was being transferred to a maximum-security jail last week when the police wagon was ambushed near Kolding, in Jutland. He hasn't been seen since."

Bolan's brows rose. "And you think...?"

"The team who got him out are tough boys. A guard was killed when the van was rammed and another—the guy to whom Wünsche was cuffed—seriously injured. They couldn't unlock the cuffs, so they amputated the guy's hand—just hacked it off while he was still conscious so that they could get Wünsche away."

"Nice guys. And this was Jaap's client?"

"I would think. After that there'd be a close watch on places like Esbjerg, Malmö, Cuxhaven, Lübeck and even Oslo. But who'd think of looking for the refugee on the Ijsselmeer?"

"Okay. But what would have happened when he did contact Jaap and found out some other guy had inadvertently taken his place?"

"I don't think he ever did find out," Brognola said. "I believe the reason for his nonarrival lies in this news item." He picked up an old copy of the *International Herald Tribune* and read: "A converted torpedo recovery boat, eighty-two feet long with sleeping accommodation for six, broke up and sank instantly when it was rammed by a tanker in ballast between the island of Terschelling and the Dutch coast last night. There was a light fog at the time of the collision, but the forward lookout aboard the tanker stated that the smaller craft was carrying no navigation lights. It is thought there were at least three people on the vessel, though neither bodies nor survivors have yet been located. Dutch marine authorities said they had no knowledge of such a craft operating in the area of the Frisian Islands."

Brognola laid the paper on the night table beside his bed. He took a cigar from his vest pocket, tore away the wrapping, removed the band and bit off the end. "That news report was dated the day I was knocked out. In other words, the collision would have been the previous night, though Conrad and his buddies wouldn't have heard of it yet.

"I'll draw your attention to three more apparently unrelated items. First, one of the courtesy blacks sent to me FYI by the Company every day. This one is dated three weeks ago. It says—" he picked up a five-by-eight flimsy from the night table "—quote, we have now received confirmation that Colonel Ralph Bellinger, the USAF flyer-turned-pacifist who vanished seven days ago from his mess near Stuttgart, West Germany, is a guest in a Soviet-staffed officers' club near Dresden, East Germany, unquote.

"Secondly there was an Interpol memo stating that a certain Ferenc Hradec, who robbed a bank in Plzen,

Czechoslovakia last month, was thought to be on one of the Dodecanese Islands in the Aegean. It adds," the Fed commented dryly, "that he was believed to have spent several days in Liechtenstein on the way. Putting the loot back in a capitalist bank and creating a tax-free company or two, I guess!

"The final exhibit is another press clipping," Brognola said, fishing a crumpled slip of newsprint from a pocket. "Here, you can read this one for yourself."

Bolan took the clipping.

PARIS, Tuesday. Bertrand Secondini, "the man they can't convict," has done it again! The stocky nightclub boss, summoned to appear before an examining magistrate today on charges concerning a gang shooting in Montmartre last month, fled minutes before detectives from the Police Judiciare arrived at his plush Avenue Marceau duplex.

A spokesman from the Quai des Orfèvres said that although a cordon had been thrown around Paris immediately, Secondini—against whom extra charges involving extortion and drugs may soon be lodged—seemed to have escaped the net. He was sure, nevertheless, that "the malefactor would be under lock and key within forty-eight hours."

Underworld sources close to Secondini were openly scornful of this claim, and said that the wanted man had already left metropolitan France. Rumors current in Montmartre hint that "the man they can't convict" may be back among his own people in Corsica, and officials at Nice airport confirmed that an unidentified light aircraft crossed the Côte d'Azur in a southeasterly direction late this afternoon.

If Secondini has in fact "gone to ground" in Corsica, informed opinion is that he will never be traced by the mainland police. Born forty-nine years ago in Bastia, he is known—despite his record and suspected links with the Cosa Nostra—to have become something of a hero to the people of the island....

Bolan whistled. "Cosa Nostra means Union Corse means Mafia?"

"It could be. And that would certainly make it our business." Brognola took back the clipping. "Look at the facts. Four movements: one south and east, from Denmark through Holland to Germany; one eastward, spiriting someone behind the iron curtain; another west, bringing a fugitive *from* the Eastern Bloc; and finally one south, from Paris to Corsica. An embezzler, a deserter, a bank robber and a gang boss. What do these cases suggest, Striker?"

"Maybe that there's an efficient and organized escape network spreading all over Europe." The Executioner frowned. "And, I suppose that it's nonpolitical, because there's traffic both ways across the curtain—and therefore nonaligned so far as the terrorist groups are concerned. I'd read it as a gang of smart operators offering a service to anyone on the run, from wherever to wherever."

"But do you think it's something we should check out?"

"Only one of the cases you quote has a Mafia connection," Bolan said, "and that's at second or third hand."

"Only he has a *visible* connection, agreed. But there's nothing to prove there may not be a hidden one in the others."

Suddenly Bolan grinned. "Okay, you win, Hal. As a personal favor to you. But I want to talk to the local law."

CONRAD WAS WAITING FOR HIM when he left the hotel. There was no question of a direct shot this time: the wrecks had been carried away and the side street, brightly lit, was full of theatergoers hurrying to make the last train at the Central Station. A crowd of kids milled around a stall on the corner, eating raw herring and potato chips and drinking Cokes through straws.

The German gunner was wearing a belted trench coat and a soft hat. There was blood on the green leather, and anyway he thought it would be too much of a giveaway with a man as quick off the mark as Bolan.

He stood on the sidewalk, half hidden by the stall, his right hand wrapped around the butt of the Colt in the trench coat pocket. Although the roads still glistened with moisture, the rain had stopped falling. Since local contacts had told him the Executioner was staying at a second-class hotel less than a mile away, Conrad's plan, hastily improvised, was based on the belief that Bolan would walk that short distance rather than compete with the theatergoers for one of the few cruising cabs.

The big guy crossed the street, towering above the kids around the stall. He strode purposefully toward the Damrak. Conrad allowed himself a small sigh of relief. Waiting until Bolan made the corner, he turned up the collar of his trench coat and followed.

Bolan passed the huge cobbled square in front of the royal palace and walked down the Kalverstraat. He looked neither right nor left as he threaded his way between groups of window-shoppers staring at luxury goods displayed in the brightly lit stores that lined the narrow street.

Conrad remained fifty yards behind, on the opposite sidewalk. The crowd didn't bother him. It was a useful cover in case the mark checked for tails. He was certain now, in any case, that the hunch had paid off: Bolan was on his way home.

The Rembrandtsplein was the city's goodtime square, with nightclubs, strip joints and twenty-four-hour bars in between the cathouses, which were legal in Amsterdam, all around a central garden. Bolan's hotel was at the end of a narrow lane running down toward the Amstel River. He would make the hit there.

Streamers of reflected neon, red, blue and green, shimmered on the polished wet road that circled the square. Bolan crossed to the garden, took the diagonal that led him to the far side and picked his way between the cars prowling in search of a parking space. An impatient driver leaned on his horn. Somewhere near the river a clock chimed eleven times. Bolan went into the alley.

The killer increased his pace, hurrying to close the gap. The Colt was a good gun, a .38-caliber Cobra Special with a powerful knockdown capacity. But leaves moving in the night wind shadowed the lamplight filtering through from the square. The illuminated sign above the hotel entrance at the far end of the lane was too high to silhouette the Executioner. In such shifting, uncertain conditions it was best to be no more than thirty to thirty-five feet from the target—if you wanted the man you hit to stay down.

Conrad took the Colt from his pocket and thumbed back the hammer. Bolan checked his stride, half stumbled, and then stopped, bending down to retie a loose shoelace. Better and better, Conrad thought. His teeth gleamed in the dark as he smiled and raised his gun arm.

Someone thumped him familiarly on the back. Well, well, old buddy! Imagine seeing you here! What are you doing in Amsterdam? The possibilities flashed through his mind in the first millisecond of total surprise. Then—what the hell?—he was aware of a hot, wet rush in his throat, a gurgling sound, a bitter, metallic taste. His mouth was full of blood.

He heard a clatter on the cobblestones. Before he realized he had dropped the gun the pain hit him and he went down, the silver haft of the knife between his shoulder blades glinting dully in the diffused light.

Bolan shoved the Beretta into its holster and ran back. He glimpsed a short, stocky figure, a barrel-chested man with a prominent jutting chin, outlined against the glare in the Rembrandtsplein. An instant later the assassin had melted into the crowd.

The Executioner let him go. What the hell. He had deliberately decoyed Conrad to the alley with the hope of getting in the first shot, maybe winging the guy and choking the truth out of him before handing him over to the police. Now someone else had done the job for him.

Terminally.

To make sure that the gunman *couldn't* talk? Or for some reason unconnected with Bolan?

He bent over the fallen gunner. Conrad was definitely dead, and the cobblestones were dark with blood. Bolan dragged the body into a recessed doorway and went back to his hotel. There was a thoughtful expression on his face as he rode the elevator up to his room. The case was more complex than he had thought. Things were heating up.

5

Yellow leaves veneered the towing path and lay thickly on the surface of the canal. From a third-floor window of the redbrick police headquarters on the other side of the road, Mack Bolan stared at a row of old houses across the water. Farther along, next to a bridge across the canal, the trees had been cut down and there was a line of cars parked with their bumpers projecting over the unprotected bank. The sky was gray and a thin, persistent rain was falling. Bolan wondered if the sun ever shone in Holland.

A paneled door opened behind him, and a tall, thin man wearing a brown suit bustled into the room. "Very sorry you had to wait, *mynheer*," he said, placing a pile of folders on the carved desk, "but it is well to have facts checked. I thought it best to verify first that my colleagues in other departments had nothing to add to the little we know here."

The Executioner murmured a polite reply. He had agreed with Brognola that if he could carry the inquiry from the Fed's own experience to the international aspect of the suspected escape network, the authorities in more than one country could legitimately be asked if they had heard of such an operation—and, if so, how strong was the evidence in favor of its existence. Then, if the consensus was positive, they could consider the next step: finding out covertly how the organization worked.

Papers rustled in the somber room. Outside, waves from an empty sightseeing launch agitated the leaves floating on the canal. A stream of cyclists poured across the bridge.

The Dutchman cleared his throat. "Yes, well . . . it seems we have very little here of what you are calling the hard facts. First, the man found knifed last night near your hotel. A German with a record of violence. Armed holdups, suspected killings. Three prison sentences. From eyewitness accounts, he might be one of the three men involved in the shootings yesterday outside your friend's hotel. A strange coincidence, isn't it?"

"Very odd," Bolan agreed blandly.

"The man who was burned died before he could be questioned, so we can find nothing that explains why they were here. As far as an escape network is concerned, we have heard from informers that such an organization does exist. However, there have been no reports of anyone in this country who would have need of such an 'escape.' And when our officers pressed the informers for details, none could supply any. It does, then, appear that the organization is very secret indeed. Or that it simply does not exist."

Bolan had turned his back to the window and was sitting on the broad radiator below the sill. "No positive link between the informers' stories and the team abducting my friend?" he asked with some surprise.

The police chief shook his head. "Nothing positive, no. We have still not found traces of a Minerva taxicab, the boatman called Wim or the mysterious Jaap. But as this country might have been only an interim stopover in the operation, maybe that is not surprising."

"And the offshore collision?"

"Oh, yes." The Dutchman opened files and rustled more paper. "The boat was salvaged. An old Nazi naval craft, reconverted. They found one body trapped inside the hull.

It was Wünsche, all right, but there was no sign of Jaap or a third man."

"I find that strange," Bolan said. "Here's a team, clearly well organized, with five distinct stages in an escape operation identified, yet the people feeding you your intel say they have no details of any escape organization."

"The 'team,' as you are calling it, is German-based. Perhaps with one or two auxiliaries from our country. It is thought to be—how do you say?—for renting, for hire. We think they were paid to arrange this first part of Wünsche's escape. Paid by the escape organization. But they are not themselves a part of it."

"But the guys involved in the shoot-out near the Central Station yesterday, the three men in leather coats—they *were* the same ones who took Hal Brognola."

"As they are all dead, who can say? But it seems a fair deduction," the policeman admitted.

"And the other guy involved in the shoot-out. Do you have a lead on him?" Bolan asked curiously.

"We think we know who he is." The voice was suave. "But it is not expected that an arrest will be made in the foreseeable future. You are enjoying your stay in our city, Mynheer Belasko? Are you expecting to stay long?"

"It's a nice place. It's called the Venice of the North, isn't it?"

"Since this city was founded long before, we Amsterdammers feel it is Venice that should be termed the Amsterdam of the South. One more thing." He opened another file and removed a sheet of paper covered with typewritten notes. "The informer who was most emphatic about this supposed escape network has just come back from Vienna. Perhaps you should go to Austria and ask your questions there."

"I'll do that."

As Bolan left the building, a camera shutter clicked in the cab of a beat-up panel truck parked by the canal. The driver, a stocky man with a jutting chin, shot two more frames as Bolan stood on the edge of the sidewalk and hailed a cab.

THE RENTED MERCEDES EMERGED from the forest and sped downhill to Vienna. Bolan's first impression of the city, as he drove along the broad highway that led from the airport, was that it had more lights than any city he'd been to.

Their brilliance mapped the city against the night, glittering along the main streets, garlanding squares, parks and promenades. Stores, theaters, hotels and public buildings were ablaze with light—and what made the spectacle even more arresting was that the lights were the same. Instead of the usual multicolored neon jungle, surrounded by flashing advertisements, yellow sodium lights and blue floods, the place was lit with regular white lamps: a firmament of silver stars coruscating against the sky in the cold, crisp air.

The warrior left the car in an elevator at a multistory garage in the old Marktplatz, where it was whisked aloft and stacked in a numbered niche someplace far above. He crossed the square and checked into the plush nineteenth-century magnificence of the Hotel Ambassador.

Later, in a steel-and-glass office overlooking the Karntnerstrasse near the cathedral, he was brought face-to-face with the present day.

The small, secret, highly efficient research unit, which dated from four-power occupation days and was attached to central police headquarters, was run by a statistician, a onetime market research genius who held a chair in psephology and had been seconded to this post at the insistence of the Ministry of the Interior. The man had met Brognola at the Amsterdam conference and was willing to help.

If there was anything to be discovered about Brognola's escape network, Bolan knew he would find it here. The quick-thinking little Austrian with the goatee and the thick-rim glasses would come up with the answers.

"Ah, yes," the computer expert said as he pushed the glasses up onto his forehead and scanned the printouts. "The computer lists five different species of escape network existing in this country—Assisted Movement Operations, if you will."

"Five?"

"Oh, yes. Five. Section One (a), positive—an organization for taking willing undercover agents east of the so-called iron curtain. It operates rather clumsily beneath the umbrella of a student cultural exchange group. And it is, of course, financed by the CIA. Section One (b), positive—a similar network for infiltrating East European operatives into countries on this side of the curtain."

"Run, I assume, by the KGB?"

The professor nodded. He ticked off two items at the top of the printout with a gold, black-tasseled ballpoint. "Section Two (a), negative—is organized by a different branch of the KGB. It occupies itself with the ferrying of *un*willing persons from West to East—and it is, not to put too fine a point on it, an agency for the kidnapping and drugging of scientists, military defectors or other fugitives they want back, for one reason or another, at secret police headquarters in Moscow.

"Section Two (b), also negative—attempts with less success to do the same thing in reverse. Except that, instead of running it themselves, the CIA employ out-of-work mercenaries, ex-paras from the Foreign Legion, retired military security personnel, people like that.

"I don't have to tell you the kind of clients these networks have. Burgess, Philby, Blake, Fuchs; the East German security boss who defected and was then kidnapped and taken back again; the Israeli spy found drugged in a trunk at the Rome airport, and the other one who gave Israel's nuclear secrets to a newspaper and was tempted away from England by a honey trap; that French colonel who was abducted in Munich and delivered, bound and gagged, to the DST in Paris; the Chinese legation people in the Netherlands. All of these, even if they didn't pass through Austria, used one of the networks that exist here.''

"But they're not exclusively Austrian organizations?''

"No, no. It is just that, because they have branches here, they appear on our computer records.''

"I get it,'' Bolan said. "And the fifth category?''

The man with the goatee riffled through the printout material. "Ah, yes. Now this...this appears to be rather a different matter. Let me see...Section Three (a), positive...it says, and I quote, 'a nameless, noncommitted and nonaligned commercial organization set up to convey malefactors illegally and secretly across frontiers; an escape chain similar to those underground networks passing along Allied escapees during World War II; an organism for removing wrongdoers from the jurisdiction of those who condemn them.' Dear me, what pedantic terminology!''

"Does the data say anything about the way it works or who runs it?''

The Austrian looked at the paper again, frowned, slid his glasses down the bridge of his nose and frowned again. He turned the paper over, as if he might find on its blank back an answer to the problem puzzling him. Finally, shaking his head, he said unbelievingly, "But, no. Nothing at all. It is amazing, but we seem to have no information whatever on this network. None at all.''

"But it does exist?'' Bolan pursued.

"Exist? Oh, yes, it exists well enough. It spirited Rudi Preisser and Otto Schlumberger away to Madrid only last week, despite the fact that the entire police force was looking for them after they had absconded with the funds of an insurance company."

"EXIST?" THE POLICE CAPTAIN in Madrid repeated. "Certainly not. There is no such organization. And I am in a position to explain to you that, if it did exist, we should assuredly have laid its workings bare and apprehended the miscreants operating it. They would be safely incarcerated in our jails, you may be sure of it. Yet there are no such persons imprisoned in Spain. You may visit the cells and see for yourself. It follows, therefore, that there can be no such organization."

"I've heard, nevertheless," Bolan ventured, "that two men, Rudi Preisser and Otto Schlumberger, are rumored to have arrived last week from Austria."

"There are always rumors," the officer replied coldly.

"Evidently. Yet these particular rumors seem to be well founded. Immigration authorities revealed to a foreign journalist—"

"Foreign newspapers frequently malign this country when the facts show the picture—the true picture—to be far from dark. It is doubtless a matter of the language difference."

"The language difference?"

"Things become distorted in translation," the Spaniard said. He flicked a speck of dust from the polished belt whose shoulder straps crossed his spotless olive-green uniform. "If it should happen that this man—Preisser, did you say his name was?—should by chance be with his companion in this country, then it must be assumed that they entered legally by one of the normal routes. Had they not done so, as I have already pointed out, they would have been discovered and the clandestine agents who brought them arrested—''

"And there are no such persons under arrest. I know." Bolan stared out the window. It was ten o'clock at night. Under the chestnut trees in the brightly lit avenue below, the crowds were strolling, shopping, pausing for a drink at a sidewalk café, gossiping with friends or merely promenading to see and be seen. Nobody had mentioned "clandestine agents" before. He drew a deep breath and tried again.

"Captain," he began, "if we might, for the sake of argument, assume that two such illegal immigrants *had* been smuggled into your country, how exactly would your undoubtedly efficient counterintelligence services start to—" He broke off as the policeman rose to his feet, one elegant hand upraised.

"You must forgive me, Señor Belasko—" his smile was charming "—but I cannot officially entertain such theories. We deal only in facts here. We cannot permit ourselves to examine such wild assumptions. Now you must excuse me. I am truly desolated, but we can help you no further."

IF THE SPANISH AUTHORITIES weren't going to admit the presence of illegals, the Executioner found no trace of this official reticence in Turin.

He called by an address not far from the Corso Alessandro, where a special police unit allied with the SID, the Defense Department, had its headquarters, and asked to see the person in charge.

The man was huge, fat and affable, with a luxuriant black mustache. "But of course it exists, this organization," he exclaimed. "It has been working for some time now— maybe one year, maybe two. Many times, too, we have been given a tip-off: raid this club, be at this house at this hour, search this apartment, watch a warehouse. But always nothing happens. Each trail is a dead end."

"But if the network is so secret—if it's one hundred percent impossible to make contact—how do people approach the organization and explain what they want?"

"I think the shoe is on the other foot, *signor*. I think—I am not certain and there may be exceptions—that the person wishing to get away quick is himself contacted by the organization. They say, 'We can help you, but you will pay much.' This way they are avoiding the small fry who have not stolen enough money to interest them."

"When was the last time it was used?"

"One week. Very embarrassing," the fat man said, dabbing his neck with a huge handkerchief. Although it was autumn, the outside temperature was eighty-five degrees and the heating was set high. "A jailbreak in Milan. Three Sicilians, mafiosi it has taken us twenty months to convict. And now they are telling me they have arrived in your country."

"Mafiosi?" Bolan's interest quickened. "Could the network itself be a Mob operation?"

The man shook his head. "I think not. I believe it was convenient for them at the time, and so they used it. But many others also, with no Mafia connections, have been helped."

"And the Mob isn't in business to help outsiders. Yeah, that figures all right," Bolan said.

"I am sorry, but that is all I can tell you."

THE SHORT MAN with the barrel chest and the jutting chin replaced the receiver carefully in its cradle. "Here are the photographs," he said to the redhead on the other side of the desk. "Find out all you can about him. Everything. Use your employer's facilities. If necessary I will myself subscribe, but I prefer to remain in the background."

The woman was big-breasted, slender in the waist, with long, tapered legs emphasized by the tight-fitting jumpsuit she wore. She stared at the three shots of Mack Bolan standing by a canal in Amsterdam. "Easy enough to pick out in a crowd," she observed. "And tall with it, from the look of him."

"Smart, too. He blew away a couple of Conrad's boys just like that. They were supposed to be stalking him, but he had the drop on them, wasted them and took off without a scratch!"

"Did you have to kill Conrad?" the woman asked. "That hasn't been our thing, Bart. You always said you'd stick to the escape routines and leave the dirty work to the hired help. And apart from the risk, making a personal appearance in Amster—"

"Conrad screwed up," Bart said harshly.

"Yes, but he didn't know that Wünsche had been—"

"He didn't know about the boat? So what? He should have checked. He shouldn't have let them pick up the first guy who happened along. And pick up some damned spook, at that! I pay good money and I expect the hired help to earn it. If they screw up that means they're inefficient. For inefficient read unreliable. And unreliable people can talk." He shook his head. "Conrad didn't know much about me," he said, "but it was too much for my peace of mind."

The phone rang. He scooped up the receiver, muttered one or two monosyllables, said "Thanks for calling back so quick" and hung up.

He pushed the phone toward his companion. "Latest on Bolan—he's heading for Paris." He thought for a moment, plucking at his lower lip, and then added, "Call Mathieu for

me, honey. Use the Montparnasse number. Tell him I want
to put out a contract...."

SUPERINTENDENT ROBICHON sat behind his desk in a dusty
office near the Palais de Justice, four floors above the Seine
River. His eyes were watering and his nose was red. He was
suffering from a cold, and he was feeling sorry for himself.
Across the room, Mack Bolan leaned against the window-
sill. Behind him, rain fell from a gray sky on the roofs of the
Latin Quarter.

Bolan was suffering from déjà vu: the same drab administration office; the same chatter of typewriters from an
outside room; the same odor of cigar smoke, sweat and
disinfectant; the same weary official with too much work to
do.

There was a different river and a different sky, but the
same damned rain and the same problem to solve.

"We got a line on Secondini quite by chance," Robichon
was saying. "He made it through the cordon in a dust cart."

"A dust cart?"

"One of those garbage disposal trucks that are the same
the world over, the kind they empty trash cans into. They
must have had a spare set of coveralls ready and he simply
joined the crew. After all, who's going to pay attention to
garbage collectors?"

Bolan nodded. "Right."

"Naturally they couldn't go far. They had to transfer him
to some other vehicle before they made the outskirts of
town, or the dust cart with its Paris sanitary department
markings would have become too noticeable. As it was, they
took a risk using it because that's how we caught on: someone noticed the truck was an old one, a model the department stopped using some years ago. But they were through

our cordon before they had to change cars, so they were home free.''

"You got a line on the next car he got into?"

"A beat-up delivery truck, in fact. Yes, we did. They took the turnpike leading south, and we traced them to the exit just beyond Avallon. After that the trail goes cold. But there is a small private airfield between Saulieu and Chagny, in the Morvan. Bel-Air, I think it's called. My guess is that they changed cars again at Avallon and then took off for Corsica from Bel-Air."

"The guy's definitely in Corsica?"

"No doubt about it," Robichon said mournfully. He sniffed and reached for a tin of anti-influenza tablets on the desk. "I'd give a lot to be there myself right now," he added. "For some reason the autumn weather this year—"

"No clues in the van or the garbage truck?"

The superintendent produced a sodden handkerchief from the breast pocket of his jacket and blew his nose violently. "Clues?" he repeated viciously. "We couldn't even locate the two vehicles. Nobody has seen them, nobody knows where they are. Not a damned trace. Which means the whole team couldn't have gone to Corsica: some of them must have been left behind to straighten up."

"Good organization."

"Of course it was good organization. You don't slip through a number one priority cordon by chance."

"This inter-European deal is a reality then?"

"A reality? You bet your life it is, *monsieur*." Robichon placed two pills in his mouth and gulped water from a glass by the phone. "I'm not saying that every *malfrat* on the run from the law, every smuggler who crosses a frontier without having his passport stamped, is a client. But certain— shall we say important?—fugitives have definitely been arranged, that is to say their transport has been arranged, by these people.''

"Including Secondini's?"

"Including Secondini's. And that of Bizel, who escaped from Fresnes after killing a prison guard. And those of Desmoulins and Valat. And of course that of Gombrowicz, whom we had arrested and promised to extradite to Moscow. Red faces all around on that one!"

"What do they have in common?" Bolan asked. "I mean, can you tell at once whether an escape is part of this network deal or privately organized?"

Robichon pushed himself to his feet and walked over to join Bolan at the window. Beyond the Quai des Orfèvres, the wash from a string of barges rolled slowly outward to fragment the reflections of trees along the left bank. Traffic, shiny in the rain, swooped along the embankment toward the Pont Royal. The superintendent sighed, sniffed and blew his nose again. "I can tell you one thing about the network jobs," he said heavily.

Bolan waited.

The Frenchman was struggling to master his feelings. "What they have in common," he said at last, "is that we have been able to find out nothing about any of them. No abandoned vehicles, no discarded clothes, no arms caches or suspicious purchases in stores. Nothing. I have men undercover in every big-time racket in the country. I have a list of informers that is the envy of my opposite numbers in Rome and Berlin. But I can't coax as much as a whisper from these people concerning the makeup of this network, the names of its members, the way it works, how to contact it, anything."

"You think they're afraid of reprisals if they talk?"

"No, I don't. They know nothing. I am convinced of it."

Bolan fell silent. He was getting tired of this tune; he wished somebody would change the record.

"I realize this is rather surprising. In the underworld, as you know, there is always gossip. Jealousy, envy, greed or a thirst for revenge inevitably make someone talk. Except in this case, where there is nothing to say."

"At least you admit it exists, and that it baffles you. It's more than your colleagues beyond the Pyrenees are prepared to do."

"Ah, but you have to take into account the Spanish character," Robichon said. "They are a proud people, anxious not to lose face. Especially now that they have been admitted to the OEEC. It is perhaps understandable that they prefer *officially* to ignore a problem until they can announce that it has been solved."

"Nothing in this case is understandable," Bolan said.

And he repeated the theme, with variations, when he called Brognola that evening on the direct scrambler line from the embassy. "I've talked with the big noises in Amsterdam, Vienna, Madrid, Turin and Paris, Hal. Most of them admit the existence of the organization, but no one has a line on it. I've put out feelers in the underworld myself. Nothing."

Brognola, speaking from his office in Washington, sounded irritable. "That doesn't make sense. You say these characters don't spring guys from jail?"

"That's what I'm told."

"Then how the hell do the cons who *have* escaped patch into the network, tell them they want transport and can pay for it?"

"If they need the service that bad—and if they can pay enough and if they're lucky—*they* get contacted. You know the line, Hal—don't call us, we'll call you...."

6

The next attempt to eliminate the Executioner came early the following morning. He had just crossed the Champs Elysées, two hundred yards below the Arc de Triomphe, when a flock of pigeons wheeling away from the plane trees suddenly changed direction and arrowed toward him. Bolan was thinking of toast and coffee. From the corner of his eye he sensed the rapid approach of something shadowy and unexpected as the birds momentarily veered his way. With an involuntary reflex he started back a pace.

The instinctive movement saved his life.

Before he had time to feel sheepish, the way people do when they have jumped away from a nonexistent danger, he was hurled to one side by a small car that had peeled off from the traffic roaring up the avenue, made a U-turn on two wheels and rocketed down the service road between the trees and the ritzy stores.

Bolan had been about to step into the service road. The pigeons had caused him to falter, checking his stride—and the vehicle that would otherwise have mowed him down struck him only a glancing blow as it raced past. Fortunately he was off balance and rode with the impact. But he was spun across the sidewalk before he dropped dazedly to the ground.

Passersby ran up as he sprawled there, panting for breath. Many hands helped him to his feet, shepherding him to a bench. A man rushed out of a restaurant with a glass of cognac, and an elderly lady kept telling anybody who would listen that the police must be called. In no time at all, Bolan was in the center of a crowd.

"It's a scandal the way some people drive!" someone said.

"No more than kids in their teens!" a woman exclaimed. "It shouldn't be allowed."

"Madame, I entirely agree," an old man cut in.

"Did you see? He shot down here like a racing driver after making a U-turn in the avenue—a thing expressly forbidden by law."

"He must have been doing sixty kilometers an hour."

"Why, only last week a friend of my uncle in Lille..."

"The foreigner didn't have a chance."

"Has anyone telephoned for an ambulance?"

"Is he hurt?"

Bolan struggled to his feet, brushing aside the offers of help as politely as he could. His head was spinning. He was bruised and shaken, but otherwise undamaged. "No, no," he said. "Thank you. I'm all right."

"Did you get the assassin's number?"

Bolan shook his head. Assassin was right. The number would tell him nothing; the car was probably stolen. What was certain was that the driver had intended to run him down and kill him.

Bolan smiled grimly as he limped to his hotel. That was just fine with him. For it proved that his investigations thus far, superficial though they were, had been embarrassing to someone, maybe even caused them to panic. Because you didn't try to commit murder in public, twice, unless you had something pretty damned important to hide. It followed, too—though he couldn't as yet see how—that he had to be getting warm, and that the organizers of the escape network were afraid he might get warmer.

The one negative point was that he was forced, for the moment, to react rather than act himself. Because while they obviously had a line on him, he had none on them. And until he did he was condemned to play a passive role.

What the hell. They would try again. He had to stay more alert than ever, every nerve, every sense at full combat pitch. Next time they made a move against him, he'd be ready. And when they did, he promised himself grimly, he'd make *his* move.

When he arrived at the hotel, the receptionist handed him a letter that had been delivered by special messenger. The envelope contained a railroad ticket and a seat reservation on the Trans-Europe Flyer that ran nonstop that evening between Paris and The Hague. Attached to it was a slip confirming a booking for a single room with bath at the Grand Hotel Terminus.

There was no message enclosed.

Bolan sighed. Brognola was acting cagey again. He had already suggested that the Executioner return to Holland and try yet again to pick up a lead on the two Dutch boatmen, this time without making his presence known to the police. Bolan had demurred. Now the Fed was insisting—in a way that implied he was no longer prepared to argue.

Bolan went back to the embassy and called Brognola's number in Washington. He was told the Fed was in conference and couldn't take a call.

Frowning, the warrior ran a mental check. He guessed Brognola must have some special reason for wanting him to be at that hotel tonight. Maybe he had instructed a contact, someone with a lead, to meet Bolan there. Maybe someone supplied with the number of his seat reservation was to contact him on the train.

On principle, he asked the receptionist to look up the times of planes. It turned out that by the time he had taken a cab out to the airport, checked in, waited for his flight, made it to Amsterdam, cleared customs and immigration, taken another cab from Schiphol into town and traveled by train or car the fifty-three kilometers to the capital, he would get there no quicker than he would by train. Maybe Brognola's assistant had checked out the planes and come to the same conclusion.

Bolan took the train.

Nobody approached him on the journey. He ate an excellent, if rather heavy dinner, read the Paris newspapers, listened to endless business conversations. In between he watched the gaunt outlines of the northern landscape whirl by through the lozenges of yellow light cast by the Pullman windows.

The Grand Hotel Terminus was a large nineteenth-century building across from the railroad station. Cheap souvenir stores, french fry stalls and car repair shops surrounded the building, but inside the revolving doors all was comfort and bourgeois respectability. The blast of overheated air that greeted Bolan carried with it the odors of food, cigars and aromatic coffee.

After he had checked in, Bolan sat in the lobby pretending to read a newspaper, a cup of coffee on a table beside him. The lobby was surrounded by a barbershop, a cigar store, restaurants and boutiques. Nobody came out of any of them or pushed through the revolving doors to contact him. At midnight he went up to his room.

The next morning after breakfast he opened the French windows and went out onto the small balcony that jutted from the hotel facade four floors above the street. Streetcar lines ran down the center of the road and groups of workers, who had arrived by train, waited on the pedestrian islands to board cars for the city center. It was cold on the balcony, but the sky overhead was at last free of cloud, and bars of pale autumn sunshine slashed the roofs and upper stories of the buildings around the station.

A barrel organ parked by the sidewalk serenaded the rush hour crowds with rollicking mechanical music. It was an enormous machine, painted all over with multicolored circus motifs and resting on four wheels. Two men worked the act, one turning the handle that moved the punched music sheets through the mechanism, the other cavorting from side to side with a battered hat held out for contributions.

Before the first tune was through, coins showered down from the hotel windows and bounced across the road from the city-bound workers. Bolan ducked back into his bedroom and grabbed some change. He leaned over the balcony rail and tossed it toward the waiting entertainers. As he bent forward, a rifle on the fifth floor of the building opposite cracked and a bullet smacked into the brickwork behind his head. Even as Bolan's mind registered the report, a second slug drilled the French window, starring the glass and sending fragments tinkling to the floor. The third shot was dead accurate. It whined across the balcony a foot above the rail, exactly where the Executioner had been leaning an instant before. But by this time he was flat on his face on the tiled floor, crawling backward into the room.

Once inside he raced to get his Beretta. He clipped on the folding carbine stock and whirled back to the window. But the figure of the marksman, dimly seen in silhouette against the sunlight reflected from a pane of glass, had vanished.

Bolan threw on clothes, ran for the elevator, sprinted through the hotel lobby and dashed across the street. The warning bell on a streetcar clanged angrily, and workers scattered as he hurtled over the pedestrian island. He jerked open the front door of the building and found himself in a dark, narrow hallway. Uncarpeted stairs spiraled up into the dark. He began to climb.

He passed an attorney's office loud with the clacking of typewriters, a private apartment with a radio playing somewhere inside, another that seemed to be some kind of rehearsal studio: he could hear the tinny cadences of an upright piano and a woman's voice counting one-two-three.

The door to the fifth floor was open.

Bolan sidled through with the Beretta cocked in his right hand. He wasn't expecting to find anyone, but Vietnam had taught him that snipers who failed to score occasionally left something to cover their retreat.

He heard a soft thumping noise, then saw a spot of bright light swinging back and forth across the far wall. An open shutter, moved by a slight breeze, was reflecting the sunlight as it thudded repeatedly against the frame.

There was nobody in the place.

A dozen cigarette stubs trodden into the dusty floorboards showed that the killer had been waiting some time. A popular brand, the cigarettes told the Executioner nothing. Three spent shells glittered beneath the window. Smallbore, high-velocity rounds: standard NATO ammunition. He looked in vain for a meaningful clue.

His face was grim as he headed back to the hotel. The hoods seemed to know his movements better than he did himself. Three times already he had escaped by chance. He reckoned that was his ration of good luck on this particular mission.

From now on every move would have to be covered front, back and both sides. And from now on, there was a new dimension to the operation: the hunt had become personal.

7

Bolan realized suddenly why Brognola had sent him to The Hague. He was passing the barbershop on his way to the elevators when a rich and fruity voice boomed out from the archway leading to the scented salon with its chairs and mirrors.

The Executioner stopped in midstride, staring through the arch. It couldn't be true—the last time he'd heard that voice he'd been in the slums of Marseilles . . . and then he hadn't believed it.

But there was no mistake about it. The third draped figure before the mirrors, sitting lower than the others, was that of an enormous man in a wheelchair. Weighing close to three hundred pounds, he sat with the great swell of his belly thrusting out the barber's sheet like a tent, the massive folds of flesh encasing his skull, almost burying unexpectedly humorous, twinkling blue eyes.

It was Mustapha Tufik, the world's leading intel broker.

Bolan stood watching the dexterous, almost balletic, movements of the barber as he guided a straight razor unerringly among the convexities of the big man's chin.

Tufik had been born to an Irish mother and a Moroccan father. After an early encounter with gangsters that had crippled him for life, he had left North Africa and set up an information service in Marseilles that was unequaled in the world. Police forces, embassy staff, military attachés, detectives, lawyers, newspapermen, crooks and secret agents from many countries had gone to him to buy the lowdown on anything from the private life of a foreign minister to the affairs of the heart of married movie stars.

For Tufik sold information. Just that. Any piece of inside knowledge required could be bought from him—for a price. He took no sides, asked no questions, played no favorites. There was only one stipulation: he refused to sell intel about one client to another.

His unrivaled sources had been built up over many years; his encyclopedic knowledge derived in part from an exhaustive cross-referencing of gossip items culled from press reports all over the world, in part from the bugging of selective meeting places, in part from plain eavesdropping. It was said that a fair proportion of the vast sums he received for his services was redeployed among the army of doormen, porters, chambermaids, reception clerks, flight attendants and cabdrivers who supplied much of his raw material.

He had enjoyed the reputation of being the most informed gossipmonger on earth—until Bolan had unwittingly involved him in a Mafia plot to smuggle stolen uranium isotopes to a secret nuclear reactor in the Sahara. In reprisal for the help he had given the Executioner, his Marseilles headquarters had been bombed out of existence. Tufik had narrowly escaped with his life.

Was it possible that he had set up shop in Holland?

As the barber drew a towel across the huge face to remove the last traces of shaving soap, the man in the next chair rose and left. Bolan slipped into the vacant seat.

"Yes, sir?" A young man with glossy black hair shook out a pink linen sheet and spread it over Bolan. The man looking after Tufik was preparing hot towels.

"Just a trim," Bolan said.

The barber fished a comb and scissors from his breast pocket.

"It pays to keep your hair well trimmed," Bolan said. "My favorite uncle always advised it."

"Just so, sir." The young man began to comb and snip. There was no discernible reaction from the next chair. Tufik was a mountain of sheeted pink surmounted by a cone of white towels through which steam rose gently into the air.

"My Uncle Brognola," he added a little more loudly.

A tremor manifested itself among the vaporous towels. A fold of the damp cloth subsided, and an eye was revealed. The eye opened and stared at the Executioner. It closed again. Bolan settled in his chair and closed his eyes. "Not too much off the back."

A few minutes later he heard a bustle of activity as the fat man was divested of his robes and towels, helped on with his jacket and flicked with a clothes brush. There was a crackle of folding money and the chink of coins changing hands.

"Thank you, *mynheer*," the barber's voice intoned unctuously. "It is more than kind. Until next week, then?"

And then the familiar, fruity tones: "Ah, think nothin' of it, Gustav, think nothin' of it. When you have it, you might as well spread it around, boy. For there's none as will give a man a sight of it when he's without it at-all. Next Friday it is, then. And now I'll be on my way. There's them as is waitin' to see me by the canalside on Sint Pietersstraat an' I don't like to miss an appointment."

There was a squeak of rubber tires, and the self-propelled wheelchair was gone.

Bolan didn't open his eyes. There was no need to. Tufik appeared to be a garrulous person, a heedless and friendly man born with the gift of the gab. Nothing could have been farther from the truth. He was a shrewd operator who planned every move: every single word in his conversation was there because he wanted it to be there, for a purpose. He had mentioned the name of a street in Bolan's hearing. That was as good as an engraved invitation.

A few minutes later the warrior was talking to the hall porter. "Sint Pietersstraat," the man repeated, scratching one side of his mustache. "Yes, of course. Here on the street plan of the city. Square D7 on the grid, see. A small street running by this canal. You'll find it off the Duikersteg, second or third after the lights."

It was only four blocks from the hotel.

The canal was narrow, its surface completely covered by leaves. There seemed to be no current and no traffic. On the far side the high walls of factories and a warehouse cut off the view. The street itself was bordered by small houses in poor repair—meaner and less imposing than the tall waterfront properties in Amsterdam—and there was a towing path below it, approached every hundred yards by a cobbled ramp.

Bolan noted with amusement that to make the Duikersteg he had to walk the length of Onkelweg—the Uncle's Way.

Once in the Sint Pietersstraat he hurried along looking for some sign of Tufik. The autumn sunshine was still bright, but there was a keen wind blowing and the shadowed side of the road was cold. Some of the two-story houses had Dutch doors at the entrance, and slatterns with painted smiles leaned over several. One flabby creature, wearing a skimpy bikini, called out something to Bolan in a dialect too broad for him to understand, and a burst of laughter echoed down the street.

How typical of Tufik, Bolan thought, to live in or near a red-light district! But where *was* he?

And then suddenly he saw him. The wheelchair was below him on the path, parked at the water's edge. The fat man, bulging massively over the chair's frail structure, appeared to be gazing along a line of stunted trees whose fallen leaves had choked the canal. Bolan quickened his pace and went down the nearest ramp.

Although his back was to the Executioner, Tufik somehow sensed his approach. Before he reached the foot of the ramp, Bolan saw the wheelchair spin through 180 degrees, so that it was facing away from the canal, and roll toward the wall separating the path from the road. Then, to his astonishment, Tufik was apparently swallowed up by the brick facade....

Slowing his walk to a casual saunter, Bolan reached the bank. He glanced across the water and then swung back toward the street. Immediately he saw how the wheelchair had vanished.

Recessed deeply in the brickwork, a series of low arches ran below the surface of the road. Behind them, he guessed, were shallow cellars, perhaps used once for storing the boatmen's equipment. Most of the arches were boarded up or bricked in, but the wooden door set in one gaped open.

The wheelchair must have disappeared through there.

Bolan patrolled a few more yards of canal bank, turned and began strolling back toward the ramp. After a little while, he veered in the direction of the wall.

He saw that the brickwork cut off the view of the houses on the far side of the street, and his movements would be invisible from the upper stories. He walked through the doorway.

Inside, beneath the dark vaulted ceiling, Bolan saw rolls of chicken wire, an iron barrow, oil drums and a stack of lumber. When he'd advanced a couple of paces into the gloom, the door slammed shut and he was in total darkness. Before he had time to be surprised electric lights blazed on, and he found himself face-to-face with a blond woman whose hair stood out like a halo.

"Mr. Mack Bolan, I believe?"

She had a fresh complexion, wore a jade-green sweater that matched her eyes, tall brown boots and a very short skirt. The Executioner estimated she was in her mid-twenties.

"I believe Mynheer Tufik is expecting me."

"Mynheer Tufik?" the woman repeated in a husky voice.

"Mustapha Tufik."

"He won't like you to use that name," she reproved. "Please remember to use his correct name when you see him."

Bolan was amused. "And that is?"

"Mynheer Hendrik Vandervell."

"I'll try to remember. And speaking of names, what's yours?"

"You may call me Gudrun. Now if you would please follow me...."

Squeezing through the wall and a stack of planking, she reached out with one arm. Evidently there was a hidden switch, for a moment later Bolan heard the whine of hydraulics and a section of wall behind the oil drums rumbled aside. A vaulted passageway beyond the opening led back beneath the road. Gudrun went through and waited for him to follow. Two yards down the passage they broke a magic eye beam and the secret door swung shut behind them.

The corridor was brightly lit, built of brick and floored with rubber tiles. Their footsteps made scarcely a sound— the wheelchair, Bolan reflected, would have been virtually noiseless. When they had gone a distance that he estimated would have taken them under the road and beyond the row of houses bordering it, the tunnel turned sharply and ended by a blank wall. The final section of tiling on the floor was outlined by a narrow crevice, as though it might be a trap-door. The woman stepped on this rectangle and motioned the Executioner to follow her.

As soon as he was standing beside her, she stretched out a hand and pressed one of the bricks set in the wall. Again there was a whine of machinery... and the section of floor on which they stood, together with the end wall and the ceiling above it, rose slowly on a hydraulic platform. They were on an open-sided elevator.

The platform lifted about twenty feet and stopped. They were enclosed by brickwork on three sides—the fourth wall was formed by what looked like an ordinary door. Gudrun pushed it open, and they walked into a luxuriously fur-nished bedroom.

Bolan calculated that they had to be on the first floor of a house in the block behind the half-door cottages—a house whose official entrance was doubtless on another street al-together. Tufik, he remembered, liked to cover his tracks.

From the bedroom the elevator now looked like a large built-in closet that happened to be empty. As he watched, the "car" sank from sight, the ceiling became the floor and another ceiling lowered itself to replace the first one.

Gudrun closed the door and led him through a screen of heavy draperies that masked an archway. In the huge room beyond, Bolan at once felt that sense of déjà vu.

Gray steel filing cabinets lined three of the walls. On a bench projecting from the fourth a computer terminal stood among speakers, transmitter chassis and spools of tape that had overflowed from an audio console sophisticated enough for a recording studio.

A boardroom table big enough to seat twenty people oc-cupied the center of the room, its polished top submerged in a tide of newspapers, magazines, press releases and infor-mation sheets stacked in piles twelve to fifteen inches high.

There were heaps of periodicals, too, mixed in with floods of newspaper clippings and dozens of sheets of paper covered with scribbled notes, on the chairs, over the coffee tables and on every inch of horizontal space in the big room. A closed-circuit television was mounted high up in one corner.

The place looked, in short, exactly like the headquarters Bolan had visited in Marseilles. Even the tape equipment, with its switches, dials and rheostats, its matched spools and twelve-channel mixer, was the same.

Like a pale spider in a corner of its web, Tufik was waiting for them on the far side of the room. "Mr. Bolan! Mr. Bolan!" he enthused as they pushed past the curtain. "A pleasant surprise indeed to be seein' you! Come on in an' sit down this minute while I see about fixin' you some liquid refreshment."

With all his old expertise, Tufik whisked the electric chariot in between tables, chairs and stacks of books to roll up to the Executioner with a pudgy hand outstretched.

Bolan grasped the fat but unexpectedly sinewy fingers. "What have you been up to? And what are you doing in Holland? I thought the Mob had put you out of business."

"It takes more than them rapscallion foreigners to keep a good man down," Tufik said, "even if he's condemned forever to sit in this contraption." He gestured dismissively at the wheelchair. "Girl, dear, perhaps you'd be good enough to furnish Mr. Bolan and meself with a small jar of the creature?"

The blonde nodded and disappeared through a doorway between the filing cabinets and the computer terminal. The only other exit was at the far end of the same wall, by the tape decks. There was one window opposite the curtained archway, which was covered by a venetian blind.

The Executioner looked for a place to sit. Every available space appeared to be covered with the raw material of the fat man's trade, but eventually he removed a copy of *Le Monde*, a page torn from *Krokodil* and a month's issues of *Der Spiegel* from a stool and sat. His host, he saw, still used his own personal system of polychromatic annotation, ringing, underlining and commenting on items of special interest in various colors.

"Why The Hague?" Bolan asked conversationally. "It seems so unlikely."

"Don't you believe it, boy! You want to keep a finger on the pulse, there's no better place in Europe. Between Amsterdam and Rotterdam, not too far from Antwerp— there's three of the biggest ports on the continent for a start. And in my experience, if you want to know what goes on, like the nice girls, you ask a sailor. The boyos working the airlines are good for a taste of honey, too, but that's the same wherever you go. Here we have Schiphol. Brussels, with connections to France, Germany and all of Scandinavia. I'm tellin' you, there's never a corner like this that gets as much shippin', that's also near an international airfield. Except maybe Marseilles—an' that's a deal too near home to be comfortable, if you take my meanin'."

"Okay, okay." Bolan grinned, holding up a hand to stem the flow. "You convinced me ... Hendrik."

"Ah, now," the fat man said chidingly, "listen, you! There's no call to make a mockery just because a fellow takes the precaution to adopt, as you might say, a trifle of protective colorin', now is there?"

"I guess not. So brief me on the setup."

"It's satisfactory. It is that. From the street you see there—" he waved a hand at the venetian blind "—the place is kind of a cheap hotel. With a bar. And though 'tis not a port itself, the town sees plenty of brave lads off the boats. From the canals too, so the bar is full—"

"And bugged at every table?"

"And bugged at every table," Tufik agreed with a side-long glance at the multichannel tape recorder inputs. "There's a heap of useful stuff on those tapes you wouldn't believe, once they're sorted. Which is why our prices are kept low and the bar is kept crowded."

"And the hotel?"

"The hotel? Why, curiously enough the place seems to be booked solid all the time. There's never a room to be had if a body tries to check in."

"You never appear in the hotel yourself?"

"Never. I use the canal bank on Sint Pietersstraat. It's easier for the chair that way, for there are steps out front here. It's discreet. And it means I'm never connected with the place at all. The hotel itself has a fourth advantage, but."

"I'm listening."

Tufik chuckled throatily. "Apart from the casuals who give with their information, er, involuntarily, via the hidden mikes, there's plenty more who come here to deliver the goods they're paid for."

"I can guess. Hotel porters and cabdrivers and—"

"Quite, quite. There's no call to be precise. Well, these ladies and gentlemen have to get in to see me. Personally. And whereas an odd crowd like this might attract attention in another neighborhood, here it's no problem at all. There's always sailors droppin' by to check out the ould girls on Sint Pietersstraat—the hotel has a rear entrance there, too—and there's always a multitude patronizin' the bar. So, between them, who's goin' pay any mind to a few extra clients here an' there?"

Gudrun came back into the room carrying a tray. Pushing aside a heap of manuscripts on the big table, she set out glasses, coffee cups, saucers, a conical copper pan full of Turkish coffee and a bottle of Izarra—the fiery yellow Basque liqueur that was the only spirit Tufik had ever been known to drink.

"I still have the sweet tooth, as you see," Tufik said while the woman poured. "Your continued good health, sir. And now let us talk business. What can I do for you this time?"

Bolan's dark eyebrows rose. "I thought you might know already." He had reckoned that, since Brognola had arranged the meeting, he would also have briefed Tufik. But the big man merely shook his head.

"No? Well, it's easy enough to lay on the line. It's information, of course, that I want. But you won't find it in your filing system, your newspaper stories or your data banks this time. You might get a lead from your microphones, if you have enough bad characters in your bar."

"Yes, Mr. Bolan?"

"There's a highly organized escape network operating in Europe. For a price it takes people across frontiers, out of reach of the law. All the police forces know it exists, but none know a thing about it. I want to know who runs this organization, how it works and how to contact it if necessary." The Executioner sat back in his chair, drained his cup and set it down carefully in the saucer.

Mustapha Tufik hadn't moved. He sat bulkily in his chair, staring straight ahead and humming a tuneless little air through his teeth. Gudrun, who had been curled up on the floor at his feet, rose to refill cups and glasses.

Eventually the fat man reacted. He spun the chair around and wheeled swiftly to the far end of the table, where he began ferreting about beneath an untidy pile of gossip columns torn from the previous week's Sunday newspapers.

"I'm always losin' that damnable phone!" he muttered. "I *know* the instrument's on this very table.... Ah!" He gave a cry of triumph and flourished an ivory-colored handset. His free hand dived back into the pile, and Bolan heard the sound of a number being punched out.

It was followed by a conversation in rapid Dutch, which he was unable to follow. Then Tufik said in English, "And you can tell the advocate that the articles he wants can be obtained in an ordinary pharmacy in Spain. In boxes of ten. That's the only country they still make them now. But warn him they're much stronger than the ones they used to sell in England: I think there's a whole cc in each." He chuckled. "Tell him too that the info won't cost him a penny. This time it's on the house!"

Tufik replaced the receiver. He spun the chair to face the Executioner. "It's not an easy thing you're askin'," he said slowly. "But if you care to come back around midnight, I think I might have something for you. In the meantime..."

"Don't tell me. In the meantime there's the question of money." Bolan reached for his wallet. "Your sources had better be good," the warrior said as he counted an extravagantly large number of bills into the fat palm.

"Always trust an old friend," Tufik said, stuffing the money into his inner pocket. "If you'd like to leave by the hotel, it might attract less attention in the long run. Gudrun will show you the way. She's going out anyway."

"Until midnight. How do I get back in?"

"The way you came. There'll be plenty of boyos about on Sint Pietersstraat after dark. Just make sure none of them see you actually go through the archway, is all."

"Will do. See you." Bolan followed Gudrun into a short passageway and then past two steel doors. Between them, a tall man with long sideburns and a dark mustache sat at a table cleaning a Walther PPK automatic. Recognizing the bodyguard Tufik had in Marseilles, Bolan nodded a greeting as he passed. The tall man looked up and inclined his head gravely.

Beyond the second steel door was a tiny office. And outside it was the lobby of a typical commercial hotel, the kind of place favored by traveling salesmen, with out-of-date theater posters on the brown-painted walls, dispirited artificial flowers and faded notices covered in food stains. Through a door at one side they could hear the brawling hubbub of the bar.

Gudrun took Bolan's arm when they reached the street. "I like dark men for a change," she said. "It's not many clients he sees personally, you know. What do you do?"

The warrior smiled. "Let's say, if Mynheer Vandervell sells information, then I collect the same commodity—preferably *without* paying for it."

"You are a detective?"

"No, just an information gatherer. There's one item you could supply yourself, Gudrun."

"Sure." The woman pressed the taut curves of her body against him as they walked. "If I can. What do you want to know?"

"I want to know what time you have to be back."

"Back with Hendrik? Not until midnight. I'm off duty as of now."

Bolan looked down into her flushed face. There was a mischievous twinkle in the green eyes, a mocking tilt to her mouth. Her whole expression was a challenge. "That's too much of a coincidence to be passed up," he said. "Are clients permitted to date the personnel?"

"I see no objection if the personnel is not on duty."

"Great." He glanced again at the eager face, the blond halo. Was he misreading the expression in those eyes? What did it matter? He had nothing else to do until midnight; he couldn't advance the operation any farther until he had the material Tufik could supply. Who was going to beef if he passed a few hours in pleasant company? "Where do you want to go?" he asked.

"Let's go to Scheveningen. It's only two miles. We can walk by the sea, and I'd like to try the food at the Bali. I'm crazy for Indonesian."

"It's a deal. We'll grab a cab right away."

"My car is here," she told him, stopping by a parked convertible with the top down. It was a low-slung roadster with red bodywork, steeply raked black fenders and a detachable windshield. Tarnished chrome lettering slanted across the radiator honeycomb spelled out the name Alfa Romeo. Bolan placed it as a model that dated back to the mid-thirties.

As Bolan slid down into a worn leather bucket seat, Gudrun asked, "Where are you staying? There's no heater in this, and there will be a wind on the coast. It gets cold after dark, too. Don't you have an overcoat?"

"In my hotel, the Terminus. It's only a couple of blocks away. If you don't mind making the detour, I'll stop off and get a windbreaker from my room."

He left the woman, looking remarkably voluptuous despite her slender build, at the wheel of the battered old roadster while he hurried into an elevator and went up to his room.

Opening the closet door, he thought at first the windbreaker was missing. Then he realized it had slipped off the wire coat hanger and was lying in a crumpled heap on the closet floor. With an exclamation of annoyance, he leaned in to pick it up.

The nylon filled with wet sand made no noise as it swung down to meet his nape. The floor cracked open into an abyss of darkness, and the Executioner fell through.

8

There was a roaring sound in Mack Bolan's ears. The world heaved in waves of blackness. Someplace far down in his skull a team of workmen with pneumatic drills were trying to blast their way out.

The warrior raised his hands to his throbbing forehead... and touched nothing. He experienced a moment of irrational panic.

Then, as consciousness gradually returned, the head came with it, and he realized he hadn't reached for it at all: he couldn't have because his hands were tightly bound behind his back.

Bound? Yeah, his feet, too. Something hard and unpleasantly dry to the taste was jamming his mouth open and was secured there with a strip of cloth. His jaws, wedged apart by the gag, ached as painfully as his head.

After a while his memory fully returned, though the blackness and the roaring continued. It took him some time to figure out that he was shut up in the back of a truck: an old, dilapidated truck, judging by the hard springs, the racket of the engine and exhaust, and the booming of the side panels.

He strained his eyes in the darkness. There wasn't a vestige of light anywhere—no cracks between doors suddenly illuminated by the headlights of a passing car, no reflections from streetlights or road signs. It must, he reckoned, be very late at night.

And if the surface was anything to go by, they were on a very minor road.

Bolan tested his bonds. His wrists were tied tightly together, but not crossed. His ankles were bound and so were his knees, but they had left his elbows free. He'd probably be able to get his hands around in front of him.

They lurched along the rough track for what seemed to be hours. At last the truck turned sharply, hurling Bolan across the metal floor like a sack of coal, then they were traveling on a smooth surface.

He heard the sucking whine of heavy-duty tires, the regular concussions of air as they thudded past cars and trailers going in the opposite direction. From time to time, as some late traveler came up behind them and waited for an opportunity to pass, cracks outlined the rear doors, limned in bright light.

Bolan occupied his mind by running over the sequence of events since Hal Brognola had involved him in this operation.

After all the legwork, the shootings, the fire, the three narrow escapes and the baffling lack of intel that confronted him at every turn, what had he come up with in the way of pay dirt?

The fact that there was an escape organization.

But he had known that before he'd started.

Worse still was the fact that the shadowy characters who masterminded the organization had not only kept up with him all the way: half the time they had been way ahead of him.

Why?

And why was it that the previous moves had all been attempts to eliminate him outright whereas this time he had merely been knocked unconscious and abducted?

Interrogation? Find out how much he did know and who was behind him? That figured.

Lastly, as far as his present situation was concerned, had he fallen into a honey trap? Was Gudrun part of the scheme, a decoy who had set him up? Or was she no more than an innocent coincidence?

He would have to leave that one on hold, along with the other questions awaiting an answer from Mustapha Tufik.

The noise of the truck's tires changed to an oily hiss. He heard the drumming of rain on the roof. Soon afterward they bumped off the road, and the vehicle groaned to a halt. The rumble of the engine died away, and the pattering of the rain grew louder. A door slammed, and Bolan was aware of footsteps squelching on wet ground. He faked unconsciousness, his breath snoring past the gag.

There was a sudden rush of damp, cold air as the doors of the rear were jerked open. An electric light flashed. Somebody grunted with satisfaction and shut the doors. Through slitted eyes, the Executioner received a momentary impression of his jailer—the upper half of a man silhouetted against a glare of light in which rain sloped down in silver lances. Then a flat iron bar was dropped across the doors, and the footsteps receded.

Bolan waited for half a minute to make certain nobody else was coming, then he forced his cramped body into action. He rolled over onto his back, gathered his strength and launched himself upward so that his pinioned feet were pointing at the roof and his whole inverted body was supported on elbows, neck and shoulders. Then, forcing the elbows as far apart as he could, he rolled himself downward, drew his knees tightly up against his chin and ma-

neuvered the hoop of his arms over his hips. All he had to
do then was pass the bound hands over his feet.

He had almost made it when the heels of his shoes fouled
on his bound wrists. Panting and cursing under his breath,
he struggled to draw his knees up still farther, to flatten his
feet against his haunches. But it was only when he pushed
his shoes off that he was able to slide his feet through and
bring his hands in front of him.

The first thing he did was reach up and tear away the strip
of cloth holding the gag in place—and then, painfully, eject
the gag itself. With his bound hands he explored his pockets, looking for a cigarette lighter. Bolan didn't often smoke,
but the lighter had another purpose: concealed in the lower
half was a small capsule of nerve gas that could knock out
an opponent and leave him unconscious for a half hour.

And, of course, the lighter would produce a flame.

Bolan located it in the hip pocket of his pants, fished it
out and sparked it into flame. The lighter wasn't self-
extinguishing: once the wheel had been spun, the flame
continued to burn inside a stormguard until it was blown out
or the hinged top was lowered over it.

Bolan set it on the truck floor, then, gritting his teeth, he
lowered his wrists toward the flame.... Two excruciating
minutes later, the last charred strand of rope parted and he
was able to give his tender flesh some much-needed relief.
Quickly he untied the knots at his knees and ankles and
freed his legs. Then, massaging his limbs to restore the cir-
culation, he took the lighter and went over the interior of the
truck to see if he could find anything that could help him
break out.

The vehicle wasn't very big—larger than a delivery van
but by no means a long-hauler, probably a two- or three-
tonner. Apart from a pile of old sacks, it seemed empty. But
the storage space continued forward, over the roof of the

cab, and here, lying in a corner with a coil of wire, a shrink-wrapped pack of four spark plugs and a twist of oily rags, he found a rusty hacksaw blade.

Bolan scrambled down to the floor again and stole to the rear doors. The lighter flame showed him that although the panels were rusted, they were still a very close fit—too close for the hacksaw blade to slip through. Grunting with the effort, he leaned his weight against the outer door, hooking his fingernails at the same time around the edge of the other, painfully dragging it inward. The crack widened imperceptibly until he could slide the blade in.

From there it was relatively easy to work the hacksaw upward until it lodged against the bottom of the flat iron bar securing the doors. Sweat beaded the Executioner's brow as he wrestled the slender steel finger up against the weight of the bar. But at last the bar was clear of its socket, and he tilted the blade away from him so that it slid off and clanked downward, leaving him free to shove open the doors.

The man he glimpsed earlier stood immediately behind the truck. He was short, bulky, barrel-chested—a dark-complected man in blue coveralls, with hair plastered to his skull by the rain. He had a ferociously jutting jaw.

Bolan recognized Conrad's murderer.

The Executioner was poised on the truck's tailgate, waiting to leap. The killer watched him with glittering eyes, hefting an outsized wrench from hand to hand. Behind him the shrouded shapes of trucks and trailers in a parking lot blocked off the neon lights of an all-night café.

The Executioner evaluated the situation in a flash. He was unarmed. He had no means of knowing how many confederates the guy might have, how many backup men could be moving in on them even now. It was no time for an in-depth investigation of who they were or why he had been kidnapped. That could wait until he had seen Tufik. Right now the operational priority was to get out.

Quick.

He would join battle as soon as he was armed, as soon as he knew the score, as soon as he had regained his own freedom of movement.

As his adversary moved forward, Bolan acted.

But instead of jumping he sank down onto his heels, pulled the cigarette lighter from his pocket and aimed it at the killer's face. Reflected light gleamed on the wrench as the guy raised it high. Bolan pressed a button in back of the lighter. A stream of gas jetted at the killer's nose and mouth from a tiny hole below the flintwheel. The killer's eyes widened in surprise and his mouth opened, but before the man could utter a sound he twisted around and fell to the ground.

With a single bound, Bolan cleared the prone figure and sped off into the rain and into the night.

When he was two hundred yards down the highway, he turned to look back. He couldn't see anyone else around the truck, and so far the alarm hadn't been raised.

The blare of a jukebox jangled from behind the steamed-up windows of the café. Cars and trucks speeding past in each direction probed the dark, wet pavement with long fingers of light. Otherwise there was no sign of life.

Bolan started to walk. A mile farther on, a glare of yellow light reflected back from the low clouds marked the position of a motel. When he got there, soaked through from the driving rain, he saw to his surprise that he knew the place. It was on a section of road in northern Belgium between Hasselt and the Dutch border city of Maastricht. He knew, too, that someplace in the vast parking lot he would be able to lay his hands on transportation.

Mercifully his papers were still in his pocket, so he wouldn't have a problem crossing the frontier back into

Holland—although it was too much to expect that he'd stumble on a car that carried its documents and insurance certificates in the glove compartment. So he'd have to junk the stolen car at Lommel, on the border, and walk through, picking up another at Bergeijksche, on the far side. Maybe he'd be more believable as a pedestrian anyway, considering the state of his sodden clothes. Taking these delays into consideration, Bolan reckoned he should make the journey to The Hague in a little over three hours.

THE CANALSIDE WAS DESERTED when he coasted the car to a halt a little after four o'clock. Nobody saw him flit down the ramp and melt into the shadows of the archway; nobody heard the faint creak as the door opened. Finding the secret switch behind the stack of lumber was difficult because the fuel in the lighter was almost gone. But at last he was standing on the elevator, ascending to the closet in Tufik's bedroom.

He turned the handle and strode in. The room was empty, but there was a gleam of light from behind the draperies. The fat man was busy marking up some papers, crouched in his wheelchair in the light from a single green-shaded lamp pulled down over a coffee table.

"I'm a little late," Bolan called softly.

Tufik glanced at his Rolex. "A little," he said. "But pay it no mind, sure, for I never sleep until six."

"Where's Gudrun?"

"She was here just before midnight for the late shift. She left at three-thirty. Said you stood her up: took her back to your hotel and walked out on her."

"That might be true," Bolan said enigmatically. "I was taken for a ride. Whether or not it was because Gudrun suggested I get something from my room, I don't know. But since the people responsible will be those I'm asking you questions about, I'm more than ready to hear what you discovered.''

"Ah, sure, you're not in a hurry at-all. Sit you down, dear man, and join us in a spot of the creature.''

"I'm in a hurry to get your report.''

The fat man toyed with a bulky sealed envelope he had picked up from the tabletop. "Now who wants to be hasty? Relax, you, and wait'll I tell you somethin'.''

"Well?''

Tufik sighed. He seemed ill at ease. Spinning the chair away from the light, he held the envelope out to the Executioner. Bolan took it, frowning, and slit open the flap with his thumb. The envelope was filled with money.

"I don't understand.''

"Four thousand five hundred guilders,'' Tufik's voice said from behind. "You better count it to make sure it's correct.''

"That's what I paid—''

"Of course it is.'' The fat man was wheeling around the room, straightening papers, making unnecessary adjustments to stacks of reference books. "Sure, it's simple enough,'' he said without looking at the warrior. "I can't help you. I can't undertake the work.''

"Why the hell not?''

Tufik was embarrassed. "Now that I've had a chance to look into it, I, uh, I find the people running this escape lark, the fellows you asked me about, are already clients of mine. So I'm sorry, but I can't tell you anything. 'Twould be contrary to me own rules.''

"You couldn't break those rules? In this case?''

"Now you know better than that, Mr. Bolan. Sure, that's me cardinal principle: there's only one kind of intel you cannot buy—the lowdown on another client. You wouldn't be after wantin' me to go against that?''

"I guess not. But—"

"But since the client protection business can work both ways," Tufik continued, "I can put you wise to one thing before you take your money and go."

"Anything would help." Bolan strove to mask his exasperation.

"The boyo you're askin' me about, he asked me a question I couldn't answer, too." There was a pause, and then he said, looking straight at the Executioner, "*He* wanted me to find out everything I could about *you*...."

9

The small man with the gray crew cut and the clipped mustache paid off his cabbie on Eleventh Street, SE, a block away from Philadelphia Row on Washington's old Capitol Hill. He looked sharply once in each direction, crossed the road and began walking toward the river. An erect man with a firm, springy step, he strode along in his belted raincoat and his pepper-and-salt tweeds as though he would be more at home in a uniform.

Ten minutes later, at the far end of a street of redbrick town houses, he went into a corner grocery store. In back of the store, behind serve-yourself shelves of canned soups and dry goods, there were two phone booths. In the right-hand booth, half hidden by a rack of newspapers and magazines, he lifted the receiver from a dial phone. Reading the figures carefully from a line scrawled on the back of a business card, he dialed a nine-digit code. A sliding door at one side of the booth slid open. Without a backward glance, the military man stepped through into the passageway beyond.

The passage served much the same purpose as the one that ran beneath the cathouses in Sint Pietersstraat in The Hague: it led secretly to a house in an adjoining street. But there the resemblance ended.

At the far end of this tunnel was the hallway of a suburban villa, all white-painted bay windows, scrolled ironwork and bay trees in tubs on the stoop. It was a safehouse used by Hal Brognola when he wanted to make discreet contact with agents whose presence would have been questioned if they had appeared at his office at Justice.

The man with the gray crew cut wasn't however, a secret agent. He had, in fact, never been to old Capitol Hill or Washington before.

Or, for that matter, the United States of America.

He was just very well briefed.

But there was nevertheless an established routine for Brognola's shadowy contacts the first time they used the secret entrance. And the man hadn't followed it.

The elderly man behind the grocery store counter pressed a button beside the cash desk, which had been installed for just this eventuality. If it had been labeled, the label would have read Provisional Alert.

The middle-aged blonde behind the reception desk in the villa hallway had already seen the stranger coming on the closed-circuit video monitor above the front door. Even without the winking orange indicator light activated by the man in the grocery, the defenses of the place would have been ready for the intruder.

Steel doors now blocked the rear entrance, the door to the garage and the way back into the grocery store telephone booth. The second-floor corridor that led to Brognola's office was similarly cut off. The power supply to the elevator and the grille between the garage and the street was shut off. And similar orange lights would be winking in every room in the house while the provisional alert lasted.

But the crew cut man wasn't there to cause trouble. He walked quietly across to the desk, clicked his heels and said in clipped, formal English, "Good morning. I should like to speak with Mr. Hal Brognola, if you please."

The blonde was trained to deal with unexpected situations, but this one threw her. People didn't usually walk calmly through the secret entrance and expect to see the boss. "I, uh, I'm afraid it's not...that is, it's usual to make an appointment," she said.

"I have not the time to waste on formalities, protocol, red tape."

"Yes, but I'm afraid... Can I have your name, please?" The woman clutched hurriedly at a straw of routine.

"I am Colonel Imre Ferenc Sujic, of a branch of the Czechoslovak military intelligence with which you would not, I imagine, be familiar." He proffered an engraved business card.

Back on home ground, the receptionist became crisp and efficient once more. "One moment, Colonel," she said. "If you would kindly take a seat, I'll call somebody who can deal with your case."

"I am not a case. I wish to see Brognola."

"Yes, Colonel. If you would just take a seat, sir...."

A minute later Frank O'Reilly, the fifty-year-old ex-FBI man responsible for internal security, was explaining in some detail why it was impossible for casual passersby, however eminent, to see Brognola, especially if they had illegally entered by a secret route. The blonde watched the exchange—O'Reilly with his pugnacious jaw, eyes watchful behind the rimless glasses, the Czech standing stiff and correct, talking with the minimum of gesture, his attitude inflexible. She'd put her money on the foreigner, she thought privately; there was an assurance about him that wouldn't admit even the possibility of defeat.

It said much for Sujic's authority that she proved right. Within ten minutes O'Reilly was all smiles, personally ushering the visitor into Brognola's office.

"I know you by reputation, Colonel Sujic," Brognola said, glancing at the card. "But why didn't you telephone to make an appointment? I must apologize for the embarrassment you must have suffered, but you appreciate we have to take certain precautions."

"Understood. I did not telephone because you might have been officially 'out' and I have little time to spare. Also, I was interested to make my way into your... fortress... by unorthodox means because it was an instructive exercise and it afforded me the opportunity to test the efficiency of our own intelligence services, who had supplied the necessary information."

"I hope you found the experience rewarding," the Fed said dryly.

"Amply, thank you. A few of the interior details were absent. I did not know about the steel doors, for example. But the briefing on the approach and the entrance itself was admirable. I found my way to the correct store and into the reception area with no difficulty at all."

"Great. I guess, just the same, that this wasn't your only reason for visiting Washington?"

"By no means." Colonel Sujic cleared his throat. "What I have to say is very strictly off the record. I would prefer it to be said in informal surroundings. I should be honored, therefore, if you would allow me to offer you luncheon. I am told there are suitable places on the waterfront in Georgetown." He coughed. "I am further briefed that the Chincoteague oysters and clams from Chesapeake Bay should be sampled at all costs."

Brognola laughed aloud. "You're on."

Thirty minutes later, sitting beneath a striped awning between a clapboard fisherman's cottage and a redbrick town house with delicate wrought-iron railings bordering the front steps, Sujic came to the point. "Our trade, as I think you will agree," he said, "is an endless chess game, an elaborate ritual of denial and counterdenial, of claim and rejection, that makes nonsense of truth as we know it. It is a convention, absurd perhaps to an extreme, but one that is imposed on us by our masters and one we must follow."

Brognola nodded. Each time he spoke, he realized that he was mimicking the colonel's speech patterns.

"If an espionage agent defects from country A to country B," Sujic said, "probably because he has a girl there or the money is better, country A will at once deny that he has defected, deny that he was a spy—and claim that, if he *was* a spy, then they knew nothing about him. Country B will in turn deny that it offered the man money and try to make out that he came because he was convinced of the rightness of that country's way of life over his own."

Brognola gazed through a screen of yellowing chestnut leaves at the brightly colored boats bobbing on the water. He nodded again.

"Within the framework of these nonreal conventions," the Czech continued, "any attempt at genuine cooperation is impossible. But when we come to the question of malefactors, lawbreakers, crooks as you call them—as distinct from ideological agents, that is—then quite another set of conditions exist, wouldn't you agree?"

"I guess so."

"It is only in the case of vulgar felons, since they cannot in any way advance the cause of our respective dialectics, that we can afford to cooperate. Am I right?"

Brognola sighed. "I can't deny it."

"Very well. I am here to cooperate. Or, rather, to make a suggestion, which you are free to accept or reject as you wish. It concerns an escape organization that operates clandestinely throughout Europe and which it would be to everybody's advantage to destroy. I assume you have heard of it?"

Brognola's jaw dropped. He paused with an oyster halfway to his mouth.

"We believe we have the means of getting in touch with this network," Sujic continued, "of putting a man, a particular man, in contact with them . . . a task that has so far baffled every police agency in Europe, as you no doubt know."

"I'm listening."

"Let me offer you three facts. One, there was in my country a convicted robber and murderer who recently escaped from a prison near Prague. He made for the capital, where he hid with a large sum of money, wondering what to do—a natural client, don't you think, for this network? Two, this man was known to have gone to ground in the old city, where his loot was cached. He was also known to be seeking a way out of the country for obvious reasons. And the third point is that he is dead."

He paused for effect. Brognola was staring at him with a puzzled expression.

"We discovered his hideout," Sujic explained, "and as we moved in to flush him out, he broke cover and fled. He was knocked down by a military truck and killed instantly as he ran across a road. The important thing about this is that nobody outside the secret police, nobody, knows that he is dead. There were no witnesses to the accident and, as far as the underworld is concerned, he is still lying low in his hideaway."

"I'm afraid I don't quite see . . . ?"

"You must remember," the colonel went on, brushing aside the interruption, "that our task is complicated by the fact that, officially, we *have* no underworld in my country. And there is one extra factor with which you should be made familiar. It is a visual one, so I shall content myself with showing you a photograph." He took a pigskin wallet from the breast pocket of his tweed jacket, opened it and separated from a neat bundle of ID papers and plane tickets one postcard-size color print that he handed to the Fed.

"That is Zoltan Cernic, the murderer who is no longer among us," he said. "And who was, incidentally, a confederate of the bank robber Hradec, who has already been spirited away by this escape organization."

Brognola looked at the portrait and gasped.

It was a typical mug shot—staring eyes, defiant expression, prison number displayed across the chest. But apart from a higher forehead and the fact that the widow's-peak hair was a flaming red, the features could have been those of Mack Bolan.

10

Bolan was back at the hotel behind Sint Pietersstraat early the next morning. "Hendrik Vandervell" was already at work, covering a huge chart with hieroglyphics as he held a telephone receiver clamped to one ear. He waved the Executioner to a seat and went on talking.

"...from that whorehouse in the Rembrandtsplein, did you say? And then out on the Arnhem parkway? Well, the devil be praised! But we have to have witnesses, mind, who saw her leave.... Sure, you do that, but first see what the chambermaid has to say."

He put down the phone and turned to Bolan with a crooked smile. "Hello, you," he said. "You wouldn't *believe* the trouble we have. There's this little fellow, a military attaché with one of the Latin countries, an' they want the lowdown on his private life. But, sure, the man's so *active*, movin' from girl to girl and from place to place so fast that my people can't tell if it's a miss he's after or a missile!"

"I won't keep you long, but I have a favor to ask."

"My pleasure, boy," Tufik replied, "so long as it has nothin' to do with that matter we discussed yesterday."

"Not directly. It's a service I can't easily call up anyplace else in this town. I'd like to use your shortwave transmitter to call Brognola in Washington."

"No sweat." The fat man waved a hand at the dials and tuners beyond the computer terminal. "And you can ask the dear lad how things are on my behalf, for I've had no word from himself for many a long month."

"You don't have to be cagey with me," Bolan chided. "It can't be more than a couple of days since you were in touch with him."

"What are you talkin' about?"

"Hell, he must have been in contact to fix our meeting."

"Our meetin'? I don't follow you at all." The Irishman was staring.

"You mean he didn't . . . ?"

Tufik shook his head.

"You didn't make it to the Terminus barbershop specially to contact me? That means our meeting was no more than a coincidence. What the hell's going on?"

And a few minutes later, when he'd contacted Brognola, he asked, "Why didn't you warn Tufik that I was on my way? I knew I had to meet *someone* once I had the railroad ticket, but—"

"Ticket?" Brognola's voice interrupted. "What are you talking about, Striker?"

"You mean you didn't—"

"I haven't made an attempt to contact you since you called me from the embassy in Paris."

The Executioner whistled softly. If neither Brognola nor Tufik knew anything about that special delivery letter, then it had to mean he had deliberately been decoyed to the hotel. Which in turn meant that someone—the guy who tried to run him down in Paris?—had changed his mind and decided to eliminate him in Holland.

Why?

If they were going to shoot at him when he was on a balcony or knock him on the head and abduct him from a hotel room, why do it in The Hague? Why not Paris? Or anywhere else? After all, there were plenty of balconies and plenty of hotel rooms in Europe.

There could only be one answer: because the person or persons who had to do the shooting and abducting must themselves be in The Hague. Having failed in Paris, they put one over on the Executioner, leading him to their next stop, so they could try again.

Why would they have to be in The Hague?

Bolan shot a glance at a newspaper on a table near the fat man, an early edition of that day's *Het Parool*.

Yeah. Affirmative.

Bannered across the front page, he read, slowly translating the Dutch: POLICE OUTWITTED IN DARING ESCAPE BID! And then in smaller type: Jailbreak Terrorist Traced to Maastricht—Then Trail Goes Cold.

That figured. It was business as usual for the network, even when they did have accounts to settle with too-curious investigators.

"...the best goddamn lead you're likely to get this side of Christmas," Brognola's voice was saying. "So, Striker, liaise with this guy in Switzerland, let him fill you in, then take it from there, okay?"

"Got it," Bolan said, his mind automatically recording the details, though his thoughts were still right there in The Hague.

As soon as the Fed signed off, the warrior turned to Tufik. "What's the strength of this, Mustapha?" He indicated the newspaper on the table.

The fat man looked evasive. "I can tell you no more than what you read in the newspapers," he hedged.

"Reading headlines is one thing, but translating six columns of Dutch is another."

"Well..." Tufik cleared his throat. He began seeding reference cards back into a box file. "It seems there was this feller, a Palestinian, who belongs to some fundamentalist group. He made a break from the courtroom yesterday after sentence was passed. He'd drawn fifteen for his part in a supermarket bomb."

"And then?"

"They had cops cordon the neighborhood in no time at all. But the feller was already through. Someone recognized him in a truck stop near Maastricht sometime after midnight, an' that was the last seen of him." Tufik chuckled. "They say he got through the police lines doubled up inside the body of some old barrel organ contraption!"

"A barrel organ?" Bolan echoed.

There had been a barrel organ below his room when the sniper had fired at him yesterday morning. And again when he was knocked out after his visit to Tufik. Was it possible that this could be a coincidence?

No way.

Maybe that was the fashion in which he, too, was spirited away from the Terminus—concealed behind the decorated panels of that antiquated machine. He could also believe that the escaped terrorist had been traveling with the tough little guy with the jutting jaws. The evidence was accumulating, but as far as hard facts were concerned, had he really made much progress?

Negative. There were still far too many questions that needed answering. Specifically, how had the conspirators fixed it so that they were always up-to-date with his own movements?

Sure, he'd had a lot of questions waiting for a reply ever since the operation had started; he had asked them in a lot of places. Many of the folks he'd quizzed had themselves demanded intel from others—and these in their turn had probably talked. But even so... If he didn't have complete confidence in Tufik's integrity, he might have thought the fat man himself was the source. However, until he could follow Brognola's lead, the only positive deduction he could make was that he had probably misjudged Gudrun, thinking her a party to his own snatch.

"I owe your girl an apology," he told Tufik.

"My girl?"

"Gudrun. I figured she engineered my return to the Terminus, knowing there was someone waiting for me in my room. It seems I drew a blank."

"Well, I don't know about that," Tufik said. "But Gudrun herself is away a couple of days. She has time owin' from last Easter, and she asked me could she take it now. She'll not be back until the day after tomorrow. Can I give her a message?"

"No. Thanks. I'll be long gone by then. In fact, I'm on my way as of now—unless you have any second thoughts about..." He jerked his thumb toward the newspaper.

The fat man's jowls quivered as the great head shook in negation. "A rule's a rule, Mr. Bolan," he said regretfully. "Even among friends. 'Twouldn't be of much use, I doubt not, even if I *could* talk. A name, a description, a probability of whereabouts, which you'll like enough latch on to soon enough yourself. You already know they were askin' about you...and, the dear knows, you've had proof of that yourself. Still, though, there is one thing I'll tell you...."

"Yeah?"

Tufik grinned. "It's a pity of him, but remember this: it's not always the new ones that travel the best!"

"It's not always the new ones...?" Bolan echoed with a puzzled frown.

But the fat man in the wheelchair refused to elaborate his hint—if hint it was—and the Executioner left with one more riddle unsolved, leaving Tufik to reach into his pocket for a fistful of colored pens as he drew a stack of newspapers toward him.

11

"Liaise with the guy in Switzerland," Brognola had said. And "the best goddamn lead you're likely to get." Okay. But there were a few formalities to get through before the liaison could be effected, before the Executioner even knew what the lead was. Such as initial contact, transport, communications. And on these the Fed hadn't been as specific.

"It's your game, Striker. Play it your way," he had said infuriatingly. And when Bolan pressed for details, for some hint on the nature of this lead, Brognola had pointed out that the long-distance airwaves weren't secure.

Bolan was left with an instruction to make his way to Switzerland, pausing at certain stated times to tune a radio to a particular frequency, waiting for a call from the contact, who wasn't yet sure of the exact time and place of the rendezvous. Once that was fixed, the warrior was to allow the contact to blaze the trail...until a given moment that the contact himself would choose. After that Bolan would know what to do.

It all seemed unnecessarily complex to him. He didn't even know the name of the contact—some spook from an Eastern Bloc country, Brognola had said—only a coded radio call sign by which he would identify himself.

Bolan didn't have to be in Switzerland until the following day, but he figured it a good idea to make it as close as he could today in case the contact wanted an early rendez-

vous . . . or favored someplace way up in the mountains. So
he left The Hague early, skirted Antwerp and Brussels and
arrived in Namur on the Meuse in time to buy bread, cheese
and beer before the stores closed for the lunch break. He ate
not far from Bastogne in the Belgian Ardennes, pulling the
rented Mercedes off the road just before two o'clock in time
for the first listen-in period.

Since the guy calling him would be far out of range of any
normal transceiver, Bolan was obliged to choose a secluded
place where he could set up a miniature dish aerial and connect that to a classic receiver about the size of a small type-
writer. Around the clearing he had selected, the undulating
country fell away in a series of interlocked, wooded curves.

Wind moaned in the pines overhead and stirred needles
around the trunks of trees farther down the hill as he ate and
drank. The sky, which had gotten more and more overcast
since dawn, was now a sullen yellow canopy stretching from
horizon to horizon. It looked as though it were going to
snow.

Bolan sat for thirty minutes with the engine running and
the heater booster turned up, the radio tuned to the frequency he had been given. Other than an occasional surge
of automatic Morse, the receiver remained silent.

He drove on into Luxembourg. Snow had already fallen
on the eastern slopes of the Ardennes. There was a thin
coating between the trees, and from time to time, along the
surface of the sinuous route near Esch-sur-Sûre, powdery
white trails snaked toward the car in the wind. Farther south
in the Grand Duchy the fall had been heavier: snow lay
thickly on branches and roofs, filling the furrows between
iron-hard ridges of plowed land.

The streets of the capital were still bone-dry, but it was
unnaturally dark, and in the chasm that divided the city into

two fairy-tale halves, light already gleamed in the dusk below the turreted cliffs. Bolan drove on toward the south.

By the time he was due to operate the radio again, he was in the center of the vast industrial complex between Metz and Saarbücken. It was like a scene from some medievalist's idea of hell. Rows of gaunt iron chimneys belched flame into the livid sky. From factory to grimy factory, huge metal pipes, twelve feet in diameter, writhed across the blasted landscape like the entrails of a galactic robot in a strip cartoon, bridging roads and marshaling yards, swerving around waste tips, linking furnaces and smelting plants and mines. Even with the Mercedes windows sealed shut, the Executioner could smell fumes from the sulfurous, polluted air trapped beneath the fiery clouds.

Small wonder, he thought, that the workless, condemned to a useless existence in this dead land, so often turned to crime. And the more the little guys turned to crime as the only way to buy a ticket out of hell, the more the predators, the big wheels it was Bolan's vocation to destroy, grew fat on the evil they moved in to organize.

Bolan shook his head. The problem was insoluble. He would continue the fight until there was no breath left in his body. Others would take up where he left off. But however much of the web of evil they tore down, however much of the rottenness behind it they exposed, however frequently the ulcers that festered on the body of society were destroyed, it seemed that they would always be replaced.

It was time to stop. He didn't know quite what to do. The road was narrow and full of traffic. The sidewalks, below high corrugated metal and chain-link fencing, were crowded with workers returning home. The few parking lots he saw were too busy. Finally he approached a stretch of dusty grass bounded by a hedge white with some airborne waste. It was too public a place to set up the radio, but at least he could get the car off the road. He steered up over the sidewalk and stopped the Mercedes beside the hedge.

Waiting until the press of walkers and cyclists thinned, he took the equipment from the trunk and looked around. A redbrick building on the far side of the road was surrounded by transformers and generator housings and gantries bristling with insulators. He could see a parking lot in front of it, bordered by tubs full of dispirited flowers. Beyond the hedge, stunted trees punctuated the rusty topography of an automobile junkyard.

He could see—beyond the stacks of crumpled fenders, the concertinaed witnesses to death and destruction and moments of fatal inattention—a wooden hut by the yard's entrance gate. It should be quiet enough in there, in the dark, for his purpose . . . as long as he could make it past the man on the gate.

Or was there, maybe, another way? A rear entrance?

Strolling by casually, he found that there was. Fifty yards farther along the highway, a lane cut up between the junkyard and the high brick wall of a foundry. And fifty more yards up the lane, Bolan saw tire tracks in the mud between a gap in the hedge. Glancing swiftly behind him to check that he was unobserved, he slipped through.

A few minutes later, cans hooped over his head, he was sitting comfortably enough on the running board of a wrecked 1930s taxicab, his aerial erected on its battered hood. He was completely hidden—from the road, from the lane and from the shack at the entrance—by the towering stacks of scrap metal.

The bigger piles consisted of metal shells from which everything of use or value had been stripped: engines, wheels, instruments, springs, transmissions, seats and even the trim from the doors. But a variety of more specific scrap was heaped between these stacks. Bolan saw a mound of radiator cores, another of bolt-on wheels, a third of bench seats, mildewed and worn, with springs and stuffing leaking from the ripped surface. Beyond these, rose a mountain of cylinder blocks from which the pistons and valves had been removed.

"Hammer calling Striker. Hammer calling Striker." A clipped voice with an unidentifiable accent rose above the hiss of static in the Executioner's phones. "Do you read me, Striker? Do you read me? Please acknowledge and stand by for time and place."

Bolan flipped the Send button and transmitted the coded acknowledgment Brognola had given him.

"Hotel Lucerne, Geneva," the voice said. "Midday."

And that was all. The static faded. Bolan heard the equivalent of a telephone line going dead.

He had questions, but although he tried for ten minutes to raise a reply, his unknown correspondent remained obstinately silent. This, the Executioner thought, was carrying security to a farcical degree. It showed, nevertheless, that the contact he was to meet was highly professional.

The guy hadn't even specified the day. He knew Bolan would have been briefed on that already and was counting on him to know. In the same way no mention had been made of recognition techniques: Brognola's contact was relying on him to play it by ear. A man who expected that kind of efficiency from others, the warrior reckoned, had to be pretty damned efficient himself. Maybe the lead would turn out to be a positive one after all.

As he packed up the components of the transmitter, Bolan continued his survey of the junkyard. An occasional intact vehicle stood out like a beacon among the tangle of exhaust pipes, sheared-off valances, overriders, side panels, rubbing strips.

There, for instance, was an American roadster that had been totaled in a head-on collision. The wheels and engine were in the driving compartment, and the long hood had been crumpled into nothing. On the other side was an Italian minicar that had been squashed almost flat in some unimaginable road drama. In contrast there were several trucks that looked as if they had died peacefully of old age. A Unic flatbed with grass growing out of the remains of its driver's seat must have been there since long before World War II. Beside it was a panel truck with scarcely an inch of its bodywork undented or unscratched, but that couldn't have been more than two years old. And nearer the Executioner was a dump truck with its back and sides literally falling to pieces.

It was crazy, just the same, how different parts of a wreck deteriorated at different rates. The engine of that dump truck was a case in point. From what Bolan could see through a gap between the cab and an engine panel, it looked in pretty good shape.

Idly he sauntered toward it, but halfway there, he stiffened. He stepped up to the derelict in half a dozen determined strides. The white dust that covered the leaves in the hedge lay thickly over everything else in the yard. Except, it seemed, in the case of this one truck.

He peered into the cab. The seat was threadbare, the rubber floor mat worn almost through, the controls shabby in the extreme. Yet there was hardly a trace of the all-pervading dust...and the cabs of the others were smothered in it.

Rapidly, silently, he circled the truck and lifted off the entire hood. The engine shone in the lamplight reflected from the street. The cylinder block glistened with oil. The spark plugs looked new, and the wiring must have been replaced within the past few weeks. Bolan unscrewed one of the caps on top of the battery. The electrolyte was topped up, and there was water in the radiator.

He checked out the other trucks he had seen.

As he had expected their engines were caked with dried grease, the insulation on the cables cracked and the top surface of everything was covered thickly with the all-pervading dust.

The dumper might only just have been acquired by the owner of the yard, but to Bolan it looked much more as if it had been there some time... and had only recently been restored to running order. It had been left looking deliberately decrepit, although in fact it could probably work perfectly well.

Why?

What use could anyone have for what was in effect a "Q-truck" hidden in a junkyard? Unbidden, Tufik's parting comment leaped into the Executioner's mind: "It's not always the new ones that travel the best...."

He dropped to his hands and knees. The street lighting didn't help much at ground level, but he could just make out the shadowed indentations of tire tracks that led from the front wheels toward the gap in the hedge through which he had entered.

The truck had been used recently.

And suddenly, in a flash of inspiration, he knew the reason why. He saw why someone could want a serviceable truck disguised and kept hidden in a junkyard. He saw why it could be important that the vehicle, however well it went, should appear to an outsider to be derelict.

"It's not always the new ones..."

Several facts, until now unrelated, jelled in his mind. The taxi Brognola had ridden in had been a Minerva—an ancient model made by a manufacturer that had ceased pro-

duction before World War II. It had taken him to a car
junkyard.

The garbage disposal truck in which the Parisian mafioso Secondini had escaped was a model the city sanita-
tion department had stopped using years earlier. The panel
truck in which the guy made it to the private airfield was said
to be "beat-up." The two-tonner from which Bolan himself had escaped was old. The car that had tried to run him
down in Paris was old. The terrorist who had bamboozled
the Dutch police had been smuggled past the cordon inside
a barrel organ that was a museum piece.

For the first time since the operation began, Bolan felt
excitement rising within him. He set up the transmitter and
its aerial again. Ten minutes later he raised the cipher clerk
in the U.S. embassy in Paris on a frequency normally used
only by field agents of the CIA who wanted to contact either
the Paris resident or the ambassador's military attaché.

"I want you to put through a priority message to Hal
Brognola in Washington," he said. "The duty officer will
give you the routing. The message is short, and it's simple.
It should be signed Striker, and it reads: I think I've found
out how they operate the network."

12

A sudden dazzle of light blinded the Executioner. "What the hell do you think you're doin'?" a voice snarled roughly. A large hand swept the miniature dish aerial to the ground and yanked free the cable linking it to the transmitter. Booted feet stamped the lightweight metal saucer into the mud.

Bolan whirled away from the mike. He must have spoken too loudly while briefing the clerk at the embassy; his voice had alerted the watchman in his shack by the yard entrance.

In the light reflected from the beam of the man's powerful electric lamp, the warrior saw that he was tall and husky, with mean, glittering eyes.

He could see, too, that the man held a gun on him.

It was an old gun, a six-chamber revolver with a rusted barrel. But it was a large-bore iron, probably a .45-caliber Colt. It would blow the Executioner to hell before he could get a hand anywhere near the Beretta holstered on his hip.

"Get to your feet," the watchman growled.

Warily, keeping his hands well away from his sides, the Executioner complied.

The man jerked his head toward the shack, and Bolan began to walk. He heard a screech of metal behind him, the snap of breaking plastic, a faint tinkle of glass. His captor had grabbed the portable transmitter and smashed it against the fender of a wreck as they walked by.

The shack, which was lit by a single oil lamp, smelled of cheap cigarettes and overboiled coffee. The guard motioned Bolan to sit at a table covered with newspapers. The warrior lowered himself into a canvas chair and placed his hands palm downward on top of the papers. The gunner looked trigger-happy, and the way he had smashed the radio suggested a low threshold of tolerance. Bolan decided to hold himself in check . . . for the time being.

There was an ancient electric heater near the door. Keeping Bolan covered, the guard tipped it over on its back and placed a chipped enamel jug of coffee on the grillwork. "Okay, now it's time for some answers," he snarled. "Who are you? Where did you come from? What the hell are you doing sending radio messages from here?"

"I wanted a quiet place to transmit," Bolan replied.

"Transmit what? Who to? Why here?"

"Find out." Bolan was relieved to see that, apparently, the watchman hadn't gotten close enough to hear the message.

"Don't think I won't," the man threatened. "We got truck generators here that run a current strong enough to make a statue sing."

"You'll need help," Bolan said affably. "Do you think I'm just going to lie down quietly while you strip me, tie me up and fix the electrodes? With one hand? You do plan to keep me covered, don't you?"

The watchman hesitated, scowling; the mechanics of his threat hadn't occurred to him. Finally, his eyes and the gun still trained on the Executioner, he backed off to a tall wooden chest, placed his free hand behind him and pulled open the door. From an untidy mass of papers, ledgers and overflowing folders, he produced a telephone, which he placed on the table. He dialed a number.

Bolan couldn't place all the figures, but from the regional and area codes at the beginning he reckoned the call was long-distance, almost certainly international.

The watchman waited a long time for an answer.

"Bart?" he said at last. "Stefan, from the yard at Montigny... I figured I might get you at home today— Yeah, yeah, I *know* you don't like me to call you, but this is important. I flushed out a guy sendin' radio messages, right here in the yard! Yeah, that's right. Tall guy with black hair. Blue eyes. Looks in shape. You want me to find— Oh, you know who he is! Well, okay, what you want me to do with him...?"

His mean eyes flicked over Bolan and then back to the phone again. "No questions. Just terminate. Whatever you say, Bart. Well, sure, there's the canal back there. Runs a reasonable flow of water about this time, on account of the sluices up at the reservoir being opened. Check. Call you back."

Stefan kicked open the door and motioned with the barrel of the gun. "Walk."

Bolan shivered as he stepped onto the muddy ground and breathed the damp night air outside the hut. He was under no illusions. Whoever "Bart" was, he had recognized Bolan from that brief description. Which meant that Bart— and the junkyard itself—were part of the escape network. It was probable too that it was the same character—the stocky guy with the aggressive chin—who had taken the Executioner for a ride two days earlier. Only this time Bart had clearly thought he could do without answers, and had cold-bloodedly ordered Bolan's execution.

They walked down a lane between towering piles of car wrecks, Fords, Citroëns, Renaults, Volkswagens and Audis, stacked in a rigor of buckled steel and rusted panels. If this was to be his last view on earth, the warrior reflected as they came in sight of the canal, it looked as if he was at the River Styx already. For no scenarist creating a twentieth-century inferno could have dreamed up a scene more hellish than the one he was looking at.

Through the heavy, sulfurous atmosphere, he saw the serrated roofs of factories above a string of coal barges moored on the far side of the polluted water. Flame seared the violet sky to the east over the belching mouths of blast furnaces. The few stars visible through gaps between the clouds were too far off to be of any help.

Bolan had reached the water's edge. He looked down at dark, scummed ripples sucking at rotted piers. A cold breeze carried the stench of decomposing skins from a tannery on the other side bank of the canal. Was this, then, the way it was all to end—no last-man-last-round defiance but a short plunge into foul and depthless water after a hammer blow that smashed the spine?

Not this time.

Light swept across the water from beyond the barges and a small motor launch angled out into the canal, putting upstream against the current. A blue light gleamed on top of the half cabin.

Stefan smothered an exclamation. "Don't move, ass-hole," he hissed as the searchlight raked the oily swell of the canal. But the warning came too late. Bolan had already moved.

Knowing the killer wouldn't fire while the lawmen on the police launch were within earshot, he hurled himself backward, cannoning into the guy's legs. The watchman went down, his arm swinging wildly as he clubbed with the butt of the revolver. But Bolan took the blows on his arm and shoulder, springing up and haring for the nearest stack of wrecks while Stefan was still thrashing in the mud.

By the time the searchlight had faded and the launch had chugged away upstream, Bolan had dragged himself, panting, among the smashed vehicles in the stack. He was seven feet off the ground, crouched on the floor of a gutted sedan whose ragged upholstery stank of mildew and decay.

He strained his eyes to pierce the semidarkness: the flickering radiance from the blast furnace across the water didn't provide enough light to show anything in detail. But he could see the watchman. He stood in the alley between the stacks, the barrel of his revolver questing right and left.

Bolan felt something hard by his knee. His fingers located the object. It was heavy—a rusty spring shackle from some outsized vehicle. He hefted it experimentally in his hand.

Many of the skeletons in the mechanical graveyard were precariously balanced on the stack: the slightest move could provoke an avalanche of steel. Bolan lobbed the shackle through the glassless window. He heard a sudden clatter, a shifting of metal lower down the stack on the side nearest the canal. The revolver in Stefan's hand roared twice and spit flame. More ironwork fell someplace within the stack.

The guy walked forward slowly, peering into the tangle of wrecks. In the silence Bolan heard a shunting locomotive puffing in a nearby marshaling yard, clattering a line of boxcars into a siding. He looked around for something else to throw.

His searching hand found shreds of upholstery, cotton waste, a twist of corroded wire too light to carry. He eased the Beretta from its holster and sprung the magazine. Carefully he pried away the top three shells from the 20-round charger and threw them as far as he could. Tinkling, jangling, they dropped down through the complex of metal.

The watchman spun around and fired two shots, almost as a reflex action. A ricochet whined past the sedan. Something heavy—a wheel? a seat? a detached fender?—displaced itself in the center of the stack. The sound could have been made by a man losing his balance, sliding, falling.

For the fifth time the flat detonation of a heavy-caliber revolver shot was batted from side to side between the wreckage.

One round left in the cylinder.

"Come out, you bastard, before I spill gasoline over the stack and fry you," the watchman rasped.

It was time for the Executioner to make his play. The gasoline threat didn't bother him, but if he didn't step up to bat now, the gunner might take time out to reload.

He stood up on the running board of the ancient, doorless sedan, the Beretta in his right hand, his left arm hooked around the car's windshield pillar.

"Up here, pal!" he called.

The watchman swiveled on his heel, leveled the heavy gun and fired all in one precise movement. The concussion of the .45-caliber round was overlaid by the sharp whip crack of the Beretta in 3-shot mode.

Bolan snatched his arm, smarting like hell, away from the windshield pillar: the slug, missing his wrist by a fraction of an inch, had sliced through his sleeve.

His own three shots drilled the watchman through the chest and hammered him backward into the mud; three dwindling streams of scarlet pulsed from his lifeless body. Bolan dragged him back to the hut, locked the door and returned to the Mercedes.

He now knew two things about the escape organization: he was wise to the junkyard connection, and knew that a member of the gang—a member important enough to order a killing—was called Bart. Plus he was on his way to see a man who had a regular lead. He started the engine and drove south toward Switzerland.

13

Imre Sujic scored nine out of ten in Bolan's book right from
the start. The Czech colonel was no buck passer: he made
his own decisions, acted upon them and was prepared to
defend those actions. And he wasted no time on nonessen-
tials. He was a professional.

There was no hesitation in his approach to the Executioner. Clearly he had studied photographs, for he strode
across the lobby of the Geneva hotel with outstretched hand,
as though he were greeting an old friend.

Maybe that wasn't all that remarkable, Bolan thought ten
minutes later, studying in his turn the mug shot of the Czech
killer he was to impersonate. It was uncanny.

"Impressive, no?" Sujic said, glancing from Bolan to the
photo and then back again. "The features are not identical, of course. That would be too much to ask. But they
have the same cast, a similar—you will forgive me, Per Bolan?—a similar ruthlessness and determination. What is
perhaps more important, the height, build and quality of
voice match perfectly. Once the hair is altered and you remember to limp a little on the right foot, you could fool even
the wardens in the jail he escaped from."

"It's the voice, the language, that bothers me the most,"
Bolan said.

"Under the circumstances, this is not important. Zoltan
Cernic was a crude man, a thug with little education and no

culture. He spoke little, and then in a kind of growl. He was excessively ill-humored. Cernic came from a peasant area in the Carpathians, the part of the country nearest the Soviet Union. Any…inadequacies…on your part will be put down by the citified characters in the Prague underworld as due to this rustic background.''

"And you have the complete lowdown on his habits?''

"Certainly. His hideout was in the old part of the city. Nobody knows he was killed except the SNB—the state security police—and my own department. We know where he bought his food, where he drank, what time he went out, everything. We even know where the loot from his robberies is hidden, for we had him under surveillance for some time. If we introduce you into the neighborhood secretly, at night, and you make it to the attic he rented right away, nobody will know he ever left it.''

"You figure that if I lie up there awhile, let certain people know I'd like assisted passage out of town, and that I can pay for it, then the guys who run the network will show up and make me an offer?''

"I should rate it probable rather than possible,'' Sujic said.

Bolan grinned. "Let's give it a try.''

A few hours later, his hair shaved back into a widow's peak and died a flaming red, his right shoe equipped with a protuberance that made it impossible not to limp, the warrior sat next to Sujic in a Tupolev jetliner, fastening his belt as they circled to land at a military airfield near the capital.

They were met far out on the perimeter track by a Tatra staff car, which drove them recklessly through blinding rain to a command post trailer parked in woods between the field and the city. Here the Executioner was provided with clothes typical of the region: wool socks, a coarse gray turtleneck

sweater and wide flannel pants with deep cuffs. Then they
set off for Prague.

They crossed the Vitava river by the Şverma Bridge, narrowly missed a late streetcar at the Na Příkopé intersection
and swung into Wenceslas Square. The main drag glittered
with light, from the intersection to the statue of Wenceslas
on his iron horse, but there were very few people about.
Soon the Tatra turned and threaded its way back toward the
river among the narrow, cobbled streets of the old town.

Sujic stopped the car halfway down a twisting lane that
led into a small square. The tall medieval houses around
them were shuttered and silent, but light from a single
streetlamp splashed lozenges of silver onto the ancient
stones through the branches of a linden tree in the center of
the square. More light streamed across the sidewalk from
the open door of a nearby tavern. The braying wheeze of an
accordion surged from time to time over the sound of blar-
ing voices.

Colonel Sujic leaned forward and opened the door of the
staff car. "Very well, my friend," he said quietly, "now it
is up to you. You know where to go. You know what to do.
Just remember that the real Cernic is known to the people
of this neighborhood simply as 'Milo.' And do not forget the
limp."

"With this lump in my shoe? You must be joking." He
got out of the car.

"As we agreed," Sujic continued, "there is too much risk
attached to any liaison between you and the SNB or myself.
If you are contacted, therefore, allow yourself to be smuggled out of the country...and then check out the best way
to eliminate the organization with your Mr. Brognola. The
only thing that interests us, after all, is the destruction of the
network. How this is done, we leave to you."

"And if I'm not contacted?"

"I am sure, Per Bolan, that it would not be the first time you crossed a frontier without papers," the Czech said suavely. "Or the first time you omitted to present yourself to the border guards."

Bolan nodded. As he melted into the shadows, the door of the Tatra clicked shut and the colonel called softly, "Good luck!" The car turned and whined away down an even narrower street, leaving the warrior alone with his new identity.

Much of the flight from Geneva had been spent, with Sujic's help, in memorizing a detailed street map of the area and learning the position of the few stores Cernic patronized. It was no problem, therefore, finding the right route, and Bolan—once the snarl of the Tetra's exhaust had been swallowed up in the distant rumble of the city—emerged from the darkness and headed for the square.

The stairs that led to the attic where Cernic had been living were on the far side of the square beyond the tavern, a bar in which the escaped con passed an hour or two at the beginning of every evening. As Bolan limped past, two men reeled out of the open door and hailed him.

"Hey, Milo!" one called. "Where the hell have you been? Haven't seen you around for days. What have you got up in that eagle's nest of yours—a dancer from the opera?"

"Yeah, how's life, you old soak?" the other guffawed.

Okay, the Executioner thought. You passed muster on the visual. But how will you make out with the words? You don't have a clue how this character articulated: all you know is that he spoke in kind of a growl.

"Life?" he repeated in the surliest voice he could manage. "None the better for your asking. It'd be a damned sight better if I could get out of this hole and finish with the likes of you." He spit scornfully on the cobblestones and stumped on toward the alley leading to his stairway.

It seemed, for the moment, that he'd made it. Then there was a burst of laughter behind him. "Who was that?" a woman's voice asked. Bolan glanced over his shoulder. She was standing in the doorway of the tavern, a slender silhouette against the smoke-filled interior: young, blond, wearing an unbuttoned trench coat.

"That?" one of the drunks echoed. "Ol' Milo, the mos' bad-tempered guy in town. What a character! Never been known to smile."

"I don't see that's anything to boast about," the woman objected. "Who is this boor, anyway?"

"Oh, some hick from the east," the first man said, tiring of the subject. "A rube. Comes from Košice in Slovakia. What the hell...it's time for another drink."

"He doesn't look like a countryman."

"Forget him," the second man said. "He probably worked in the bauxite mines or something. Come *on*, Nagy, move your ass."

"If you ask me, he looks more like a crook. He probably came here to escape the police—"

"Then he's safe here, ain't he?" the first drunk interrupted. "For you don't catch *them* down here often. They'd rather wait until we make it to the bright lights and put the arm on us then."

"Well, if you ask me..." the woman started again. But the rest of the sentence was lost in a fresh burst of laughter, mixed with drunken singing, as more patrons of the tavern spilled out into the square. Somewhere beyond the linden tree, a window frame squeaked open and a voice called angrily for quiet.

Bolan limped on. Beyond the forced gaiety of the square, darkness and silence closed in on him. The rain, which had stopped falling while the Tatra was navigating the city center, started again. Down the alley, turn left across the courtyard and go through the arch. Walk up three stone steps and take the second cul-de-sac on the right... There it all was, exactly as the colonel had described it.

The old buildings leaned together across the passageway, so that from the leaded windows of one projecting top story to the peeling shutters of the one opposite, the gap was narrow enough for a man to jump. Ancient, bowed beams cradled tile, brick and crumbling plaster. At the corner, a turret with a conical slate roof was etched against the night sky by light from a lamp set in the stonework of the arch. And ahead, zigzagging up the wall blanking off the end of the alley, a wooden staircase led to a door beneath a sagging dormer. Behind it was Zoltan Cernic's hideout.

Bolan climbed the stairway and thrust the iron key he had been given into the lock. It turned silently, and the door swung open. He felt inside for the cracked porcelain cover of a light switch. The feeble illumination from a single forty-watt lamp showed him a large room with a varnished pine floor, a bed, a table and two wicker chairs, one on each side of a dark mahogany closet. Cans of soup, dried food in packets and a bottle of milk that had gone sour jostled for position on top of a cheap trunk.

Bolan crossed to a small window beneath the sloping ceiling, opened the shutters and leaned out into the dark. Rain pelted down on the chaos of roofs, gurgling in the gutters and misting a distant curve of lights that marked the embankment by the river. But the air was fresh, cold and tingling. In a few minutes the musty, stale atmosphere in the room had dispersed.

In his role as the escaped con in hiding, Bolan had no papers, no firearms, and no clothes other than the shabby garments he was wearing. He had decided against carrying a gun because, if it was seen by anyone who knew Cernic—and knew where he had come from—his cover would have been blown at once. The only weapon he had permitted himself was the small throwing knife, which was strapped to the inside of his left ankle.

The room had a skylight, and through its grimy glass an agile man could reach a slant of massive curled shingles beneath which was hidden the equivalent of three hundred and ninety thousand dollars.

With these two rather differing assets as the only entries on the credit side of the ledger, the Executioner installed himself in his hideout and settled down to wait.

14

It rained incessantly in Prague for two days. It was raining all over Europe, but the downpour was heavier, more relentless, and seemed somehow even wetter in the Czech capital.

Mack Bolan sat in Cernic's attic room, listening to the ceaseless drumming on the roof and wondering if the damp was penetrating beneath the shingles and damaging the hoard of bills. He had been told not to touch the cache until he was contacted by the escape organization, then he could take enough to pay for the ride and leave the Czech security forces to recuperate the rest.

Each morning he took a raincoat from a hook behind the door and battled his way through the deluge to a general store on a corner in the lane below, where he bought beer, black bread and *parkys*—the succulent local sausages that he cooked on a battered electric ring that was the attic's sole means of heating. In the evening he went to the tavern on the square and, as Cernic would have, drank steadily, speaking to nobody in particular and keeping his general remarks surly and pessimistic.

Presenting a tough, villainous and boorish facade was the most difficult part of the operation for Bolan, who—except in his dealings with the savages of the world—was usually a mild-mannered guy. Indeed, in Nam he had been dubbed Sergeant Mercy because of his compassion for civilians caught up in the horrors of war.

The first time he went into the store, the owner—a stout red-faced man in round spectacles—called out, "Ha! So you made it back again! What happened to you yesterday and the day before? We were scared you'd been run over or something."

Bolan took the cue. "What has it to do with you where I was?" he shouted. "You should learn to mind your business, friend. And your business is selling people what they want, with no questions asked. *My* business is…well, that's my business."

"All right, all right," the storekeeper said hastily. "No need to bite a man's head off. I was just passing the time of day."

"Well, don't pass it prying into other people's affairs," Bolan growled. Then, since it might be wise to account for Cernic's two-day "absence," he added, "I was laid up with a dose of influenza, if you must know."

He told the same story to the proprietor of the tavern. "This bloody climate," he said, scowling. "I wish the hell I could get out of here. Your damn dirty city air—it fouls up the lungs of a man used to the country. Now in Slovakia, where I come from…"

It wasn't a bad idea, Bolan reckoned, to answer questions before they were asked—and the storekeeper's crack about being run over had come scarily close to the truth.

Bolan had been told that Zoltan Cernic always sat in a particular corner of the tavern, and he conscientiously carried his drink over to that seat each evening. But however gruff and unapproachable he was, there was always one thing he couldn't guard against: the arrival of an intimate friend whom he might not know he should recognize and welcome. As it happened, however, his first real test related to an adversary rather than a friend.

While he was at the bar ordering his second drink, someone took his seat. He turned around to see a large mustached man with ham-sized fists sitting at his table, nursing a tankard of beer.

Judging from the baggy pants and peaked cap, the man was some kind of manual laborer. Bolan had no doubt he had taken the seat quite innocently and had no idea it had been occupied. But he realized from the suppressed giggles and covert winks all around that Cernic would be expected to react. A sudden silence fell as he stamped across, set his shallow glass of apricot-colored *baracz* on an adjacent table and stood staring belligerently at the man. "I think you're mistaken, friend," he said in an unfriendly voice. "That's my table."

The big man looked up. "*Your* table? You bought the place, maybe?"

"I was sitting there." Bolan jerked a thumb over his shoulder. "Now beat it."

"Well, *I'm* sitting here now," the workman said shortly. He tugged a creased newspaper from his pocket, unfolded it and began ostentatiously to read.

Scowling ferociously, Bolan snatched the paper away and hurled it to the floor. "I said that's my seat. Out."

The man half rose threateningly. "What the hell do you think you're doing?" he yelled. "I've a good mind to—"

He broke off as the Executioner swept his tankard from the table with a crash. He drew a deep breath and erupted into action, trying to overturn the table onto the warrior.

Bolan slammed it down on its legs again, pinning the man behind it. The workman was a giant, half a head taller than Bolan and rugged. The warrior would have no problem taking him, but Cernic's reputation as a tough was almost

certainly based on straight roughhousing and fistfights, so
Bolan would have to hold back on the martial arts he knew
so well. In the split second his opponent was frozen against
the wall, he decided to try to cripple him with a single sharp
blow…and then add some fancy punches afterward for the
benefit of the gallery. And of his cover.

Leaning forward swiftly, he seized the man by the collar
and jerked him facedown across the tabletop. Then, before
the man could recover, he linked his hands and brought
them hurtling down on the unprotected neck. The fight was
effectively over at that moment: the man's reflexes were
paralyzed. But the window dressing had to be put on for the
customers.

Bolan growled with simulated rage, threw aside the table
and thrust the guy up against the wall. Steadying him with
one hand, Bolan drove three blows into the pit of his stom-
ach, allowed the guy to slide to the floor and finally helped
him on his way with a couple of contemptuous rabbit
punches. The man was out before he hit the ground.

Abruptly the place was loud with chatter again. The
owner stood the table upright, dusted it down and brought
Bolan another drink. Waiters dragged the unconscious man
outside. Bolan sat down and stared morosely into his glass.

The clientele was a rough bunch. Among them were the
two drunks who had accosted him the night he had arrived.
Several times he saw the blond woman who had been with
them staring at him covertly. But the majority seemed to be
the Czech equivalent of small-time grafters. There wasn't
the opportunity for organized crime here the way there
would be in a Western city, but such criminals and black
markets as there were, he guessed, hung out around this
quarter and this particular bar.

He was proved right sooner than he expected.

There were four of them. They sidled out from behind the
archway as he left the courtyard and made it toward the cul-
de-sac that led to his room.

They closed in before he could react, one on each side to
pinion his arms, one behind to close a viselike grip on his
neck, the last one in front to lead the way to the rickety
wooden staircase that climbed to the attic. For an instant
Bolan toyed with the idea of fighting back, but the man with
the grip on his neck produced a gun and rammed the muzzle against his spine. "What's going on?" he demanded.
"You guys buddies of that man I busted in the tavern?"

"You know better than that, Cernic," the man on his
right said.

"What's with this Cernic? My name's Milo. Anyone will
tell you that. You guys are making a mistake."

"No mistake," the man in front said. "And no talking.
Until we get you inside, and then you'll talk plenty. Because we're going to get that loot before we leave."

"Loot? What loot? I don't know what you're talking
about. I tell you I—"

"Shut up."

"But you got me wrong. I don't know—" Bolan broke
off with a gasp as the point of the front man's elbow drove
backward into his belly.

Inside the attic he got a good look at his captors. They
looked the way small-time chiselers look the world over—rat
faces, mean little eyes, cheap suits. The leader, with red-
rimmed eyes and pig-bristle hair, looked like a failed prize-
fighter.

Bolan didn't believe for a moment that they had anything to do with the escape organization he wanted to contact. They weren't intelligent enough. He figured them for
hustlers who had somehow gotten wise to the real Cernic's
identity and determined to carve themselves a piece of the

action. He knew he would have to deal with them fast if the evening wasn't to go sour on him. These guys meant business.

He ran quickly over the options as Pig-bristle looked around the shabby room. The two flankers still held his arms. The man with the gun—it looked like a Walther PPK—stood with his back leaning against the door. The gun was held loosely, the barrel pointing at a spot on the floor halfway between the gunner and Bolan. The guy looked as if he knew how to use it.

Should he fake cowardice, pretend he was caving in and start blabbing in an attempt to stall and have them relax their vigilance? No way. He was known, both as Cernic and as Milo, as a hard man, too tough for that kind of behavior to ring true. Should he continue denying there was a connection between Milo and Cernic? Negative. They were well informed, maybe they knew the bank robber by sight, they wouldn't believe him anyway. And, hell, the whole aim of this Prague stakeout was to convince people that he *was* Zoltan Cernic.

"Keep him covered," Pig-bristle said to the man with the Walther, "while we tear this rat's nest apart." He turned to Bolan. "Unless you want to save us a lot of time and yourself a heap of trouble and strife."

"The dialogue's threadbare," Bolan said. "You want to change the disk." And then, contriving a crafty note: "Suppose, just suppose, I was this character you think I am—Cernic, did you say—and just suppose I did know something about some kind of loot, what did you have in mind?"

"Tell us where the stuff's hidden, and you get to keep twenty percent. We take the eighty. After all, there's four of us and only one of you," Pig-bristle said. "But if we have to beat the shit outta you to learn the secret, you get nothing. Take my tip, Cernic. Get smart and take the twenty.''

Yeah, Bolan thought. And a bullet in the back as soon as the money is uncovered.

Aloud, he said, ''The terms don't interest me. *I* take the eighty. But it's worth twenty percent to get you guys off my back.''

The hood gritted his teeth. ''Okay, if you want it the hard way.'' He opened the door of the cupboard where Bolan's meager food supply was stored. ''Mischa and me will get started. You two strip the son of a bitch and tie him up.''

One of the thugs pinioning the Executioner stepped forward. He wrenched the cupboard away from the wall and threw it to the floor, scattering the supplies over the floor. He began ripping away the flimsy wood panels at the back while Pig-bristle took a short jimmy from his pocket and pried up a floorboard near the wall.

The gunman moved away from the door and the fourth man relaxed his grip on Bolan's arm. ''Okay, drop your pants,'' he growled.

Bolan unbuckled his belt, unbuttoned the fly and pushed the thick woolen pants to his ankles.

''All right—step out of them,'' the man with the Walther ordered.

They were the last words he uttered.

Bolan straightened as he kicked one leg free, the short, squat throwing knife that had been strapped to his ankle in one hand. Before he was fully upright the razor-sharp blade was buried in the gunman's throat.

The guy choked, gurgling blood as he fell. His hands spasmed open, flying instinctively toward his savaged neck. Bolan hurled aside the fourth man and dived for the Walther, fielding it before it hit the floor.

He whirled toward the smashed cupboard, pumping out
two rounds at Pig-bristle, whose hand had flashed between
the lapels of his jacket. Both 9 mm flesh-shredders scored—
one drilled the back of the guy's hand, riveting it to his rib
cage, the other smashed through the heart, bursting out
through a shattered shoulder blade. Pig-bristle spiraled to
the floor, spewing scarlet.

Bolan staggered sideways as the fourth man cannoned
into him, seizing his gun arm in both hands and forcing it up
toward the ceiling. The Walther spit flame again; a third slug
plowed through the rafters. Then the Executioner twisted
violently sideways, throwing the thug off balance. A knee
zeroed in on the guy's crotch, folding him forward. But he
still had a hold on Bolan's gun arm, pumping it up and
down with a nerve hold on the wrist, so that the automatic
flew from the warrior's fingers and skittered beneath the
trundle bed.

For an instant the adversaries seesawed back and forth,
then Bolan kicked the guy's feet from under him and they
went down with a crash that shook the room. Bolan rolled,
freeing his arm to wedge the palm of his hand beneath his
attacker's chin. The hood fought furiously to keep the warrior's other hand from circling behind his head. But Bolan
was bigger, stronger and in better shape. Inexorably he began to exercise pressure.

The thug writhed beneath him, uttering unintelligible
cries. His fists pummeled, scratched, gouged uselessly. Then
there was a terrible, dull snapping noise and he went limp.

Bolan thrust away the body with its lolling head and up-
turned eyes, and clambered to his feet. He was panting.
Mischa stood by the ruin of the cupboard, trembling with
terror, his mouth open and his eyes wide.

"All right," Bolan said, jerking his head at the door. "get out of here. And remember—if I ever see you again, you're dead."

Mischa's forehead was dewed with sweat. He gabbled some reply and bolted. Bolan heard his panicked footsteps clatter down the staircase and out across the cobbled courtyard.

He wasn't worried about repercussions. Not in this quarter. And leaving the surviving thug free to run wasn't a bad idea: it would bolster Milo-Cernic's reputation as a hard man, once the guy started talking. Word would get around. And if the people running the escape network hadn't heard of him before, they would now.

Bolan maneuvered the two men he had shot through the skylight and down a slanted roof. They dropped seventy feet onto a stone stairway that led up from a different street. He pushed the man with the broken neck over the rail of the wooden stairs outside his own door. Too bad he missed his way in the rain.

The fight had created a lot of noise, but there was no reaction from either side or below. The lower floors of Cernic's old house were entered from the stone stairway where the bodies dropped, and the buildings flanking it were used as offices and stores. Bolan locked his door and went to sleep.

When he awoke he realized he could no longer hear the rain on the roof. He threw the shutters wide and looked out on a different city. The downpour hadn't been over long, but the sky was now an impeccable blue and pale sunshine sparkled from a million droplets of moisture beading the chaos of roofs, gutters and chimneys outside the window. In the narrow streets of the quarter shopkeepers and their customers wore cheerful smiles, and several food stores displayed crates and baskets of fruit and vegetables on the sidewalk. There was no sign of the body beneath the wooden staircase, or the dead thugs on the stone steps six floors below Bolan's skylight.

He felt justified in making a break with tradition: he went to the tavern at midday, passing off ribald references to this lapse with a snarl a little less surly than usual. The blonde wearing the trench coat—her name, he had discovered, was Mariella—even favored him with a half smile when he came in, and the proprietor was quite cordial.

"Better, isn't it?" he asked, taking Bolan's order. "Makes the world a happier place, I always say, when there's sun around."

"For those that have time to notice," Bolan replied sullenly. "Me, I wish I was a thousand miles away."

"Why, comrade? It's not such a bad city. At least there's life here."

"Life? I'd give a lot to get out of it, life or no life. And I mean right out. The place stinks. All I want—"

"Well, if you hate it so much," the proprietor interrupted reasonably, "why don't you *get* out? There doesn't seem to be anything to keep you here. You've no job, no family—"

"You mind your own damned business," Bolan shouted, thumping the bar. "It's got nothing to do with you why I stay here. What I do is my own affair, and I don't want any interfering snoopers meddling." He drained his glass and walked out, leaving the man staring.

Anyone at the bar who didn't suspect by now that "Milo" was a criminal on the run, the Executioner thought grimly, had to be pretty dense.

That evening he returned to the tavern and took his usual table, but he affected anger and kept more than ever to himself. In any case there was none of the customary "Hey there, Milo!" routine. He wondered if word about the fight had gotten around. If so, the sooner the contact he expected was made the better; otherwise he might have awkward police questions to parry.

It was several hours after he had returned to the attic that the soft knocking on the door penetrated his consciousness. He got out of bed, drew on his pants and opened it a crack. In the light of a half moon he saw a woman standing at the top of the stairway.

She wore an open trench coat, and the moonlight glinted on her pale hair.

It was Mariella.

"What do *you* want? What the hell's the idea, waking me at this time of night?" Bolan snapped ungraciously.

"Let me in," the woman whispered. "I have something to say to you. It's important... Oh, come *on*. The longer I stand here, the more likely someone is to notice."

Grumbling and growling, the Executioner opened the door wide and stood aside to let her pass. Once she was inside, he closed it and turned the key before switching on the light. Mariella, pushing thirty, was thin-faced and had large gray eyes.

"You're Zoltan Cernic, aren't you?" she asked.

"Zoltan who? Never heard of him." Bolan didn't ask her to sit down.

"Look, don't waste time denying it. I *know* you are Cernic."

"I tell you I never heard—"

"Oh, forget it, then! You're not Cernic. But you keep on beefing, saying how much you want to get away from here, don't you? Obviously you're on the run, or you would just go, right?"

Bolan ran his tongue over his lips. "Supposing I was on the run?"

"If you wanted out of the city unseen, without the risk of identity checks, with no chance of being asked for papers, if you wanted to get out of the country even..."

"Well?"

"Well, I think—if you have money—I think I know someone who can arrange it for you."

15

At ten-thirty the following evening Bolan stood on a corner of Wenceslas Square and watched the crowds thronging the wide sidewalks beneath the trees. Glittering with lights, bordered by stalls selling hot *parkys*, the square pulsed with the gleam of fast-moving traffic. In a few minutes the Executioner would have to act, but for the moment he was content to stare and take in the scene. There was no telling when he might have to return to Prague on some other mission.

He had argued and protested the previous night for a credible amount of time before permitting himself to be persuaded to talk seriously. He had guarded his suspicion and hostility until the last possible moment. But finally he had given in and allowed the woman to make her proposition.

After blustering and bargaining for an hour, he had at last agreed to pay what he considered privately to be an incredible sum for the privilege of being secretly transported to Zurich, Switzerland.

Mariella had refused to provide any details regarding how this was to be done. She had merely told him that the organization was known well enough to need no references. And she had made a rendezvous for the following night and told him to bring the cash with him.

Since then, he had made it onto the roof again and removed the correct amount from the hoard beneath the
shingles. He had also—in case the network was keeping him
under surveillance—pretended to take the balance and mail
it to himself in Zurich. But the three bulky envelopes had in
fact been stuffed with newspaper. The police would no
doubt, as arranged, collect what remained and return it to
its rightful owners.

The police, too, he was sure, would be keeping him under surveillance. But it would be just for the record . . . and
in any case, when the cards were finally on the table, they
could hardly have acted against the woman and her accom-
plices for transporting a citizen of the United States from
Prague to Zurich!

Clutching a cheap document case to his chest, Bolan
stood among the crowds, watching the minute hand of the
huge clock beneath the domed tower of a building across the
street. When it moved to 10:35, he shifted the document
case to his left hand and walked fifty yards up the hill to
where the streetcar lines forked into double tracks. He
crossed to a traffic island and stood as if waiting for a
streetcar.

At 10:37 precisely a car—a Skoda Octavia in anonymous
beige—stopped beside him. A door opened, and Bolan
climbed into the passenger seat.

Mariella was driving, her slender hands and feet expert
about the controls as she whisked the car in and out of the
traffic clogging the great square. "Where are we going?"
Bolan asked suspiciously. "Surely we can't drive out of town
openly like this? There are too many cops around. We could
be asked for our papers anytime . . . and my face is known."

"Relax," the woman replied. "It's all under control. But
it is best to start with a short car ride, in case anyone is fol-

lowing. We have a rendezvous not far from where you were staying."

"Then why the hell drag me all the way to Wenceslas Square when we could have—"

"I told you to relax." Mariella sighed.

She turned toward the Charles Bridge and then right along the embankment. Soon she doubled back, drove into the old town and stopped by the long, blank wall of a warehouse. The building had once perhaps been some civic center, for there were turrets at each end and the high wooden gates were enclosed by an ornamental arch. "See," Mariella said, "we are beside the repository you see from your window. The entrance to the lower floors of your building is just around the corner."

She pointed to the archway. "And there is where you have to go now. There is a small pass door in the left-hand gate. Soon, the night watchman leaves to fetch his beer. After he has gone, go through the pass door. It has been…arranged that it will be open."

"And then?" Bolan kept a tinge of suspicion in his voice.

"Inside there is much furniture, stored on all the floors. But there is also a loading bay with a big Tatra semi and trailer. They are already packed full. Get into the semi—not the trailer—and squeeze as far forward as you can. Right at the front you will find a clothes closet, facing away from the rear doors. You climb into this—it will be quite comfortable, with rugs and pillows—and you wait."

"For how long? I don't like vague arrangements like—"

"Me, neither. But here we have no choice. There are, as you say, many police. And you are very much wanted. Besides, the people arranging this may make good business out of it, but they must also take risks. So they have the right to state the terms. You understand me?"

"Very well, very well," Bolan growled. "But I still don't like it."

"Now," Mariella said briskly, "we must act. See, the watchman is leaving to visit the tavern." She waited until an elderly man wearing coveralls had walked from the gates to the corner, and then vanished, before she continued, "You have the money with you? So. Good... No, no. Keep it. They will ask for it when it is time. You may go now, quickly, while the man is away."

Her long face creased into a smile and for a moment, in the lamplight, she looked quite beautiful. "Perhaps I will say one thing more," she added. "I wish you luck." She leaned across and opened the passenger door.

"It's a damned nuisance, not knowing how long," Bolan muttered under his breath. He got out of the car and limped off along the sidewalk, the document case still clutched to his chest, without a backward glance.

The pass door, as Mariella had promised, was unlocked. As he stepped through, he heard the Skoda's engine start, and then the whine of gears as Mariella turned the vehicle in the narrow street and drove back the way they had come.

Inside the warehouse, a light burned behind the glass windows of a hutch where the watchman obviously sat between his rounds. Sausage, black bread and pickles were laid out on a newspaper, awaiting the arrival of the beer. Off to one side, a low-power electric lamp hung above the platform at the rear of a loading bay. Otherwise the huge furniture warehouse was in darkness.

The truck and its trailer looked enormous—two leviathans of the road silhouetted against the sheeted stacks bulked in the dark. Bolan paused to listen. Very distantly he could hear the sounds of the city—a roar of far-off traffic, shouts and a snatch of music from another street, a siren on the river, bells. But nearer at hand there was nothing—no footsteps, no demanding voice, just a scuffle and a squeak as a rat scurried away down one of the aisles...and the thin, high singing of silence in a large space.

Satisfied, the Executioner walked to the rear of the semi. The double doors were ajar. Pulling one open, he climbed into the interior and edged his way between chairs, tables and crates exuding straw toward the front of the vehicle. The closet was deep and wide. He made himself a kind of nest in the dark and settled down to wait.

Ten minutes later he heard faint sounds, suggesting the watchman had returned. Later still—a church clock somewhere had just chimed midnight—voices echoed under the high roof of the loading bay. The doors at the rear of the semi were opened and then slammed shut. Retaining bars dropped into place.

Bolan was reminded of his forced journey in the old two-tonner driven by the guy with the jutting chin. He hoped the man wouldn't be part of the team on this run: that would be the ultimate test of his disguise.

There was a clatter of mechanical activity as the Tatra diesel whined and then coughed to life. Then, after the body of the semi began to vibrate as its engine settled into its normal idling speed, the vehicle jerked into motion and rolled out of the warehouse into the night.

It was no sweat for Bolan to distinguish between cobblestones and asphalt; between city blacktop with streetcar lines and country byways with potholes; between the paved surfaces of city and suburb. But he soon lost all sense of direction and stopped trying to work out which compass point they were heading for. After a while, in the darkness, the monotonous rhythms of the semi and its trailer lulled him to sleep.

Sometime later he was awakened by a bright light shining in his eyes. He struggled to sit up in his nest of pillows.

"Ah, so it's you all right," a gravelly voice pronounced. "You better come outta there. We switch horses here, and we have business to transact, too."

Bolan knuckled the sleep from his eyes and followed the guy with the flashlight past the stacked furniture and out into the dark. The night air was cold and moist, but it wasn't raining. The semi and its trailer were drawn up beneath a canopy of trees at a turnpike rest area.

But as soon as they were standing on solid ground, the warrior's guide rapped twice on the panels and the starter whirred. The engine growled, the headlights were switched on and the double juggernaut lumbered back onto the road and disappeared down the tunnel of light that it carved out of the dark.

Bolan stared around him. The half moon showed him hills on every side, most of them heavily wooded. A pale ribbon of road twisted down into a valley, where water gleamed by a bridge.

The man with the flashlight was short, stocky, a powerful figure wearing overalls and a peaked cap. His face, half seen in the reflected light, was seamed and wrinkled and, as Bolan had feared, it was marked by a pugnaciously jutting chin.

For the moment, however, there was no cause for alarm. The man who led with his chin was expecting to see a Czech fugitive, an ill-tempered man with close-cropped red hair. He saw a character eager to quit Prague, who had close-cropped red hair, and Bolan was quick to pile on the boorish bit. There was no particular reason, after all, to connect this tall man on the run with another tall man, a dark man, who had been making himself a nuisance asking questions in another country.

"What's going on?" Bolan asked suspiciously. "Where are we? Why did we stop? Why the hell did the truck go on without us?"

"We are not far from Çeský Krumlov," the hoarse voice told him. "Southwest of Çeské Budĕjovice. We bypassed the town. That's the Vltava you see down there in the valley."

"How far to the border?" Bolan demanded, looking at his watch. He had slept nearly three hours.

"Less than twenty miles. Then it is only about the same distance again to Linz, Austria."

Bolan figured it was time to seed in more character. "That's all very well, friend," he grated. "But how the devil are we to get there now that you've sent the transport away? Just what the hell are you playing at?" He hugged the document case to his chest and glared at the stocky man.

The guy laughed. "Keep your cool, comrade," he said. "I only paid for Jan and his truck to get you clear of the city. He has work to do. That's a genuine load that has to be delivered. He has to get back to Kralovice, beyond Plzeň, by daybreak."

"That's not my worry. Let him look after himself, whoever he is."

"He's looked after *you* well enough, friend. Do you think we could have gotten you past the three roadblocks between here and Prague without that regular load, complete with bills of lading and other papers, and an authentic moving truck?"

"I tell you, that's not my affair. What I'm paying you for—"

"Ah, yes," the man interrupted. "Paying. Speaking of which . . . let's have it." He held out a hand for the document case.

Bolan hesitated, then passed it over.

The stocky man counted the money carefully in the flashlight beam. Then, dividing it roughly into two, he stuffed one half in his pocket and put the other back into the case, which he handed to the Executioner. Bolan stared at him.

"Matter of faith," the guy explained. "We've always had a good reputation. Based on mutual trust. You don't seem too happy. Okay, to show you we're on the level I'm giving you half back. You can hand it over when we get you safely to Zurich. Right?"

Bolan nodded, reflecting with a wry smile that if by chance the man *was* treacherous and aimed to kill the client and keep the money, it didn't matter who held the money at the time of his death.

"Time we moved our asses," his guide was saying. "We cross the border at a very small frontier post, on a dirt road nobody ever heard of. There's only two night men on duty, and they'll be half asleep by now. I want to get there before they freshen up to meet the 6:00 a.m. relief."

"Yeah, but twenty miles—"

Placing a finger on his lips, the tough little man walked a few paces to one side and parted a screen of bushes in back of the rest area. Hidden by the leaves, a panel truck stood facing the highway. Bolan could just make out lettering on its sides that announced the name of a firm of electrical suppliers in Linz.

"They're used to seeing this heap go through," his guide said. "At this time of night? Piece of cake. They probably won't take a look in the back, but we took precautions just the same. Get a load of this."

He opened the rear doors. In the small delivery space were two half dismantled television sets, a few old-fashioned radios, a brand-new electric cooker and a huge refrigerator.

"The freezer is empty," the guy went on. "We took out all the shelves and like that. When we near the border, you better squeeze in there, just in case. I'll wise you up in plenty of time. Until then, you can sit where you like here in the back."

He handed Bolan into the truck and then, with a curt nod, slammed the doors, hurried around to the cab and started the engine. A moment later the truck bumped out onto the road and headed for the Austrian frontier.

In the black interior, Bolan made himself as comfortable as he could among the rattling, banging, bouncing items of electrical ware. The longer he could stay out of that refrigerator, the happier he would be.

16

His name was Bartolomeo Baracco, and he was Corsican. Bolan found out at once that he rated himself a very tough character indeed. Maybe he was right. But if he had a fault—and for the Executioner this was a plus point—it was that he found himself unable to resist telling anyone who would listen just how tough, tough was.

It was crazy, a compulsion to blab on the part of a key man in an organization that owed its success to the fact that nobody ever talked—and he had to be a key man because it was obvious that this was "Bart," the guy who had cold-bloodedly ordered the watchman at Montigny to liquidate Bolan. But whatever the reason, Bart craved an audience, and it suited the Executioner just fine to pin back his ears and take in everything that came his way.

They had plenty of opportunities to talk. The escape organization preferred to move its clients in short, sharp bursts, changing vehicles often and working mainly at night. Since abandoning the electrician's panel truck somewhere south of Linz, they had traveled in a dilapidated hearse, a cattle truck and a motor home that must have been at least twenty years old. Each time they switched, it was in a car junkyard, and that tied in with Bolan's theory of how the network functioned and why it worked so well.

He ran over in his mind all the points that had occurred to him in the Montigny scrapyard. The Minerva...the Paris garbage truck...the two-tonner he had escaped from...the wreck that had taken Secondini from Avallon to the air-field...the dump truck in Montigny...the transport they had used since Linz—every single vehicle in the escape chain except the genuine moving truck that had spirited him away from the Czech capital. All of them old, all of them fit only for the junkyard. Except that beneath the decrepit exterior they were mechanically sound.

There were two more points to consider: one, none of these trucks, vans or cars had ever been located; two, there were wreckers' yards every few miles along all the main trunk roads in Europe.

Yeah, it stacked up. What better place to conceal ancient vehicles than a junkyard? What was more anonymous than a wreck apparently heading for the scrap heap? What was more serviceable to the network than one of those wrecks with an engine tuned to showroom standard?

And if there were a chain of these yards spread across Europe, each with a doctored "Q-truck" waiting some-place among the write-offs...?

It would be a near-perfect blueprint for a clandestine transport service.

The client was picked up near the point of his escape and driven away in a wreck on wheels—but only as far as the nearest junkyard. There he was transferred to another jal-opy, indistinguishable, apart from the engine, from the beat-up carcasses surrounding it. And like that, from yard to yard, each time the organizers reckoned they were pushing their luck or wanted to switch for security reasons.

Bolan had to admit it was a smart idea. One wreck looked much like another, so who was going to notice the substi-tution in a car cemetery where there were hundreds of ve-hicles—especially if the men on the gates were in on the deal?

Right now, Bart and the Executioner were in a used-car lot behind a truck stop less than twenty miles from Salzburg. They were still only seventy miles from the Czech frontier, waiting for nightfall so that they could run a delivery truck out from the lot and make it to the next yard, in Innsbruck.

The little man with the big jaw had bought a newspaper at the truck stop. "They suspect you made a getaway from Prague. But Baracco is too smart for them—" the Corsican favored the braggart's third person, which was often used by monomaniacs "—and he has been cunning enough to get you this far without them once seeing you. But he has to be careful. From now on Baracco must use all his skills, for the paper says you are heading southwest and again it is suspected you will try to reach Switzerland. It is *suspected*!" He laughed contemptuously. "They will need more than suspicion to match the guile of Baracco!"

Bolan laughed, too. He elbowed open the door of the truck's cab and spit into the dusk. "I'd like to see the frontier guards who could stop *me* getting through once my mind was made up," he boasted.

"The question will not arise. Baracco has arranged it so that no guard will see you."

"You arrange things well. You seem to have a talent for it," Bolan observed. "But tell me. Such things cannot be arranged in a day. It takes time to organize. You could not do all this without planning. Even I could not. Tell me, how did you and your friends start this thing?"

He hoped the question would start the Corsican off on another ego trip, for he was becoming increasingly tired of playing the ruthless killer—a vainglorious, self-vaunting role it seemed essential to play if he was to command the little man's respect.

The ruse paid off. His eyes gleamed in the half-light. "To many," Baracco began, "I would say mind your business. But you are a man. You have done such things as a man might do. So I will tell you."

He leaned his head against the rear of the cab and went on. "I was born in a small village near Venaco, in the center of Corsica. My family was very poor. We never left the village. But once a year I was asked by the local curé to go with other kids to the coast to see the sea. We would climb into an old motorbus and go for the day to Aleria, to Folleli, or even perhaps to Corso, near the Capo Rosso. It was very beautiful. And all the time when I was a child I wanted nothing more than to be near the sea.

"I would have liked to have been a fisherman, or worked on the boats that went from Bastia and Ajaccio to Nice and Marseilles. But for folks like us that was impossible. You had to work on the land all the hours of daylight to get enough to eat. So, as a young man I became just another peasant in the mountains. But I never forgot the sea. Always in my heart I longed to live beside it, to see the sun rise over the horizon, to watch how the colors changed all day long, to listen to the fury of waves in wintertime. And then, when my parents died, I did go to the coast. But I could get no work.

"So I stowed away on a boat and I made it to Marseilles. But still there was no work for me on the sea—I had no experience, I did not know the right people. The best I could do was work as a mate on the *poids lourds*, the great transport trucks that hauled merchandise from the Marseilles docks to Paris and the north.

"I became a driver. I had my own trucks, and I made some money. I saved. But still I could not find what I wanted. It is not much, you would think, for a man to want.

I did not desire riches. All I wanted was a cottage from which I could regard the sea, a place to retire.

"But the sea has become a preserve of the rich. Every inch of coast—at least where the climate is acceptable—is parceled out. Each stone has its price, and the price is too high for people such as us. But I swore, just the same, that I would have my rich man's morsel one day. I would get my cottage on a cliff or die in the attempt."

Baracco stopped talking and stared out at the angular shapes of the old cars parked in the lot. "Three years ago," he went on slowly, "I found the piece of land I wanted. It was secluded. It was covered in olive trees. It looked out over the Mediterranean between Cannes and St. Raphael. There was already a cabin where I could live, but I could build more if I wished. It was, of course, expensive. Unbelievably expensive. I put down all the money I possessed, and that only bought me a twelve-month option.

"Then I realized that however hard I worked, even if I could persuade the owners to wait, it would take me years to raise enough to complete the purchase. So I decided to... find other means. If a man's work is not enough to bring him the small thing he wants out of life, then life must be manipulated in such a way that he is satisfied in an alternative fashion."

"You decided on your present occupation?"

The determined jaw swung toward Bolan like the prow of a ship. "It seemed right that Baracco's salvation should be through the salvation of others, the less fortunate ones such as I had been. Also, through my experience in transport, I had the means to carry it out."

"You weren't afraid of the law?"

"The law?" The Corsican spit scorn. "The law is an abstraction. Which side of the law you are on is a matter of chance. On the right side, you lie, cheat and steal and they call you a smart businessman. Do the same things on the wrong side and they call you an embezzler and put you behind bars. If you are on the right side and you kill, they give you medals. If, like yourself, you are on the wrong, they execute you or shut you up forever. Don't speak to me of the law."

Although there was a grain of truth in Bart's outburst, the Executioner was in total disagreement with his conclusion. Bolan wasn't a determinist: for him, the side of the law you were on was a matter of choice, not chance. And he rejected a moral relativist approach to life: for him, right and wrong, good and evil were absolutes. But he had to remember the role he was playing. It went against the grain, but he said, "Yeah, a curse on the law. Let a man take what he needs, and the hell with those who would try to stop him."

"In addition to that," Baracco rasped, ignoring the warrior's contribution, "they refused to renew the option at the end of the year. The property was sold to a famous attorney who was also a senator, a man with more money to spend than Baracco. Now the olive trees on my land have all been cut down and there is a flashy villa with a pool, a sauna, a Jacuzzi and a Cadillac in the garage." He thumped the wheel with his fist. "So much for the law."

"But you'll find another property?" Bolan prompted.

"Oh, sure. Two years have passed—fifteen months since I helped my first client. But if I keep up a flow of operations like yours, friend—" the Corsican glanced at Bolan's document case "—I could probably make enough to buy something similar in another three or four years."

"So long? At the prices you charge? You must have your eye on something exclusive!"

"I do. It would have been twenty years if I hadn't started in this business. But no sweat, friends. Nobody need worry on my account. If things go well in certain directions, Baracco will not even have to wait the three or four years."

"But you just said—"

"I said three or four years with clients like you. In the case of people paying more, much more, evidently it would take less."

"Impossible! Nobody would pay more than I have. No one!"

"No *one*, perhaps," Baracco said craftily. "But an organization might, an organization that was all-powerful."

"An organization?" Bolan echoed, trying to mask his excitement.

"Certainly. An organization with an interest in helping unfortunates on the wrong side of the law to avoid the spitefulness and malice of the bloody do-gooders. An organization that might have an interest in keeping contact with certain clients, making use of their special talents, progressing their careers instead of just removing them from danger temporarily. Such people would pay more."

Bolan scented pay dirt. Maybe, after all, Hal Brognola had been right. Deciding to take a risk, he played a hunch. "Might such an organization have connections with your Corsican friend Secondini?" he asked.

Baracco started. Through the darkness, his eyes gleamed suspiciously at the Executioner. "How the hell did you know about him?" he demanded.

"In our world," Bolan said, "good news travels faster than bad. There is much admiration, even in the East, for the way you got him out of Paris."

"It is deserved," the man conceded. "But what is this about connections?" His tone had become aggressive.

"Everyone knows that Secondini was associated with the Union Corse," Bolan said. "You mentioned an organization that was 'all-powerful,'—and, in my book, for Union

Corse you can read Mafia." He avoided carefully the direct question: was the Mob offering to take over the network and use it as a recruiting center as well as an illicit transport service?

He had read the Corsican well. For Baracco said, "It is…better not to speak of these things. And you don't want to bother yourself with such thoughts. A man like you—what need does a strong man have for others?"

"You are right," Bolan said. "But talking of others, what about your associates? Are you the boss of the organization? Or do you have to consult them before decisions are taken? What do they think of your money-making plans?"

He stopped. Beside him in the darkness of the cab there was a wheezing, rasping noise. Baracco was laughing.

Bolan waited.

"Why do you think, friend," the Corsican said at last between chuckles, "that the escape service has always been a hundred percent success? Why do you think there is not a single police force in Europe that knows one damned thing about it? How is it that there has never been a leak, never a hint of underworld gossip? How come nobody ever talked, nothing was ever given away, the organization was never penetrated?"

"You tell me."

"Because Baracco was too clever for them." He paused for effect. "Because there was never anybody *to* talk…because there is, in fact, *no* organization!" Baracco laughed once more. "The famous trans-Europe escape network is strictly a one-man show. And I am the man.…"

"But that's crazy!" Bolan exclaimed. "It's incredible."

"What do you mean—crazy?"

"You say a one-man show, but that's not possible. There may be nobody in the underworld to give away secrets, but people still talk. And even the little I know…" Bolan had to be wary of showing how much he knew. "Even the little I know involves many other people. The watchmen at the breakers' yards, the men who crewed the garbage truck in Paris, the driver of the furniture van. And there was talk of an escape that went wrong in Holland. Of a boatman, of sailors lost in a collision at sea..."

"I said there was no *organization*, as such. Baracco has no gang, no hired heavies to spill his secrets. I didn't say nobody ever helped him."

"Okay, but—"

"But Baracco never uses professional underworld help. That is why there is no gossip. He recruits his helpers from all over, and the really crazy thing is that they have no idea what they are doing! None of them knows he is part of a service carrying crooks beyond the reach of the law!"

"How can that be?" Bolan needled.

The Corsican swallowed the bait as his boastfulness took over. "Baracco has invented clever and often involved reasons," he said proudly. "He has painstakingly built up elaborate covers to account for the presence of the clients. The helpers never get wise to who they are. Baracco himself owns some of the junkyards. He is a licensed scrap metal dealer, and some of the older vehicles are driven from one country to another *as* scrap. But the other yard owners, for example, mostly think they are turning a blind eye to some minor racket involving the reregistering of stolen cars. Those whose yards are near frontiers believe they are being paid to help with the smuggling of a few bottles of liquor, a few cases of cigarettes, in an untraceable vehicle. The helpers on each side of the iron curtain are convinced they are aiding political refugees."

"And the Dutch operation? *That* sounded professional." Bolan remembered Brognola's boatman, who complained that clients using the escape chain were always in a hurry. He wondered how far he dare push Baracco without revealing his own knowledge.

"The Dutch operation did involve a network, admittedly, although it had nothing to do with me. And it was the only one that fouled up. I paid an existing organization run by a man named Conrad—an ultra-right-wing group that occupies itself smuggling ex-Nazis back into Germany, using a few of the greedier Dutch as hired help along the way. Baracco made a handsome contribution to their funds for the privileges of using their service just that once. From Denmark, it was very convenient, you see."

Yeah, Bolan thought. Except the client was drowned at sea, the organization was blown, and the boss man was wasted by Baracco himself—presumably because he knew too much.

On the whole, though, it *was* a damned original idea. Planning carefully, choosing and spacing out his clients to the best advantage, selecting only those he knew he could handle, the Corsican could dodge from city to city, from country to country, like a freighter taking on and discharging cargo from port to port on its way around the world. And, as a one-time haulage man, he'd be known to people all along the route anyway. Half the customs and immigration men at the frontiers were probably his old buddies.

Baracco's revelations explained why nobody in the underworld knew how to connect with the escape service, why nobody ever knew if they were acceptable as clients until *he* contacted *them*: there was nobody to contact unless Baracco happened to be in the area; and he'd only make contact if he thought the case was worthwhile, and if it worked in geographically with his other commitments.

So when a hit misfired in Paris, he decoyed the mark to The Hague, back in Holland, because he promised to be there to pack a terrorist into the inside of a barrel organ. A cigar for the gentleman with the prominent chin!

Bolan wondered which junkyard the organ was in now. But he wondered, more urgently, if it was true that Baracco had been approached by the Mafia via their Corsican associates, or was that just another piece of bragging? It might be nothing more than wishful thinking on his part, an idea of his own that he hoped to sell to the Mob. Whichever, if the big wheels of organized crime stateside *were* interested, Bolan could see that the escape network would be of unrivaled value to them.

Interpol had a thick dossier that listed every capo and most hit men and enforcers…information available by telex and computer links to every police force in the Western world. And even if there was nothing hard enough to warrant an arrest or an extradition demand, the activities of those men were logged, checked out and reported on wherever they went.

With the increased interest the Mob was showing in European rackets, what an advantage if such men could be moved secretly from country to country in their efforts to organize crime into a worldwide conspiracy! What an opportunity to move mafioso who had a price on their heads out of reach of the law, to switch planners from one theater of operations to another without alerting the police. And, as Baracco himself had hinted, what a great way to co-opt or recruit specialist talent from among the ex-cons and jailbreakers who had nothing to lose….

"Time to make a move if we want to hit the border between shifts." The Corsican's hoarse voice broke in on Bolan's thoughts.

A gust of wind shook the truck as Baracco climbed out of the cab to hand-crank the engine, and before they rolled out of the lot the windshield was spattered with large rain-drops.

"Damn," the Corsican complained. "If it rains, we'll take all bloody night to make it through the mountains. We'll forget the Innsbruck yard, cross the frontier into Germany and then take the tunnel beneath Lake Constance to make Zurich."

"All the way in this truck?"

Baracco shook his head. "There's a yard off the freeway near Oberammergau. We'll make the switch there."

The rain was much heavier now, bouncing high off the road and veiling the windshield more quickly than the ancient wipers could clear it. Ten minutes later it turned into driving sleet.

Cursing, the Corsican pulled off the road and cut the engine. "We better wait here until this eases off. We can use the time wrapping you up for the frontier crossing."

The delivery truck was loaded with rolls of carpet and linoleum consigned, according to the fake bill of lading, to a decorator in Zurich. Bolan was to pass through the border checkpoint inside one of the rolls.

Turning up his collar, he left the cab and joined Baracco at the rear of the truck. The Corsican had already opened the double doors. Bolan helped him manhandle the heavy rolls into position, rearranging them on the floor beyond the tailgate. It didn't take them long, but by the time they were through, the Executioner was drenched from head to foot. Grasping his jacket by the lapels, he shook it violently to rid himself of some of the frozen sleet before he got back into the cab. At the same time he shook his head to clear his face of the streams of moisture running down from his hair.

A truck rumbled past on the road, the headlights brightly illuminating the parked delivery truck and the two men who stood hunched against the sleet by the rear doors. In the vivid light, Baracco's face, with its staring eyes and jutting chin, abruptly changed into a mask of murderous rage....

Before he realized what had happened, Bolan found himself hurled backward into the body of the truck as the Corsican shoulder-charged him with brutal force. The doors slammed, and a bar dropped into place. A moment later the engine roared, and the vehicle accelerated back onto the road.

Bolan didn't get it. What the hell had gone wrong? He picked himself up and hammered on the partition separating the rear of the truck from the cab. He shouted. There was no reply. Slewing from side to side on the wet roadway, the truck careered ahead at a dangerous speed.

They should have arrived at the German frontier in less than twenty minutes, but it was almost two hours before the delivery truck shuddered to a halt. Bolan heard running footsteps, voices shouting commands.

Light flooded into the dark interior as the doors were jerked open. Facing him across the striped barrier pole of a minor frontier checkpoint were half a dozen uniformed men with leveled rifles. Behind them he could dimly see an officer and Baracco.

The Corsican was waving his arms. "You see!" he shouted. "Stowing away in my truck! There he is! That's Zoltan Cernic—the murderer who broke out of jail and escaped from Prague.... I'd know that face anywhere. His picture has been in all the papers. Arrest him! Take him away! He was trying to make it across the border in my truck."

Keeping away from the rifles' line of fire, the officer motioned Bolan to jump down from the tailgate. Cold steel embraced his wrists as handcuffs clicked shut. It was then that he realized the uniforms were Italian and not German:

instead of militiamen from the Bundeswehr, he was in the hands of the carabinieri.

Bolan allowed himself to be led through the sleet into the guardroom. What had happened? What had given him away? For if Baracco had denounced him as the killer Cernic, it could only be for one reason: because he had discovered that the Executioner was an imposter.

At that moment he caught sight of his reflection in a mirror hanging over an old-fashioned mantelpiece behind the duty officer's desk. He knew at once what had betrayed him. In Prague, each time he had gone out into the rain, he had worn a Czech workingman's peaked cap. For the escape he had worn no headgear. This time, the cheap dye that had transformed his dark hair into Cernic's carrot thatch had run... and now his face was grotesque, streaked from one side to the other with the orange stain.

17

Now that he was wise to the mechanics of Baracco's one-man escape service—and now that he was certain there must be some Mafia connection as Brognola had feared—Mack Bolan felt justified in throwing the Corsican to the wolves.

Whether it was the Executioner that eliminated the wily ex-trucker or the forces of law and order was immaterial; what was important was the timing. The service must be dismantled, finished, stamped out before the Mob got involved.

But posing as a killer on the run, Bolan was in no position to denounce Baracco. The guy was smart enough to talk himself out of it, and Bolan had no proof. Also, as a common criminal rather than a political refugee, the Executioner would probably be handed over to Eastern-Bloc representatives or sent straight back to Czechoslovakia under escort. And by the time he had gotten through to Colonel Sujic and straightened things out, Baracco would have vanished and the trail would be cold.

So he'd have to come out into the open now and tell the carabinieri who he really was. Except that he had no proof of that, either.

As soon as the Corsican had left the guardroom, Bolan turned to the officer and said, "You've got to stop him."

The young man stared at him. "What are you talking about?"

"I'm not Zoltan Cernic. I'm—"

"Be quiet. Of course you're Cernic."

"I'm *impersonating* Cernic—why else would I have dye running down my face? I was investigating an illegal transportation racket. The man believes he is smuggling Cernic out of reach of the Czech authorities."

"You're talking nonsense. If he was doing that, why would he hand you over to us? Why would he call in the military of all things?"

"Because he discovered I was an imposter, that I am *not* Zoltan Cernic."

"Now you're talking in riddles. That's enough."

"He's running an escape service for criminals. Every police force in Europe knows about this service, but nobody knows he's the one organizing it. Now that he knows I'm not a criminal, his organization is in jeopardy, so he wants me out of the way."

"Enough! It's time you were taken to the cells. *Sergeant!*"

"You're making a big mistake—"

"Silence! Sergeant, take this man to the cells and place a close guard on him. Transport will be arriving soon to take him to Rome. Until then he isn't to be left alone."

And so, until some time after midnight, Bolan cooled his heels in a brightly lit room with barred windows and a peephole in the door through which guards kept constant—and curious—watch. He guessed from scraps of dialogue he could hear that the border guards were attached to an important frontier post on a more frequented road nearby. But his escort was clearly coming from farther away.

During the long wait, Bolan wrestled mentally with the latest and most puzzling mystery since the mission had begun. If they had been within a few miles of the West German frontier when Baracco had unmasked him, why had he turned around and driven fifty or sixty miles through the foothills of the Tyrol before he had denounced the Executioner? If the aim had simply been to rid himself of the warrior, to hand him over to the military, why not make it directly to the Federal Republic and get it over with? What was so special about a mountain border post in Italy that Baracco rated it worth a two-hour drive in lousy conditions to make his play there?

There could be only one answer. And, yeah, it tied in with the guy's thinking... like the tactic he used to decoy Bolan to The Hague: once he knew Bolan was a phony, there were urgent reasons for Baracco to have him in Italy... and not in Germany.

So why denounce him to the authorities at all?

There was an answer to that, too, and the implications were chilling. But before Bolan could work through them in his mind there was a rattle of keys, the door of the cell crashed open and he was led back to the guardroom.

An escort of a half-dozen soldiers with submachine guns—Heckler & Koch MP-5s—was drawn up outside the door and beyond them, frosted with the sleet that was still falling, he could see a mesh-covered Fiat riot truck with a canvas top.

The young lieutenant in charge of the escort was receiving his orders from the carabinieri officer Bolan had argued with before.

"You will proceed south through the mountains to Udine and Padua. From there you take the autostrada through Bologna to Florence. It has been arranged that a civil police escort will rendezvous with you at the pay station complex south of the city, and they will complete the journey to the Czech embassy in Rome. You will deliver this envelope to the commanding officer at the same time as you hand over the prisoner. Is that understood?"

"Yes, Captain." As the lieutenant saluted and reached for the brown manila envelope, Bolan exploded into action.

He had seen the Walther automatic that had been taken from him at the time of his arrest lying with the document case on top of the guardroom table. He knew there were still five shots in the magazine.

He knew, too, that the remainder of the money that was to have been paid to Baracco when they made Zurich was still in the leather case. And he was relying on the fact that the Italians would think that was what he was after to give him the second's advantage that he needed.

It was a good try—and it almost worked.

Bolan twisted away from the guards flanking him and dived for the table. Snatching up the Walther in his manacled hands, he hurled himself into the corner of the room as his finger wrapped around the trigger. "All right, drop the guns and put your hands in the air. Tell the soldiers with the SMGs that you're dead men if they open fire."

The lieutenant barked an order. The captain, who had, as Bolan hoped, started a protective swoop toward the document case, stopped with a hand halfway to his holster. The guards who had brought Bolan from his cell remained frozen in astonishment. Handcuffed prisoners just didn't behave this way....

"One of you step forward," Bolan growled. "You—" he indicated the lieutenant "—turn around with your back to me. I'm going out of here, and this gun will be six inches from your back. If anyone makes a single move, I'll blow you apart. Understood?"

The captain looked beyond the Executioner's shoulder and raised an eyebrow. "All right, Rinaldi," he said quietly. "Take him now. But make it fast and make it sure."

It was the oldest gag in the world and Bolan wasn't buying it.

But Rinaldi *was* there. He was big and he was strong. He had silently opened a door that led to an inner office, and now he was immediately behind the warrior.

Rinaldi's linked hands dropped smoothly over Bolan's head and shoulders, and the circle of his arms tightened around the Executioner's biceps, darting lower to force the warrior's forearms toward the floor. The barrel of the Walther no longer pointed at the officers.

Bolan's finger contracted involuntarily, and the automatic spit flame. A 9 mm slug plowed into the floor. Then men were flying at him from all directions: gun butts thudded into his back; hands tore at his thighs and shoulders; a fist cracked against the side of his head and a practiced hand wrenched at his wrist so that the Walther fell from his fingers to be kicked away under the desk.

He fought like a tiger, but the sheer weight of numbers was too much for him. Heaving manfully against odds, he was finally subdued. A few minutes later, bruised, bloodied and only half-conscious, he was dragged out to the riot truck and shoved into the rear with the escort.

"What about the gun?" the lieutenant asked.

His superior plucked his lower lip. "It's not ours," he said finally. "You better take it with you. Hand it over to the Czechs when you give them the money."

The young man saluted again and climbed into the cab. The riot truck lurched back onto the road and headed down through the mountain passes toward Udine.

18

Bartolomeo Baracco wasn't a man who did things himself if he could persuade others to do them for him—especially if they didn't realize exactly *what* they were doing, or why.

Having no forged papers suitable for a north-south crossing of the Austro-Italian border, and doubting whether he could make it anyway with a captive yelling in back of the truck, he had therefore decided to denounce not the man himself, but the character he was impersonating...and allow the authorities to ferry him into Italy for him.

Once he was some way into the country, a rapid change of ownership would have to be reaffected—because Baracco had to lay hands on the imposter himself...fast.

There were three reasons for this. The most important was to stop other, more influential people hearing the man's story. And it wouldn't be long before he was able to gain at least some credence for his protests that he wasn't really Cernic.

Second of all, he had to have the man to himself so that he could find out who he was, who he worked for and how much *they* knew. And thirdly, the man had to be silenced. Permanently. He knew far too much about the network to stay alive, even in a Czech prison.

Neither Germany nor Austria were suitable for taking care of his priorities. Italy was. It was perfect, and thanks to the military, the hardest part was over already. All he had to do now was to get the prisoner back.

Waiting for the escort to arrive, he had driven to a junk-yard near Tolmezzo and traded in the delivery truck for a military jeep, which was hand-painted a bright yellow and equipped with a 1951 civilian registration. The jeep's soft top flapped dismally, the garish paint was flaking off all over, and the tires were almost bald. But there was a highly tuned engine beneath the hood and it went like the hammers of hell.

Baracco picked up the riot truck at a quarter to two, soon after it passed the yard. The downhill route ran in a valley, twisting left and right as it followed the curves of a river. In those conditions it was all right for the jeep to stay behind, but as soon as they hit a long, straight stretch, the Corsican accelerated and took the lead. He knew where they were going, and it was too much of a gamble staying in sight of alert soldiers in a vehicle as conspicuous as his.

Twenty miles from Udine the truck was joined by four motorcycle outriders. Baracco cursed, pushed the jeep to its limit and shot ahead until the lights of the convoy dwindled and then vanished in the dark of his rearview mirror. If his plan was going to succeed, he had to hit the convoy before they quit the country road and joined the high-speed autostrada that ran from Udine to Padua.

The superhighway ran close to the road, but it was a good fifteen miles before the next cloverleaf. Baracco took a side road, bounced along a narrow lane and came eventually to a dirt road that led to a wrecker's yard—a large field piled high with the remains of cars that had come to grief on the autostrada, whose embankment formed one boundary of the yard. There were several ragged gaps in the hedge shielding the place from the dirt road. Baracco chose the smallest and least used and steered the jeep in among the mounds of scrap metal.

Toward the back of the graveyard, just beneath the embankment, he drove close to a towering stack of metal and stopped the jeep, canting it over an outsized hummock of grass. From a distance, slanting drunkenly toward the mountain of wreckage, it would be indistinguishable from the derelicts surrounding it.

He switched off the engine and jumped to the ground. Sleet blowing through the open sides had soaked him to the skin, but it wasn't even raining now and the clouds had momentarily withdrawn. By the light of the waning moon, he threaded his way through the scrap to an old East German Wartburg three-tonner that was parked among waist-high nettles near the hedge.

It looked barely capable of remaining erect on its wheels, but the engine turned sweetly, and there were papers in a secret place behind the gaping glove compartment—insurance certificates, bills of sale, an agreement to buy the vehicle for scrap from an East German cooperative and permission to bring it into Italy for breaking up, which had been easy enough since he was a licensed scrap dealer and the yard was his own.

He drove the Wartburg into the lane, willing himself not to glance at his watch. Time was running out on him and each second counted. Once back on the highway, he floored the pedal, staring anxiously ahead in search of the convoy's red taillights.

They were only three miles short of the cloverleaf when he caught up with them. The road was twisting through hilly, densely wooded country, and that suited him fine. It was a bonus, too, that all the bikers were riding in front of the riot truck.

Bolan was sitting with the six soldiers on a bench that ran the length of the truck's rear. No one paid any attention to the ancient East German truck as it rattled abreast of them. The nerve gas from Baracco's expertly lobbed grenade worked so fast that they wouldn't have had time to react anyway.

All seven of them were out for the count before the Wartburg pulled in again to the right-hand side of the road after passing the Fiat. The men in the cab had noticed nothing.

Two of the outriders were fifty yards ahead, the leading pair another hundred in front of them. Baracco passed the first couple, gunning the Wartburg's reconditioned engine, and approached the second. He waited until the road dipped into a valley and then he drew level. As soon as he couldn't see the rest of the convoy beyond the crest, he lifted his foot and swung the wheel violently to the right. The nearside fender crunched against the man riding on the outside, smashing his arm and leg. With the handlebars wrenched from the rider's grasp, the bike slewed sideways and cannoned into the second machine, knocking the second rider off balance.

The second motorcyclist dropped his right foot to the ground, fighting the steering, but the sideways thrust of the collision, added to the momentum of their forward speed, was too much for him. The tires skidded on the wet pavement. Pivoting on his foot, he spun the bike and skated off the road into a screen of bushes, where his left leg was trapped beneath the bike's hot cylinders.

Ahead of them the Wartburg screeched to a stop. Baracco leaped from the cab, holding a mini-Uzi machine pistol—another of the secrets concealed inside the wreck's decrepit body. Amid the tangle of machines and riders, the guy with the broken arm and leg was pushing himself to his knees, groaning. Beside him the four-cylinder BMW engine, freed of its load, howled up the scale as the rear wheel of the capsized bike spun faster and faster. The engine of the other bike had stalled. The cop was dragging himself out from under, unfastening the flap of his holster with his free hand.

Baracco was down among the bushes twenty yards away, his 9 mm weapon primed. Light beams probed the night sky, silvered the branches of trees overhanging the road, then swung down to send twin reflections wavering along the rain-wet grade. The second pair of bikers had breasted the rise.

Baracco was taking a chance. He wanted all four of the outriders in a single group. If he finished off the two fallen cops before the others braked, the second pair might have time to swerve off into the trees and make trouble for him. Waiting, on the other hand, might give the guy going for his gun time to zero in on the Corsican. Because he knew damned well the spill had been no accident.

Baracco waited.

The riot truck lumbered over the crest. There were four headlights now, illuminating what looked like a nighttime pileup: the fallen riders, the blood on the road, the damaged bikes and a truck angled crazily into the soft shoulder some yards ahead.

The second pair of cops skidded to a halt beside the guy with the smashed side. As they dismounted, the man in the bushes yelled a warning. Orange light flickered among the leaves, and a stream of slugs whipped through the branches above Baracco's head. Twigs and fragments of bark were still raining on his head when he opened fire.

The blast of the mini-Uzi cut through the single reports of the fallen cop's Browning. Both new arrivals were going for their guns when Baracco stitched a lethal figure eight looping from the dismounted cops to the man in the bushes by way of the wounded biker in the road. He triggered the entire 32-round magazine in a single deadly burst, raising the Uzi's barrel at the last minute to pump the final shots through the riot truck's windshield. Behind the starred glass, the driver and the young lieutenant leaned together in a crazy embrace and then slid to the floor of the cab.

Beyond the Wartburg, the road curled away to the left. But the riot truck went straight on. It bumped over the shoulder, tore off a fender against the trunk of a tree, lumbered into a hollow and then, gathering speed, slammed into a rock outcrop and fell over onto its side.

Baracco was running noiselessly toward it before the echoes of the crash had died away among the sighing branches overhead. He knew he didn't have to worry about the bikers. He had seen blood and bone splinters in the illumination spilled across the road by the BMW's headlight. But although it was a country road, although it was an isolated area, although there was another hour of darkness before dawn, there was always a chance that an all-night driver, an early-rising farmer, a police patrol, perhaps, might pass. And he had work to do before he split.

He crawled into the space beneath the truck's crumpled mesh covering and tried to drag Bolan into the open air. A pocket flashlight showed him that there was a bruise on the unconscious man's temple, but otherwise he seemed to be unhurt. He was, however, handcuffed to the guards flanking him, and the wiry Corsican was unable to maneuver all three out together.

Baracco cursed. He lifted his head and listened. Was there a faint hum of traffic in the distance? Sure, but it was a continuous hum, rising and falling; it was heavies on the mile-away autostrada. Not a single vehicle was approaching along the country road.

Backing out from beneath the mesh, Baracco loped around to the cab and went through the pockets of the officer and the driver. No keys. He tried the soldiers in back. Negative.

He bit his lip. Should he simply waste the man here and go home? He shook his head. He hadn't worked his guts out all this time to see his meticulously planned racket collapse at the first push of the first person to penetrate it. He had to get the son of a bitch away and choke the truth out of him, find out how many more snoopers were in on the Cernic deal. Because he knew damned well it wasn't something the guy could have dreamed up all by himself, whoever he was.

And Baracco had to find out who the others were so that he could eliminate them, too. Find out, as well, just how they had gotten onto him in the first place. Yes, he had to free the imposter so that he could work him over. First, though, get him out of the damned truck and away from the men he was manacled to.

A memory stirred. The Cernic deal was the first time he had ever fouled up on an escape. Well, not fouled up, but been fooled by some smartass. But it *wasn't* the first time an operation had gone wrong. No fault of Baracco's, but Conrad and his team had laid an egg with Wünsche, the embezzler from Denmark.

Baracco flashed his light around the riot truck. He hadn't guessed wrong. There was salvage gear clipped to the back of the cab: a foam fire extinguisher, a shovel, a pick, steel shears. And a small ax.

He unshipped the ax and crawled back beneath the mesh. Four minutes later he was dragging Bolan into the open air. The Executioner was alone now, but with an empty, bloodstained handcuff dangling from each wrist.

Baracco dragged him to the Wartburg's cab and propped him up on the passenger side. The dim light from the instrument panel illuminated the unconscious man's dye-streaked features. What *was* there about the man that seemed so tantalizingly familiar?

Until he saw the murderer's mug shot in the papers, Baracco had never laid eyes on Cernic. This man looked like Cernic, but he wasn't Cernic. So why, now that he knew that, was the face still reminding him of... Who?

He fished a rag from the glove compartment, moistened it in the wet grass and wiped the dye from the man's face. He frowned. With one hand he covered the close-cropped hair. With the other forearm he blocked the view of the cheap Czech clothes. He was staring at a determined chin, a strong nose and lips that could be set in an implacable resolve. He thumbed open an eyelid.

The eye was a cold, hard blue.

Baracco's breath hissed through his teeth and he swore. The realization hit him with stunning force—Bolan! The bastard who had wasted Conrad's team, poked his nose into the archives of half the police forces in Europe and bested Baracco himself—with a nerve gas just like the one he used himself—after he had lifted him from his hotel in The Hague and ferried him away with the Dutch terrorist.

Why the hell hadn't he realized before?

Damn, because he was expecting a tough character with cropped red hair and that's what he got. Because, if he'd thought about it at all, he'd figured Bolan was five countries away.

And after he had discovered the switch?

This was the first time he'd really looked carefully. The moment he'd seen the dye, he'd slammed him into the delivery truck, and after that it was all action at the border checkpoint. Baracco couldn't blame himself for that! Baracco could never blame himself for anything. And now that he knew who he had, it was more urgent than ever to get him away from here and make him talk.

But there was one more chore to handle first. Baracco didn't know how much, if anything, Bolan had said to his guards on the trip south. But he couldn't afford to take chances. It was possible that he had spilled the whole story in an attempt to establish his true identity. And even if they hadn't believed him, a fragment of the real story might stick.

The Corsican wasn't going to allow that. Those men must die.

He left the Executioner in the Wartburg's cab—the gas from the grenade would keep him quiet for at least another hour—and hurried back to the riot truck. He recovered the document case with the money in it and the Walther PPK that had been taken from Bolan. Might as well sow the seeds of suspicion that he had somehow overcome the guards and then taken off with confederates who had ambushed the convoy.

Quickly and efficiently the Corsican strangled two of the unconscious soldiers. Birds flapped angrily away from the treetops in the predawn gloom as the remaining four shots in the Walther disposed of the remaining quartet.

Baracco threw the gun beside the truck. He was wearing gloves, so the weapon would be covered with Bolan's prints. As an extra hint to the investigators, the Walther, like the mini-Uzi that had eliminated the bikers and the men in the cab, was chambered for 9 mm parabellum rounds.

On the way back to the Wartburg, the Corsican heard a low, bubbling groan from beneath the trees. He pushed hastily through the bushes and found that the cop who had opened fire on him with his Browning was still alive. His guts had been blasted apart by the killstream from the mini-

Uzi, but his chest heaved in agonized gasps, his lips were moving and the beam of Baracco's flashlight struck a gleam of light from his wide-open eyes.

He was trying to say something, mouthing some plea, but the Corsican didn't have time to translate. "Friend," he said genially, "I'll do you a favor."

When the riot truck had fallen on to its side, the impact had split away parts of the rock outcrop. Baracco came back, hefting a ten-pound fragment, and crushed the dying cop's skull.

By the time the first farm truck stopped by the slaughter that half covered the road, he was four miles away, heading east into the sunrise and aiming for the next junkyard.

19

It happened that way sometimes in the hill country north of the low-lying marshes around Venice—storms that had ravaged the mountains all the way from Yugoslavia to the Alps withdrew placidly to the west, leaving a clear sky behind them.

Bolan opened his eyes and stared upward into limpid blue. His temples throbbed, there was a lump on his forehead and he felt like he was halfway through a king-size hangover. But only halfway.

He was lying on wet grass. He moved his limbs experimentally. They were free. There were handcuffs on each wrist, but the wrists weren't handcuffed together. He frowned, bending his arms so that the bracelets came into view. An empty cuff dangled from the steel circlet on each wrist, and there was dried blood on the steel.

Without moving his head, Bolan slid his eyes from side to side. He could see stacks of twisted, rusting metal, an ancient automobile with wide footboards and a rectangular body. There was an odor of diesel and hot engine oil carried on a gust of wind that stirred his hair. Behind him he could hear the ticking of cooling metal.

Something moved by one of the heaps of wreckage. Squinting—still without moving his head—he located the figure of a man. He was strolling up and down, methodically feeding rounds into an ammunition clip.

A stocky man with powerful shoulders and a jutting chin. Memory flooded back.

Bolan remembered everything down to the smallest detail, up to the time he was hustled into the Fiat riot truck. He had no recollection at all of the night journey, the Wartburg three-tonner or the gas grenade; he assumed his aches and pains were due to the beating he had received from the carabinieri.

But what had happened? How the hell had he ended up in Baracco's hands?

The magazine was loaded. The Corsican shoved the clip into the butt of a mini-Uzi, ramming it home with the palm of his hand. He turned to approach the Executioner's prone figure.

Bolan decided to play possum, which saved his life.

He assumed he was expected to be unconscious; he didn't know how he'd gotten where he was or how he'd been knocked cold, but he guessed Baracco was making one of his transport switches. He *should* have been unconscious: only a man with the Executioner's great reserves of strength, his battle-honed resilience, his determination to keep in shape would have been conscious in that junkyard at that moment.

After he had eliminated the escort, Baracco had reckoned the nerve gas would keep Bolan out for at least another hour. He miscalculated by fifty percent. It was only thirty minutes since he had steered the Wartburg back onto the country road. Daylight had returned, but the sun hadn't yet appeared over the rim of the mountains to the east. The Executioner was as mentally awake as he had ever been, but he displayed no outward sign.

As Baracco passed within three feet of Bolan's head, he took in his slack mouth, his stertorous breathing, and went on walking. He circled an old rectangular sedan with the wide running boards, then unlatched and lifted the hood. After manually flooding the carburetor beneath a gravity gas tank, he bent down in front of the radiator and cranked the handle projecting from the front of the engine, which wheezed and choked.

With shoulders heaving, the Corsican bobbed up and down, spinning the heavy crankshaft. No dice. He went back to the door and moved one of the quadrant levers. When he hauled up on the crank handle this time, the engine caught with a rumble and a roar.

Once it was idling smoothly, he returned to Bolan, but the Executioner had vanished. Baracco stood stock-still and cursed. It couldn't be possible! Bolan should have been out cold for—automatically he glanced at his watch: strict timetables were the essence of his racket—another twenty-five or thirty minutes.

Could somebody, some ally, perhaps, have followed them all the way from the frontier and lifted the guy while the Corsican's back was turned? No way. Could one of the guards, a biker cop, have climbed in back of the Wartburg to surface here in this yard and take back the prisoner? Negative. Remembering the roadside carnage, Baracco knew those men were dead.

Okay, so the impossible must have happened. He had underrated Bolan; the bastard had overcome the effects of the gas quicker than expected.

The guy had been shamming. So what? He still couldn't be far away. No engine had started, nobody had passed the sedan on the way to the gate. Bolan had to still be in the yard.

The jaw jutted more aggressively than ever. Baracco thumbed the mini-Uzi onto full-auto and started to patrol the aisles between the stacks of wreckage. It shouldn't be too difficult: he knew Bolan was unarmed. All he had to do was locate him, flush him out and press the trigger. Nothing permanent, though. He wanted that creep alive. A short burst across the legs should do it. See how far the smartass could run then! But the pain from shattered kneecaps would be nothing, the Corsican thought grimly, to what he had in mind for the Executioner once they reached the end of their journey....

The machine pistol's stubby muzzle questing left and right, he walked briskly and openly down the center of each aisle. He had nothing to fear. The only defense Bolan would have, could have, would be a length of jagged metal torn from a wreck, or something heavy—a brake drum, a starter motor—that he could throw. And for either of those, Bolan had to be at close quarters to be effective, far closer than the little stuttergun.

Baracco made a circuit of the whole yard, but found nothing. Okay, he could play the waiting game, too. He had all the cards. He halted near the old sedan. Should he cut the engine and listen, wait to hear some tiny giveaway sound, a shifting of metal, the tinkle of a displaced washer or bolt?

The hell with it. The heap was difficult enough to start as it was. Why make trouble for himself? Why go through the rigors of swinging that damn engine? Why risk flooding the damned carburetor and have to wait fifty minutes or more while the thing dried out? He left the engine running.

Bolan had to be *somewhere* in the yard. He couldn't have made it to the shack at the entrance. True, the watchman wasn't there yet, but Bolan would have had to pass Baracco to get there.

And he couldn't have left any other way. Unlike some of the car graveyards, this one was surrounded by a high wooden fence, which was quite new. There were no gaps. None of the scrap heaps were near enough to the fence for a man to make the top in a single leap. And climbing it, even if his hands could reach the top, would involve noise as his feet scrabbled for a hold.

Baracco started his second circuit, more warily now, slitted eyes scrutinizing each mass of tortured metal for a shadow, a movement. Beyond the high fence, the mountaintops glowed suddenly against the pale sky as the sun hoisted itself above the eastern peaks.

Bolan was determined not to repeat the hide-and-seek routine of the Montigny junkyard. He had no weapons, no papers, nothing but the clothes he wore—and two sets of handcuffs. And although his physical stamina had fooled the Corsican, allowing him to fight his way back to consciousness ahead of time, the effects of the gas had left him well below his usual strength.

So he wasn't going to fall for any eyeball-to-eyeball heroics. Baracco was all muscle and immensely strong: even if the man was taken completely by surprise, Bolan doubted he could best him in his present condition.

Right now the Executioner's only aim was to get out. And on this one he had no options. There was no way he could quit the yard without Baracco seeing him. He had to neutralize the Uzi, then slip away before the Corsican could reactivate it. Not the easiest brief for a man facing a trigger-happy opponent with thirty-two rounds of 9 mm parabellum ammunition at his disposal. But Bolan figured he could make it.

He wasn't holed up among the mangled sedans and flattened convertibles this time. He had gone to ground near the boundary fence in a towering rampart of used tires. Crowning the stack was a pile of four heavy-duty covers that had once shod a farm tractor or maybe the front wheels of a bulldozer. Bolan had slid down the sinkhole the tires had formed and now, crouched out of sight, he raised the top one an inch and peered through the gap. Baracco was fifteen yards away, approaching the tires. His face was set in an aggressive scowl, his right forefinger curled around the Uzi's trigger.

Bolan decided to utilize one of the smaller tires strewn around his hidey-hole. He would have to work superfast, and his choice had to be perfect. If the one he chose was too small, it would bounce off the target. If it was too big, it would drop uselessly to the ground. And if the section was too wide, the tire would be too heavy to place accurately. As an additional hazard, the mound of obsolete rubber was unstable: it quaked with every move Bolan made.

Baracco had drawn level. The Executioner held his breath as the man's burning gaze raked the tire mountain. Then the Corsican's belligerent jaw swung back toward the wrecks, and he moved another pace forward.

Bolan rose swiftly, still buried waist-high in heavy-duty rubber. He leaned forward and grabbed the tire he had selected from the stack. It was bald, the canvas showing through the smoothed-out tread, but it was narrow-section, the sidewalls were rigid and it had the right diameter.

Baracco was six or seven feet below him, about two yards past the center of the stack. Bolan leaned out as far as he could, the tire held flat in his two hands, and spun it forward and down. His aim was true. The old tire dropped neatly over the gunman's head and shoulders.

At the last moment something—a displacement of air, a movement within the stack—telegraphed the Corsican an alarm signal. His head jerked back, and his mouth opened as the inner edge of the tire lassoed past his eyes.

He swore, seeing the Executioner and attempting to raise the barrel of the Uzi at the same time. But the tire had angled down his body, pinioning his arms to his sides even as his finger tightened on the trigger. The machine pistol fired a burst into the ground, and then Baracco was overwhelmed by a cascade of rolling, bouncing, spinning rubber. Leaping down, Bolan had swept the top layer of discards from the pile and sent them hurtling toward the Corsican.

By the time Baracco, screaming threats, had struggled upright, freed his arms and stepped out of his prison, Bolan had rounded the nearest stack of wreckage and was racing up the aisle toward the yard entrance. The Corsican made the aisle as Bolan turned the far corner. A burst from the Uzi slammed into twisted steel and with splinters of metal stung the warrior's face before he was out of sight.

Pelting after him, Baracco reached the corner, only to see Bolan vanish behind a flatbed transport truck still loaded with wreckage from an autostrada pileup. The veteran sedan with the wide running boards, its engine idling, was on the far side of the transport.

Baracco was scarlet in the face and gibbering with rage. He shouted furious threats, circling the massive cab of the transport, his finger itching to release the killstream that would annihilate the man who had fooled him. But his brain urged caution because the bastard had to be taken alive.

In any case, the choice became academic. Bolan leaped into the sedan and slammed the heavy lever into first. The old car lurched toward the gate and began to accelerate.

Baracco dropped to one knee and hosed lead after it, slugs thunking into the custom-built bodywork and drilling the rear fenders. The oval window in back shattered; a side-view mirror flew into fragments that glittered in the early-morning sun. But the tires remained intact, and Bolan kept his foot to the floor.

By the time Baracco had emptied the Uzi and then run back and coaxed the engine of the Wartburg into life, the sedan was a mile away down the dirt road and heading for the autostrada.

20

Bolan didn't take the autostrada. His first priority was to lose Baracco, his second to contact the Rome embassy, alert Brognola and equip himself with an armory, an identity and unmanacled hands.

For the second, he figured a small town would be best. And, as for the first, it was simply a question of doing the unexpected.

He turned off the dirt road, maneuvered the sedan along a trail separating fields of rice and alfalfa and steered through an access tunnel that ran beneath the freeway. There was a vineyard on the far side, and beyond that a country road lined with Lombardy poplars.

Bolan turned left, heading back into the hills they had traversed during the night. He reckoned that was the least likely course for a fugitive from frontier guards to take.

He realized the rear fuel tank had been hit when the needle of the gauge bounced to empty and the engine choked into silence. He coasted the vehicle in behind the trees and climbed out. After the racket of the ancient six-liter engine—the car was an Austro-Daimler, dating back to the late twenties—it was very quiet beneath the poplars. The highway ran, together with the railroad and a river, along the floor of a narrow valley that twisted up toward the foothills of the Dolomites. It was probably, Bolan thought, the old road leading to Venzone, Malborghetto and the

Austrian frontier. Udine and the plain would be ten miles or more downstream and to the west.

He closed the door of the car and began to walk northward in the direction he had been driving. Each time he heard a vehicle approaching from behind, he left the road and ducked behind the undergrowth under the trees. But in thirty minutes he was passed only by a tractor hauling a load of hay, a clapped-out flatbed piled high with crates of live chickens and a couple of locally registered Fiat sedans. In any case, he wouldn't have recognized the Wartburg if he saw it.

He stopped when there were no more poplar trees to provide cover and the sun was high in the sky. He could hear a tremble of sheep bells, the shallow river babbling over stones, a breeze hissing through the roadside grasses. Shading his eyes with one hand, Bolan looked around him.

He had to be quite high up by now, but thin skeletons of vines still clung to stony terraces rising above the road on one side. Beyond the tracks and the river on the other, he saw the gray slate roofs of a village among the trees on the edge of a chestnut forest. At the head of the valley the mountains stood bare and brown against the blue sky.

Bolan deliberated. Should he cross the river and try his luck in the village? Or would the small-town mentality, always suspicious of strangers, be a hindrance, delaying or even preventing any chance of making contact with a foreign embassy in far-off Rome?

A bigger place would be better, but he hadn't passed any signposts and he hadn't seen anyone working in the fields. He had no idea how far the nearest town would be. He made up his mind—the village.

The river flowed fast between banks of shingles, but Bolan had no difficulty wading across. On the far side he found a footpath curving toward the village. Halfway there he noticed a length of twine caught on a brier. He grinned: that could be the solution to one problem!

He stripped off his jacket. Then, freeing the twine, he tied one end to the empty handcuff attached to his left wrist, pulled it and the circles manacling the wrist as far up his arm as possible, passed the twine around his neck and then down the other arm to secure the second pair of cuffs in the same way. The handcuffs weren't visible when he shrugged back into the jacket.

He continued along the footpath. Second problem: how to make a long-distance phone call in a remote Italian village with no money, no ID and not a single article of value on him? The village wasn't exactly the hub of the Western world. It had a wide, dusty piazza, an arched colonnade that ran beneath the ocher facade of a block covering one side of the square, several smaller houses with stained stucco walls, and a barn with open doors.

Bolan strode toward the colonnade, scattering chickens, ducks and a mongrel dog. Beneath the arches he could see old men sitting in cane chairs outside the village store, and beyond the block a dirt road curled past a church and then vanished among the trees.

From the shadowed colonnade he could sense eyes watching him. He guessed the smart thing to do would be to ask for some official and explain the problem. His car had been stolen and his papers and money had been in a wallet on the front seat. Would it be possible to arrange a call, collect, to a number in Rome?

Maybe the priest would be a better bet. He would have been to some kind of college; he might be in a better position to grasp the problem.

A hum of conversation ceased as Bolan approached. He was aware then of a different hum, not too far distant. It was a mechanical noise, rising and falling, altering its pitch and cadence but signaling all the time a single unalterable, unmistakable fact: high-speed traffic—a lot of it—moving somewhere beyond the trees.

He changed direction and headed for the dirt road. A woman cranking water from a hand pump lowered her pail and watched him with her hands on her hips. He turned a corner in the road.

Check.

Carving an arrow-straight swath through the forest, the new turnpike linking Klagenfurt in Austria with Udine and Venice ran within five hundred yards of the village. Above the Armco barriers, the roofs of cars, trucks and buses hurtling past in each direction glinted in the sun. Maybe he could hitch a ride up to Carnia or back down to Udine. He quickened his pace, heading for a bridge that carried the dirt road over the autostrada. Halfway up the grade he halted. This time he had really hit pay dirt.

A quarter of a mile to the south there was a rest area with parking lots, a multipump gas station, a cigar store and newspaper kiosk...and a Pavese cafeteria built over the twin three-track motorway like a glassed-in steel-and-concrete bridge.

The Executioner had a hunch he would find a sympathetic ear. Vaulting over a fence at the side of the road, he ran down a grassy bank and hurried along the shoulder toward the rest area.

It was in the parking lot nearest the stairs that led to the cafeteria that he was hit by that day's biggest surprise. A low-slung red roadster whose battered bodywork dated back to the mid-thirties stood among the bulbous, shining products of the automotive age. There was a yellow Dutch license plate below the tarnished chrome Alfa Romeo lettering on the radiator honeycomb.

Bolan didn't believe in coincidences. Not in coincidences with an arm *that* long—an arm stretching over six countries, seven if you counted Luxembourg, with a reach of some 950 kilometers.

He ran up the steps and into the crowded cafeteria. The woman was sitting alone in a pitch-pine booth. Her elbows were planted on the red checkered tablecloth, and there was a cup of untasted coffee between them. Bolan slid into the vacant seat on the other side of the table.

"The trout with almonds is quite good," she said without looking up, "and they have an Orvieto in half-liter flasks that's a must."

"Sold to the man with the hungry eyes," Bolan replied lightly. He realized he hadn't eaten since Baracco had brought a liverwurst and a can of beer to the panel truck twenty-four hours before. And talking of hungry eyes...

He stared at the woman. Hell, yes. He knew there was something different. The green eyes were the same, but the halo of blond hair was gone. He was looking at a woman with a voice he knew, who was stacked the way he remembered. Only now she was a redhead.

"Which one is the wig?" he asked.

"You're looking at the real me."

"What are you doing in this neck of the Italian woods?"

"Waiting for a guy to offer me a brandy. A gentleman who doesn't aim to get fresh with me."

Bolan held up a finger to summon a waiter. He continued staring at her with raised eyebrows.

"Okay, I'll answer your question if you'll answer mine first," she said at last. "What are *you* doing here, Mr. Bolan?" Her uptilted nose was slightly red at the tip. She looked as if she had been crying.

"You know what I'm doing here. I'm trying to catch a man who runs an escape service for criminals and break up his organization."

Gudrun caught her breath. A tear welled from her right eye and rolled slowly down her cheek. She sniffed.

Bolan had a flash of insight. "It's him, isn't it? He cut you loose."

"How do you know?"

"It's a fair deduction. Someone was asking questions about me in Tufik's office. You had the run of the office, so you knew who I was. Then you engineered it so I would return to my hotel. A nice girl like you doesn't make a habit of arranging for a total stranger to be knocked out...unless a guy you're in love with asks you to. So you have the hots for somebody in the organization. And now, since I know it's a one-man show, it figures you're in love with Baracco. You had some time off due you, and you went to see him. But something, evidently, went wrong."

"The bastard!" Gudrun said venomously. "Oh, the lousy son of a bitch! After all he promised me...and it's only for some thin-faced cow from Czechoslovakia. I could *kill* him!"

The waiter brought Bolan's order and set a brandy in front of Gudrun. "How did you get me out of the hotel?" Bolan asked.

She brushed the back of her hand across her eyes and then rubbed her thumb against her fingers in the universal sign of money changing hands. "They have very large laundry hampers at the Terminus that go down in the service elevator and then get dumped in the yard."

"Where's the boyfriend now?" Bolan asked.

"You tell me. He had some job. Ferrying a jerk from Prague to Zurich, I think. If that wasn't just a stall to hide the fact that he's there with that woman."

"That was no stall," Bolan told her. "Meet Joe Jerk."

"You mean you'd horned in on the...? You'd passed yourself off...?"

Bolan nodded. "But it turned sour. Something loused up our beautiful friendship, too."

"He figured you out?" Gudrun guessed. "He's smart. But he's a very dangerous man. Is he after you? Is that why you're here?"

Bolan nodded again.

"He was probably taking you to his base. He was due there last night. That's why I'm here—to have it out with the swine."

"His base?" Bolan remembered the phone call from Montigny.

"It's not far from here. In the chestnut forest. The craziest place you ever saw—kind of a cross between the world's most comprehensive junkyard and a medieval castle!"

"Is this the birthplace of your roadster?"

"It *was* the graveyard. Bart reconditioned the engine, but he won't touch the rest of it. He's got a thing about beat-up cars."

"I've noticed," Bolan replied dryly.

Gudrun gave a bitter laugh. "And now he's got a thing about beat-up women. That bitch is years older than me. And it's all because her damn father is a big wheel in the American Mafia. Bart's hoping to talk them into some kind of partnership deal."

"The Mafia?"

"Sure. The woman's mother was a Slovak, but the father was born in Sicily. He's been in America for hundreds of years. I'll bet that cow was born before Czechoslovakia was even a *country*!" Gudrun said viciously.

Bolan grinned. If Mariella was the go-between linking Baracco with the Mob, the mission was finally shaping up nicely. "I guess you wouldn't mind getting a little of your own back?" he suggested. "On Bart, I mean. Pay him back."

"Would I ever!" The redhead was emphatic. "You don't realize what that rotten bastard has done to me. He forced me to break the law, cheat on people I like, risk going to jail, you name it. And he's not just my ex-boyfriend. We were going to get married. God knows how many times I've been sold that line about the cottage on the cliff, the hot Mediterranean sun, the sound of the sea."

"The wind through the olive trees? The changing colors?"

"He shoveled that crap your way, too?"

"And more."

"The number detailing his childhood in that village in the mountains of Corsica? Well, it's all lies. There's not a word of truth in it. He was born in a Bastia slum. He was leading a street gang when he was eleven, terrorizing old ladies with switchblades. There was never any option on any piece of land overlooking the ocean. Bart's the vainest man you ever met. He has to justify himself—in his own eyes particularly—so he's made himself into the biggest liar in Europe, inventing stories to account for the way he lives."

"This base of his," Bolan said casually. "Could you take me there?"

"Of course I could. If you intend to clobber his damn escape network, it would be a pleasure."

"I have to ask your help another way first."

"Offer me another brandy, and I'm your girl."

"I can *order* you another," Bolan said ruefully, "but I can't *offer* anything. I can't even pay for what I've eaten myself." He explained his predicament, and added, "If I can borrow enough money from you to pay our bill and make a call to Rome, I'll stick around until a friend contacts me with the gear I want. After that we can be on our way."

"We'd have to wait anyway," Gudrun replied. "I just remembered—Bart will be in Venice until tomorrow. He has a job to do."

"A job in Venice?" The Executioner's interest quickened.

"That's right. I guess that's why he didn't have more time to pull out all the stops looking for you. The way I heard it, there are three Red Brigades killers who come up for sentencing tomorrow. Friends on the lunatic Left have collected arms from other extremist groups and they aim to spring them from the courtroom. Bart's being hired to get the men away once the opposition has been liquidated."

Bolan reached across the table and touched her arm. "Sunset over the lagoon. Gondoliers singing along the Grand Canal. High life in the Gritti Palace. What would you say to a trip to the Amsterdam of the South?"

21

Hal Brognola was in Paris, attending the second session of the terrorist summit, this one covering the side of the drug trafficking business that financed the buying of illicit arms for terrorists.

There had been more than fifty bomb outrages and random automatic weapon killings in the French capital within thirty months, some of them with death tolls as high as sixty, so the security chiefs and leaders of the antiterrorist squads at the summit figured they knew as much about the terrorist scene as any man—and more than most.

For the second time, Brognola was unable to deliver the major policy speech that was expected of him. But since Bolan's relayed SOS was concerned with the Red Brigades—perhaps the most cynically ruthless of all the terrorist groups—he reckoned that was a good enough excuse to take a rain check on the speech. His panic run to Italy was directly concerned with the conference, he told the organizers. It might affect what he had to say; he would report to conference the moment he returned.

He arrived at Treviso International Airport, fifteen miles north of Venice, at dusk on the day Mack Bolan contacted him. Bolan was waiting for him in the VIP transit lounge. The French antiterrorist chiefs and their Italian counterparts in Paris had fixed it so that the Fed didn't have to pass through immigration or customs at either end of the flight.

He carried the equipment Bolan had requested in a plastic Alitalia airline bag.

Brognola was irritable. His eyes were red-rimmed, he had slept in his suit, he was still suffering from jet lag after his transatlantic flight twenty-four hours earlier and he was missing the special banquet laid on to welcome the conference members in Paris.

"What gives, Striker?" he growled. "What's so damned important it couldn't wait at least until tomorrow morning?"

Bolan filled him in.

"You said murder," the Fed said when he had finished. "How many cops and security men will they have to kill to spring these guys from the courtroom?"

"Around forty," the Executioner told him. "Not counting the people who get caught in the cross fire. The law was afraid there'd be a demonstration or even some kind of rescue attempt when the sentences were handed out, so they switched venues. The trial's been held in a specially built court on the island of Murano, north of Venice in the lagoon. The place is stiff with guards, but I don't think they're prepared for a full-scale commando assault."

"And that's what they're going to get?"

"That's the way it was told to me." Bolan took possession of the bag. Neatly packed inside were the Beretta and AutoMag that had been returned to Brognola by Colonel Sujic, a Heckler & Koch caseless assault rifle, Bolan's blacksuit, two sets of ID papers—one in his own name, the other identifying him as Mike Belasko, a news photographer—a miniature throwing knife and a few more arcane tools of his trade, plus keys to unlock his handcuffs.

"I don't have details of the raid on Murano," Bolan added. "My intel relates strictly to the getaway plans fixed by Baracco, and even that's only a generalized rundown."

Brognola fished a cigar from his vest pocket and bit off the end. "Do you aim to horn in on the raid," he asked, "or wait until Baracco is operating and hit him then?"

"There's a moral question involved."

The Fed spit the cigar end into a cuspidor. "A *moral* question?" he repeated. "Since when did antiterrorist activity and morals figure on the same printout?"

"As of today," Bolan said. "I'm in this to nail Baracco and waste his network before the Mob takes it over. And in practice that means wasting Baracco, too, because the Mob would for sure want to keep him in the driver's seat. He's the only one who knows one hundred percent how the organization works."

"And so..."

"So from our point of view it would be best to lie low and let the terrorists do their courtroom number. Then we could move in and catch the Corsican red-handed once the guys who'd been sprung were handed over to him."

Brognola nodded, but said nothing.

"On the other hand," Bolan said soberly, "if we let the terrorists go ahead so we can do our own thing, there's going to be a lot of people dead. People who might stay alive if we tipped off the Italian authorities. At the moment they don't know a thing about this rescue deal. They only suspect there might be something somewhere along the line."

"Do we have the right to sacrifice those guards, those passersby, in the interests of our own operation, important though it is—is that what you're asking yourself?" Brognola said. "How do you read it yourself, Striker?"

Bolan sighed. "I want to get this Baracco deal wrapped up—it's become personal. But I can't justify the death of a single innocent person, whatever the circumstances, if there was something we might do to prevent it." He shook his head. "No way."

"I guess you're right," Brognola replied heavily. "Okay. So we tip off the Italians there's a plan to spring these bastards. We don't know the details, anyway. And then we make our own dispositions—I can't say in the *hope* that the Italians screw up, but let's say in case they do. In which case we do our damnedest to get the terrorists back and eliminate your Corsican friend, right?"

"I guess that's about it."

"You said you had no details, only a generalized idea of what Baracco aimed to do. What exactly do you know?"

"I know the ultimate aim is to get the three Red Brigades terrorists to Albania, where anyone with ultra-Left, Maoist ideas is welcomed with open arms."

"That figures." Brognola nodded. "The Russians wouldn't want to know, but the Chinese might and the Albanians certainly would. It's only a couple hundred miles down the Adriatic, anyway."

"Across the Gulf of Venice...and nearer 350, parallel with the Yugoslav coast," the Executioner corrected. "I know there's a chopper involved and a powerboat, but I don't know which is to lift the guys from the island and which is slated for the Albanian trip. I only know some kind of switch is planned, which will take place in Venice itself."

"How do you know even this much? Can you verify it?"

"Yeah. Let's just say the intel comes from an ex-colleague Baracco betrayed."

"And the terrorists come up for sentencing tomorrow? I guess I better stop over and see it through," Brognola said. "What do you say we go into town and you show me the layout?"

"I have to familiarize myself with it first." Bolan grinned. "I only just got here, remember?" He led the way out to the parking lot.

"Jeez," Brognola said, staring at the battered Alfa Romeo. "You want *me* to ride in *that*? Where the hell did you get it?"

"I borrowed it from a friend."

"How old's the friend? Someone in the antique business? Or did you unearth it from one of Baracco's dumps?"

Bolan didn't reply. The Fed's last remark was a little too near the truth for comfort, and for reasons of his own he wanted—at least for the moment—to keep the source of his information under wraps.

He breathed life into the ancient engine and took the highway south to Venice.

Night had fallen by the time they arrived. The moon hadn't risen yet, and the dark waters of the lagoon surrounding the city were ablaze with the reflections of millions of lights. They checked into a hotel in the Calle del Barcaroli and made their way to the waterfront by San Marco. Although it was out of season, tourists still drifted in the huge floodlit square beneath the basilica's five great domes. Bolan and the Fed threaded their way through and found a free *motoscafo* by the landing stage.

It was little more than a mile to the island of Murano, but a wind blew shoreward from the southeast and the lagoon was choppy. It didn't take them long to make the crossing.

The small town on Murano, once the scene of Casanova's wilder excesses, was famous for its glassblowing. There was a great deal of glass, most of it bulletproof, in the heavily fortified temporary courtroom built for the Red Brigades trial. The courtroom had been improvised inside a disused casino between an eighteenth-century convent and the Church of San Cipriano.

There was already an unusual concentration of police and carabinieri as the two Americans stepped ashore. If Brognola hadn't been supplied with special passes by his Italian counterpart before he'd left the conference in Paris, they would have been refused permission to land.

Brognola asked to see the officer in charge of security. There were two: one looking after the island as a whole, the other with special responsibility for the courtroom, the prisoners and safety of the officials.

"The whole trial," the man told the Fed, "has been, as your countrymen would say, kept under glass. Armored glass separates the dock from the rest of the court. It protects the judges, the lawyers, the ushers, and keeps the press, the witnesses and the few members of the public admitted in separate compartments. Everybody can see everybody else but the testimony, the pleading and the judgments have all been through microphones."

"You tell us that a rescue attempt is planned," the first officer said, "with a powerboat and a helicopter involved. Naturally we have expected—and been on our guard against—such an eventuality. But I cannot see—"

"That's all I know," Brognola interrupted. "That and the fact that the getaway arrangements have been put in the hands of a second organization. It was an underworld tip-off. With no details." Bolan was keeping discreetly in the background. This was strictly administration material: he would step up to bat when they knew where the action was at.

"I don't see how they can hope to get away with it," the *commendatore* pursued. "All entries and exits to and from the court are heavily guarded. There are twenty men in reserve at the Church of San Cipriano, with automatic arms, grenades, even a rocket launcher loaded and ready. There will be an escort of half a dozen armored cars when the police van brings the prisoners from the cells on the other side of the island. And they will keep their engines running while the sentences are pronounced, in case some kind of break did succeed and they make for the waterfront.''

The island security chief continued, "Even if they get that far, there will be six high-speed police launches equipped with machine guns and 40 mm cannon on constant patrol around the island. Everybody will be in constant radio contact, and naturally all persons landing or in the neighborhood of the courtroom have been—and will continue to be—closely screened.''

"The only conceivable way," the *commendatore* said, "would be to use the helicopter—a direct assault on the courtroom roof, and then lift them out of there. It's been done twice in France. But we already have a dozen men posted on surrounding rooftops, expert marksmen with express rifles and Ingrams for short-range work. In view of what you say, sir, we'll add a team with a bazooka, and perhaps have a couple of choppers of our own on patrol above. Other than that, I can't think..." He shook his head in disbelief.

"I'm only passing on what I've been told," Brognola said. "And you seem to have covered all the angles.

"I don't understand about the powerboat," the first police chief said. "If they used that to escape from the island and the chopper was waiting someplace else for Phase Two, that would make sense. But since we agree they'd never get as far as the waterfront and they'd have to leave by air, why the boat?''

"Maybe it's a decoy." Bolan spoke for the first time.

"Or maybe it's the chopper that's a decoy," Brognola put in.

The *commendatore* shook his head. "I tell you again, Signor Brognola, it is impossible for anyone to leave the island by water while the court is in session. Impossible.''

Maybe, Bolan thought, both the powerboat *and* the chopper were decoys. But he said nothing: it was what happened *after* an escape that commanded his attention.

"We're all assuming an attempt would be made while the court is in session." Brognola tried a new tack. "But suppose it's planned for some time before—while the guys are still in their cells, on the road between the cells and the courtroom, or even on the way back, after sentences have been passed?"

That would make it even tougher for the would-be rescuers, the two officers agreed.

And when Bolan and the Fed made a tour of the tiny island, it certainly looked that way. Carabinieri covered every inch of the waterfront; armed police stood silhouetted against the floodlights on rooftops, behind balustrades, in windows commanding every street. "Most of them seem kind of jumpy, too," Brognola observed. "We'd all have egg on our faces if the breakout was scheduled for tonight, eh?"

"It won't be, Hal." The Executioner was adamant. "My source was quite definite: the getaway is planned for tomorrow morning, after the court appearance. And they're not going to have those terrorists hanging around for hours after some earlier breakout. Besides, Baracco couldn't have had the time to organize anything for tonight. He was still chasing after me at breakfast time!"

"Okay," Brognola said. And then added, "What's bugging you, Striker?"

"I don't know." Bolan was frowning. "The little we do know doesn't stack up with Baracco's usual MO. Not in my book. The lead-up to the getaway, I mean. This guy's specialty is ancient machinery, all along the line. Powerboats and 350-mile flights over the open sea... For my money, they're written into a different scenario."

"Then you better check back with this mysterious source you're so cagey about," the Fed replied tartly.

Ten minutes later Bolan rapped a code knock on the door of a fifth-floor room in the same hotel. "There's nothing, not the smallest, unimportant detail that you can add? Nothing else at all that you can remember?" he asked Gudrun when she had let him in.

She shook her head. "It wasn't finalized the last time I saw him. All I know is that the changeover is in Venice itself, near San Marco."

"The changeover from what to what? That's what we need to know."

"I can't help you," the woman said. She looked very desirable—tan leather jeans with a loose honey-colored sweater that only touched the seductive curves of her body where it mattered. "He usually spends some time checking over the wrecks he's going to use. But the only time he spoke of this job, it was too far ahead. He hadn't made up his mind."

"But he knew about the job some time ahead? That doesn't sound like his usual routine. He usually waits until people are holed up and then *he* contacts *them*, right? Are you telling me that he's been hired for this job, that someone contacted him first?"

She nodded, the gold threads woven into the sweater mirroring the highlights in her red hair and green eyes. "It was that pig in Prague. It was the first time I heard of her. *She* put him up to it. She was the go-between." Gudrun's green eyes flashed fire. Bolan took note of the information: it was something that could come in useful later.

Back in the American Bar with Brognola, he said, still keeping Gudrun's existence secret, "It seems a hundred percent certain that the escape itself is a Mafia-organized job, and that this time Baracco is the hired help rented by the Mob.''

"With the support they can count on in this country," Brognola observed, "that could mean the breakout is a big-time deal—lots of troops, unlimited funds, the latest weaponry."

"That's what I'm afraid of," Bolan agreed. "So we watch the island, the waterway, the sky, and we note every arrival and every departure, every single movement, suspicious or otherwise . . . as of now."

"Counting those they built the city on," Brognola said heavily, "there are 120 islets on this lagoon. The city itself is subdivided by 117 separate canals. You figure we can keep all that water under surveillance throughout the night and tomorrow morning?"

"Look, we can forget all of those islands except Murano and the city ones, because the operation has to start on Murano, and we know the rendezvous with Baracco is someplace in the city. Okay, that leaves just your 117 canals. With the help of the police, they shouldn't be impossible to cover—given that we finger the prisoners the moment they leave Murano. That way we can pinpoint their direction and narrow down the areas they could be heading for. For us the vital thing is to stay mobile."

"Suppose they leave the island on the far side and head *away* from the city?" Brognola growled. "Switch transport on one of the smaller isles and come back to Venice for the rendezvous by land?"

"It's a thought," Bolan admitted. "Let's hope they don't."

The nightwatch was aboard a brass-railed, teak-decked cruiser with 240 horsepower available to spin the two titanium screws beneath the sloping stern. There was a Trilux night vision scope attached to Bolan's Heckler & Koch G-11, and the bag Brognola had brought from Paris offered up IR binoculars and a helicopter crewman's helmet equipped with the latest HNVS nightsight apparatus, including a B&W binocular display on the visor.

The launch itself, cajoled from the anti-drug-smuggling squad attached to the Italian coast guard service, was fitted with a "black hole" engine exhaust suppression system that drastically reduced the craft's own infrared signature in the event of attack by guided or self-seeking missiles.

They cruised the lagoon all night, circling the island of Murano close inshore every fifteen minutes, but they saw and heard nothing. Fog blanketed the lagoon at dawn, leaving the baroque roofline of San Cipriano and the towers and domes of the buildings on neighboring islands riding ghostlike on the ocean of white that lay above the oily swell of the gulf.

"Damn," Brognola said. "Don't tell me the Mob is strong enough in these parts to lay on *this*!"

Bolan throttled down the engine and allowed the cruiser to ride the swell. He looked up through the veil of mist. "Sky overhead seems cloudless," he said, "as far as I can see. If the sun's not hidden this should disperse by eight-thirty, nine. It's part of the scenery at this time of year."

"It won't be too soon," the Fed grumbled. The hearing was now scheduled for nine. It had been put forward one hour at the last moment, in the hope of foiling any Mafia plans that depended on split-second timing— "Although," the *commendatore* had observed acidly, "you can be certain that someone on their payroll, one of the few people here who know about the change in plan, will have informed them within ten minutes of the decision being made."

At a quarter to nine the sun broke through as Bolan had forecast, and the mist rolled away, thinned and then vanished. According to the baton transceiver Brognola carried, all was quiet on the Murano front. Nothing unexpected had happened; no suspicious characters had appeared. The armored convoy was about to transport the three Red Brigades prisoners from their cells to the converted casino-courtroom. Bolan and his companion could clearly hear the crackle of exhausts across the calm water as the escort vehicles warmed up their engines.

The noise was lost seconds later when the six police launches put out from the main landing stage and resumed their patrol around the island. Two helicopters appeared from the direction of Mestre and circled the improvised courtroom at a height of five hundred feet.

"At least the locals are taking this thing seriously," Brognola said. "Those Nightstalkers carry a seven-tube rocket launcher and twin 7.62 mm machine guns in their pods!"

Bolan had flipped the lever into neutral, allowing the engine to idle while he kept the cruiser head-on to the swell with deft turns of the wheel. "Let's hope they don't totally annihilate everything they get in their sights."

The third helicopter appeared at 9:05, flying over the water from the northeast and skimming the sandbanks that sheltered the land on the inner shores of the lagoon. It was a large twin-rotor machine with civil markings that Bolan couldn't identify. The cabin looked spacious enough to carry twelve to fifteen people.

The two army choppers soared away from the island to intercept it, and for several minutes the three aircraft hovered in close formation. Bolan could imagine the exchange, by radio and by gestures: interrogation, protestation, commands, expostulation. Eventually the army choppers forced the interloper down on flat land beyond the sandbanks.

The police launches had intercepted and were about to board a 120-foot ocean cruiser creaming into the lagoon past the Lido.

"For my money," Bolan said, "there'll be fifteen blue-chinned dudes with shotguns in that third chopper. They'll look as suspicious as hell, but they'll say they're on their way to an innocent duck shoot on the marshes. And they'll be right. A crowd of similar hardcases will be on the cruiser, and they'll have an equally plausible excuse for being there. The Mob has always been pretty good on alibis."

"You mean the chopper *and* the boat are decoys? You think none of those men have anything to do with the heist?" Brognola demanded.

"That's the way I read it—that's what I always thought. They've probably been paid by the Mob to act as decoys, but who can prove it? And how can you jail a guy for going on a duck shoot?"

"Then who the hell springs the prisoners?"

"Wait and see," the Executioner said cryptically.

Before the Fed could reply, his radio crackled to life and a voice said urgently, "Signor Brognola...? Something is wrong! Something has happened in the courtroom. Transmission has been interrupted. We are no longer in radio contact with the trial."

"Shit!" Brognola exploded. "This is it! Get your men in there and start rolling. Block every route to the waterfront...and keep in touch, okay?"

"I don't understand why—"

The voice broke off abruptly, and the radio went dead. Two seconds later the sound of three dull, flat detonations echoed across the water. They were followed by a confused rattle of automatic fire and several single rifle shots.

Brognola shouted into the mike, his thumb jammed on the Send button. Bolan touched his arm and gestured seaward. An oil tanker, bound for the storage depot and refinery at Venice's Porto Marghera, was lying off the lone spit of land on which the Lido was built, waiting to steam into the lagoon.

"There's the attackers' base," Bolan said as he raised his binoculars. "Iranian registration. No sweat stowing a command of guerrilla terrorists aboard that baby. Finance courtesy the Mafia, killings by permission of Khomeini or Khaddafi."

There was a lot more shooting now, the rapid-fire volleys punctuated by cracking explosions from mortars or grenades. But no smoke spiraled above the seminary or the old casino; the action seemed to be concentrated on the far side of the island.

"You think we should speed around there, see if we can lend a hand?" Brognola asked.

Bolan shook his head. "Wait. It would take us farther away from the city, and that's where Baracco is. Either the cops can handle it or they can't. If they can't we're in a better position to help staying where we are."

The Fed was no longer listening. He was staring out to sea, a finger pointing at the tanker. "What the *hell...?*"

Bolan swung around. There was movement aboard the ship. On the long foredeck that covered the storage tanks in front of the superstructure, groups of men maneuvered curious spidery objects about five feet high that moved on small wheels. Bolan raised the binoculars again.

The wheeled devices were moving faster than the men. They headed for the bow of the ship, increasing speed, then suddenly took to the air. There were three of them, triangular batlike shapes swooping up over the tanker and then down to glide over the ornate roofs of the Lido on their way to Murano.

"Son of a bitch!" Brognola breathed softly. "You have to hand it to them!" He was looking at a trio of ultralights—in effect, powered delta wings, hang gliders driven by engines no larger than those of lawn mowers.

A helmeted pilot sat at the controls in the spiderweb of struts beneath each wing, and beneath each pilot's seat hung a webbing harness something like a ski lift chair.

"Scoop up the terrorists somewhere on the far side of the island, lift them off without having to land," Bolan said, somewhat impressed. "God knows what happened to the guards, but the ultralights wouldn't be airborne if the cargo wasn't ready. Then dump them behind some tall building in the city while the choppers are still grounded with the duck shooters and before the police water patrols can reembark from that cruiser. A crack operation."

"What do we do? Try to intercept?"

"We wait," the Executioner said again. "Then, if they get away with it, we follow."

The ultralights dived over the ramparts of the island fortress of Sant' Andrea, vanishing behind the buildings on Murano. Then suddenly the put-put of their diminutive engines throbbed again and they flew out from behind San Cipriano, soaring upward on a thermal to head for the city. A man now hung suspended beneath each hang glider.

"They used the deck of that tanker like an aircraft carrier," Brognola said. "There'll be a few questions for the master of that ship to answer!"

"If they catch him before he makes the three-mile limit," Bolan replied dryly. He jerked his head toward the Lido. Beyond the spit of land, the tanker had put about and was hightailing it for the open sea, its smokestack trailing a long plume of diesel fumes blown landward by the breeze.

There was frenzied activity among the police patrol boats, cops swarming back from the big cruiser as whistles blew and the outboards started to roar. A Nightstalker chopper clattered into view above one of the inner sandbanks.

The leading ultralight was halfway to the city, no more than one hundred feet above the surface of the lagoon. "They'll never make it," Bolan shouted, slamming his own throttles wide open. "Those wings can make anything up to fifty, sixty. They'll be out of sight behind San Marco or the Doge's Palace or one of the museums in half a minute. All they have to do then is slow down, allow the passengers to step off, then junk the wings somewhere on the mainland beyond."

"Unless that's where they meet Baracco anyway."

Bolan shook his head. "It's in the city," he insisted.

The crew of the helicopter shared Bolan's doubts. Two of the hang gliders were nearing the thirteenth- and fourteenth-century palazzi that rose straight from the water at the entrance to the Grand Canal, when the chopper opened fire on the third.

A spurt of flame exploded from the helicopter's right-hand pod, a streak of white against the blue sky, and a 2.75-inch heat-seeking rocket arrowed toward the defenseless ultralight. The pilot didn't even see it coming. The harnessed fugitive, dangling in the webbing below, windmilled his arms frantically as the missile zeroed in on the tiny engine.

A blinding white flash momentarily dimmed the early-morning sunlight, and a ball of orange fire daubed with brown boiled over the lagoon. Dark fragments trailing spirals of smoke arced through the air, and part of the wing canopy, still blazing, hissed into the water. The remaining hang gliders were out of sight before another missile could be launched.

"Are *we* going to make it?" Brognola asked, glancing at the creaming bow waves of the patrol boats a quarter of a

mile astern and at the other chopper soaring above the
sandbanks.

"We're going to have a damned good try!" Bolan returned.

The engine howled, the deck shuddered beneath their feet
and the stem of the launch rose high out of the water as he
hurled them toward the great waterway looping through the
city.

22

The assault on the island of Murano that sprung the jailed prisoners was as daring—and in its way as simple—as the aerial operation that spirited them back to Venice.

The problem facing the Mafia planners was simple, too: how did they rescue three hardmen from an island courtroom bristling with guards when the place was surrounded by heavily armed reinforcements and both air and sea approaches to the isle were totally blocked?

The Milan-based mafiosi and their Camorra friends in Naples had decided that they had to lay a false trail to lure away the air and sea cover. Then they had to neutralize the people in the courtroom and eliminate the reinforcements. The hardmen could walk into the open air free and be picked up.

But how could they neutralize the courtroom without affecting the prisoners? And how could they lay enough firepower on to block the opposition when the approaches were being policed?

They had to have an accomplice inside the courtroom of course, and they had to put the bite on someone. Phase Two was no more than a matter of tactics. Those things could always be arranged.

The bite was put on an attorney—one of the prosecution lawyers, ironically enough—on account of certain irregularities concerning clients' money held in escrow, and certain photographs that linked the attorney intimately with the son of a high court judge.

The court was neutralized by a lethal nerve gas pumped into the room through a sabotaged radiator in the steam heating system. The gas, developed by chemical warfare experts and stolen from a secret biological research station in Lombardy, was a less virulent derivative of Tabun. It oxidized rapidly in the open air and was rendered harmless in less than fifteen minutes—but by that time its deadly work was done.

All the attorney had to do was twirl the wheel on the doctored radiator that allowed the gas to escape, and then whisk four lightweight gas masks from his briefcase. Three masks were to be tossed over the armored glass partition to the prisoners; the fourth was for himself.

It was left to him to find an explanation of how he came to be the sole survivor, although there would, of course, be no witnesses to explain what had actually happened.

The signal for the assault on police and carabinieri outside the courtroom was the detonation of three stun grenades lobbed into the seminary to put the reinforcements out of action.

The mobsters who opened fire had been on the island since before dawn. Off-loaded from the Iranian tanker on inflatable rubber rafts, they had landed on the spit between Punta Sabbioni and the Treporta Bridge, carried the rafts across to the lagoon and paddled between two of the islands to Murano. Too low on the water to register on a radar screen, with no heat-producing engines to print an IR signature, they had landed under cover of the fog and stolen away to await the signal to attack.

The battle was short and fierce. By the time the three hang gliders winged in from the ocean to pick the escaped prisoners off the ramparts, only the *commendatore* and two of his men were left alive, and all of them were wounded. Four surviving mafiosi left their automatic arms, grenade launchers and mortars on the quayside, pushed off one of the rafts and headed for Torcello in the northern sector of the lagoon. The last act of the last man aboard was to put a bullet through the head of the attorney. "No witnesses," the capo who had organized the escape had said, "means no witnesses."

BARACCO STOOD IN THE STERN of a gondola, dressed as a traditional gondolier. With one hand he held on to a striped mooring post that projected from the water by the door of a house on one of the narrowest canals in Venice. The gondola was high-prowed with a curtained center section, an eighteenth-century replica designed to attract tourists.

The canal ran behind the city's famous clock tower and crossed the Grand Canal near the Rialto Bridge; then it twisted between older, poorer buildings, eventually leading into the Grand Canal again opposite the railroad station.

And at the station, waiting to be loaded onto a baggage car, were three laundry hampers similar to the one he had used to smuggle Mack Bolan's unconscious body out of the Grand Hotel Terminus in The Hague. The hampers were consigned to Mestre, and each one was large enough to accommodate one escaped Red Brigades prisoner.

Baracco stole the obligatory glance at his watch. They should be climbing into the harness below the ultralights just about now—Cristoforo Zanussi, the brains behind the Bologna railroad station massacre, Giuseppe Ognano, the muscle man, and Alex Delrenzio, who had gunned down three United Nations diplomats in Rome.

The Corsican listened, his head tilted to one side. Was that, very distantly over the lapping of water and the hum of the city, the rumble of distant gunfire?

He stooped to pick up the gondola pole with his free hand. The canal was perfect. There were no promenades on either side: the tall houses with their stained stucco and rotting brick facades rose straight from the gray-green water; no footbridges arched over the surface, and there were no picturesque squares full of rubbernecking tourists to break the monotony of those towering walls. The waterway could have been designed to baffle pursuers. Throughout its sinuous length there was never more than an eighty-yard reach without a corner, and most of the deeply recessed windows above were barred.

Baracco nodded his satisfaction. He always could pick them. He let go of the hitching post and began to pole the gondola toward the stone staircase where his clients were due to arrive.

A sharp double explosion cut through the air. He didn't know it, but there was going to be one empty hamper making the rail trip to Mestre. Ognano, stronger but slower than the others, had paid the price of a fumble with the harness that had caused his hang glider pilot to lag behind his companions.

Baracco frowned. He looked up at the narrow strip of sky above the canal. No sunlight penetrated these canyon depths, but the sheets, shirts and underwear hanging from laundry racks that projected from windows on the upper floors were bright against the blue.

There was no doubt about it now: he could hear the rasp of ultralight engines. He poled the gondola more powerfully ahead.

"THEY LANDED THEM on a *roof*!" The two hang gliders appeared from behind the domes of San Marco—without their passengers. The launch was two hundred yards away on the Grand Canal, and Bolan sent it surging forward between the river traffic.

Gondoliers and the pilots of water taxis shouted abuse. A pleasure boat loaded with sightseers veered dangerously near the bank as the wash from the powerboat rolled forcefully out to slap against the worn stone walls. In the center of the canal a bargeman standing in the stern of a heavily loaded sail-freighter lost his balance and shook an angry fist.

Brognola was scanning a large-scale map of the city waterways. "They must have put them down somewhere between San Zaccaria and the Querini Stampalia Palace." He snatched the transceiver from the padded seat. "Police headquarters is less than two blocks away, across the water from the Campo San Lorenzo. There's a network of narrow streets around there. I'll tell them to throw a cordon around the whole area and call up those choppers."

"Baracco's a specialist at avoiding cordons," Bolan said. "There's also a network of very narrow canals, and several derelict blocks that are either condemned or waiting to be restored. My guess is that the terrorists have been lowered to the roof of one of those, with Baracco waiting below with some kind of transport—I'd say a boat."

Brognola was speaking rapidly into the mike, checking out tactics with the carabinieri liaison office that had been set up. "They'll be under cover by the time the choppers are positioned overhead," the Executioner called from the wheel. "Tell them to question every last person in the streets. People always look up at low-flying aircraft, especially offbeat ones like those hang gliders. Someone must have seen those guys put down."

It was 350 yards from the Querini Stampalia Palace to the Rialto Bridge. For Bolan's big cruiser—obliged to follow the course of the Grand Canal on its huge loop through the city—the distance was more than two thousand. To the observers in the two choppers hovering above the city center it was no contest. Contradictory police messages crackled through their earphones—the fugitives had been seen on the roof of an abandoned palazzo; they had climbed down a stairway into a canal; they were trapped on the "leads" between the domes of San Marco; they had been sighted by the Colleoni statue a quarter of a mile to the north. But it was impossible for them to distinguish two escaped prisoners and a would-be rescuer among the antlike thousands crowding the squares, bridges and promenades below; impractical to separate one boat from the hundreds waterborne between the canalside spires and colonnades. They were unable to chart the progress of the race—the launch zigzagging at full speed between the craft jamming the water; the phony gondolier desperately poling the short distance that remained to the Grand Canal, in the hope of crossing it before the pursuit closed in.

A squad of police was gesticulating on the Rialto Bridge. The radio confirmed the presence of the fugitives on a stairway above an extra-narrow canal. Someone reported a vintage gondola with a curtained center section in a similar canal. The choppers had come down to within fifty feet of the rubberneckers thronging the Riva del Ferro quayside.

Bolan and Brognola saw it at the same time: one gondola among many, but the only one with a curtained pavilion.

And the only one propelled by a stocky man with wide shoulders and a prominent jaw.

The craft was three-fourths of the way across the Grand Canal, weaving skillfully among the small vessels dawdling near the bridge. Bolan wrestled with the wheel, feeding the engine brief bursts of power to jockey the cruiser nearer the narrow opening—little more than a water-filled alley—for which Baracco was clearly heading. But he was too late. The gondola glided out of sight while he was still fifty yards away.

Bolan raced for the opening, throttling back and throwing the engine into reverse at the last moment as he saw that the alley was too narrow to take the cruiser's broad beam. The bow crunched against stone piles at the entrance to the canal.

"Tie her up!" the Executioner called. "Brief the choppers and wait for me here."

Springing over the low glass screen, he ran to the stern and dived into the polluted waters of the canal. He was wearing his blacksuit and the H&K G-11 assault rifle was slung over his back. The weapon, with its smooth, sealed, plastic casing, was completely waterproof. The tiny 4.7 mm slugs that it fired were set into solid blocks of propellant, with no empty shells to be cleared or ejected.

Bolan's crawl arrowed him through the water after the slow-moving gondola.

Because of its ornamentation, the replica was heavy and sluggish. Plunging in the pole with redoubled energy, Baracco looked back at his pursuer, his features twisted into a snarl of hate. Was he never to be rid of this son of a bitch?

Bolan was forty yards behind now, and gaining, his muscular frame cleaving the water with scarcely a splash. His arms scythed through the surface as cleanly as the titanium screws of the launch.

Baracco was in a quandary. His mini-Uzi was slung over one shoulder, but although it was small enough to be fired with one hand, he needed both hands to punt the gondola. And if he once lost his way... well, he might not waste the blacksuited bastard with his first burst. Plus the damned helicopters kept passing and repassing the thin strip of sky above. Plus there was a good eight or nine hundred yards to go before he made the Grand Canal again opposite the railroad station. Cursing, he called out to the two Red Brigades terrorists hidden behind the curtains.

Delrenzio's swarthy face appeared in the gap as one of the drapes was edged back. "I thought you told us not to show—"

"Forget it," Baracco rasped, thrusting the pole with all his force. "I didn't expect they'd be so smart—or onto us so quick. I didn't figure on this bastard behind us and I didn't think I'd need to risk bringing guns for you people. But here—" he plucked a Beretta automatic from a holster beneath his jacket and tossed it to the terrorist "—kill him. Then maybe we can start making time to the damned station."

"I thought you were the one who was paid to be smart," Delrenzio growled. But he sighted the gun two-handed and fired.

The reports were loud in the narrow space between the high stone walls, two 3-shot bursts. But the gondola was rocking as Baracco heaved it forward; a head-on target almost totally submerged wasn't the easiest thing to hit, especially when it twisted and moved fast in the water.

Slugs smacked into the surface in front of Bolan's face and whipped small spurts of spray from the ripples on either

side of him. He sensed a slight jar as part of the assault rifle's plastic casing was smashed away, but he was un-
touched. Swiftly the warrior changed direction and swam
behind a flight of stone steps that led to a brassbound oak
door four feet above the canal.

He dragged himself from the water and lay along the ancient smooth-worn stones with his elbows resting on the
platform in front of the door. The Heckler & Koch was unslung, with the butt pressed to his shoulder. He squinted
through the optical sight incorporated in the carrying handle above the gun's pistol grip, and his forefinger tightened
around the trigger.

Bolan shot very carefully. He didn't want Baracco
dead...yet. There were still too many things to find out. He
aimed for the hull of the gondola, just below the waterline.
The craft wouldn't sink, that was for sure, but he could
punch in enough holes to let in water and slow it down.

The Heckler & Koch G-11 was capable of firing 3-round
bursts at a rate of two thousand rounds per minute, each
ninety-millisecond trio clearing the muzzle before the recoil
began. The Executioner ripped out four bursts.

Baracco shouted with fury as wood splintered by his feet
and water began to well into the gondola. Curses from inside the curtained pavilion testified that Bolan's groups had
been artfully spaced. Delrenzio poked the Beretta through
the curtains again, and the weapon chugged out another
burst. But Bolan had already ducked behind the top step,
and the killstream only chipped away stone.

It was then, perhaps for the first time since he had started
his getaway business, that Baracco lost his cool. Suddenly
it was all too much for him, the dice were loaded, and he
panicked.

He ran the gondola in to another flight of steps on the far side of the canal and leaped ashore. "Come on! Move your asses," he shouted at the terrorists. "We'll make it quicker and safer on dry land."

"What do you mean, dry land?" Zanussi grated. "There's God knows how many canals between here and—"

"I know a way across the rooftops. There's an arch over one of the canals, high up. Then a bridge. And a backup boat." The Corsican ran across a courtyard at the top of the steps and led the way along a twisting lane that curved around the rear of a church.

Bolan slung the G-11, dived into the water again and swam to the second flight of stairs. On the top step he looked back to the entrance to the canal. The cruiser was moored, and Hal Brognola stood on the foredeck ahead of the screen, shading his eyes with one hand as he stared down the narrow waterway. The gondola had swung out from the steps and was drifting slowly backward toward the Grand Canal.

Bolan waved to the Fed and plunged across the courtyard in pursuit of the fugitives. If Brognola used the radio, there should be cops all over the area within minutes. He could already hear sirens in the distance.

Beyond the church was a rubble-strewn vacant lot where an old building had been demolished. Only the steel girders that formed the skeleton of a new structure had been erected. A cement mixer, several truckloads of cement and a stack of lumber had been delivered, but no construction crew was working the site.

The three fugitives were swarming up the tubular scaffolding that covered two sides of the five-story girdered frame. Shielded by the metal crisscross, Baracco and his clients were poor targets for a man with a small-caliber rifle. Determined not to waste time—for he could see that it was an easy jump from the top girders to an adjacent building—Bolan raced to an open-sided service elevator on the far side of the lot.

Gunshots reverberated from girder to girder as he flung himself down behind the grillwork of the elevator gates. From somewhere above, Baracco had opened fire with the Uzi. A ricochet whined off the counterweight and splatted against a quarter-inch steel stanchion.

Bolan rose to his knees and reached for the control panel. When he thumbed the button, the pulleys and cables remained stationary—the electrical supply had been disconnected.

Two heavier reports from Delrenzio's Beretta rang out as the warrior ran for the scaffolding at right angles to the complex the gunners were climbing. He leaped for the lowest tubular crosspiece and pulled himself up.

Bolan used all his tigerish strength in a supreme effort to overhaul Baracco and the terrorists before they made it to the plank walkway that circled the block above the fifth floor. But he was still six feet below the fourth level when he heard their footsteps clatter on the boards.

Baracco shouted something and one of the terrorists replied, but Bolan couldn't make out the words. They vanished over the crumbling balustrade that topped the facade of the old house adjoining the site.

Above the warrior's head an H-section girder that would one day support the building's floor slanted diagonally out to join the scaffold wall Baracco and his companions had been scaling. Bolan reckoned it was a quicker way to close in on them than continuing vertically to the walkway. He dragged himself up, sat astride the ironwork and began to work himself out over the fifty-foot drop.

He was less than halfway over when Delrenzio's head and shoulders appeared above the balustrade. The Beretta in the terrorist's right hand spit fire. Sighting through the close-meshed network of steel, it was tough drawing a bead, but Bolan knew he would be a sitting duck once the gunner maneuvered himself into a position where his sightline was unobstructed. None of the slugs in the first burst made it as far as the crosspiece girder, but there were plenty more in the magazine....

Marooned on his six-inch steel strut with nothing but space between him and the ground, Bolan did the only thing he could do: he drew up on one knee, then the other, pushed himself upright and ran.

His feet were still slippery from the weed-slimed canal, but he sprinted for the far wall of scaffolding. Lungs pumping, eyes staring—and refusing to look down—legs pistoning, he hurled himself along the narrow girder.

Delrenzio fired two more single shots. One whistled past the Executioner's head; the other slammed against the girder and jarred it when Bolan was no more than a yard from his goal. The slight shock was enough to make his foot slip just as he placed his weight on it. For a dizzying moment he overbalanced and hung in midair, then his outflung arm hit the scaffolding tubes, his hands clenched around smooth steel, and he dropped to the full stretch of his arms with a shock that jolted the breath from his body. By the time he made it up to the walkway and crossed to the balustrade, Baracco and the two Italians were nowhere to be seen.

On the far side of the stone barrier he found himself in an unreal landscape of tiled slopes, chimney pots, television aerial, and laundry drying on wooden frames. Here and there the rectangular bulk of an elevator housing lent a touch of modernity, but the great domes of San Marco and the bell towers of more than fifteen churches within a radius of a quarter mile emphasized the antiquity of the fabled city.

There were many houses crowded around the construction site, and Bolan was suddenly aware of the interest his private war was provoking. Over the sound of music from a dozen radios he heard shouts and cries. Men were gesticulating on flowered balconies. Somewhere a woman was screaming. He unslung the G-11 and advanced cautiously.

Between two chimneys he saw the blue of the lagoon...and a sudden shadow that fell across the slates between them—a bulky shadow with a short, stubby projection that slanted his way. Bolan flung himself to the slope as Baracco's mini-Uzi ripped a deadly 9 mm hail his way. Stone splinters fountained from the balustrade and cracked the slates. Bolan fired a short burst from the assault rifle, but the Corsican had already pulled back behind the stack: the slugs only stained the sky with a cloud of pulverized brick dust.

Scrambling to his feet, the Executioner felt the sodden blacksuit chill against his skin as the rotor wash from one of the choppers swirled through the laundry lines. The machine roared down to hover above the roof.

A rope ladder swung below the open hatch at one side of the bubble, with a carabinieri gunner wearing a bulletproof vest clinging to the lower rungs. A harsh voice shouted something unintelligible through a bullhorn.

From behind an elevator housing fifty yards away, Bolan saw a wild eyed, bearded figure—Zanussi, the terrorist who was unarmed—dash for the far side of the roof and gather himself for the six-foot leap that would carry him over an alley and down to the coping surmounting the facade of a building with a lower roofline.

The helicopter sank farther, and the man clinging to the ladder gestured with his gun. Zanussi panicked and jumped before he was ready. He made the sandstone coping, but his weight wasn't far enough forward. Feeling himself about to topple backward, he made a desperate grab for the open window of a dormer projecting from the steeply shingled roof next door. His fingers clenched around the frame, but the wood was cracked and rotten. Glass flashed in the sunlight as the window disintegrated, and he dropped with a wild cry into the void.

A woman in a flowered housecoat ran to the window, her mouth open in astonishment. She leaned out and looked down, one hand flying up to stifle a scream when she saw the terrorist's broken body crumpled across the edge of a stone basin in a fountain. Water spilled from the basin, staining the flagstones of a small patio red.

Bolan was standing between two lines of drying sheets. The crack of Delrenzio's Beretta was simultaneous with the three holes that appeared in a quilted bedcover within inches of the warrior's head. He dropped to one knee and swung around in time to see the Italian himself drop out of sight behind an improvised barrier that had been erected to protect a cracked skylight from the wind.

That was Delrenzio's mistake. The barrier was made of tin roofing material, a strip of corrugated iron popped up between a chimney, and a small stack of lumber. The Heckler & Koch G-11 caseless assault rifle was capable of punching its high-velocity, small-caliber rounds through a steel helmet at a distance of five hundred yards. That made the terrorist's cover about as useful as the sheets hanging on the line above Bolan.

The Executioner hosed a stream of death up, down and across the corrugated strip, emptying the rifle's magazine in a single lethal burst. For a moment the roar of the shots and the clangor of tortured metal drowned out the rotors of the second chopper, which was now hovering above the building.

There were no more shots from the Beretta.

Bolan pushed himself upright and walked over to the skylight. Behind the drilled metal sheet, Delrenzio had been torn almost in two by Bolan's skullbusters. Thin slivers of splintered bone pricked whitely through a mess of steaming organs in the center of a great fan of blood already congealing in the sun.

The choppers had landed two men. "Good work," one praised. "The state should be grateful. The treasury will be saved the expense of feeding these bastards for thirty years."

"It's the third man I'm interested in," Bolan stated.

"He was blown apart by one of our rockets," the other cop replied.

"Not him. The one with the Uzi."

They looked at each other and shook their heads. "We got the three terrorists," the first man said. "I didn't see anyone else up here."

Bolan cursed. He ran to the edge of the roof and looked out across the alley beyond the patio. There was no sign of Baracco, but he saw another skylight propped open on a roof two houses away. Beyond the fountain where Zanussi's body lay, Byzantine arches flanked a paved passage that led to a street market bright with vegetables, fruit and flowers.

Bolan swore again. He jerked open the cracked skylight near the remains of Delrenzio and dropped into the building below. Fifteen minutes later he was standing at the corner of the Grand Canal where he had left Brognola and the powerboat. The cruiser, efficiently hitched, was nudging the mooring post as it bobbed on the swell. The gondola, which had been drifting back down the narrow waterway, had disappeared. The Fed was nowhere to be seen, but the windshield of the boat was shattered, and three bright medallions of blood stained the polished timbers of the foredeck.

23

Mack Bolan played his hunches. That was an integral part of his character. They were of course a minor part of his mental armory. "But," an intelligence analyst had once written, compiling a dossier on the warrior, "these hunches are no wild, off-the-cuff guesses: they are based on the instinctive interpretation of data stored and retrieved without conscious effort by that most sophisticated of computers—the mind of a natural fighter."

It was a hunch—programmed perhaps by his continuing belief that the whole Venetian operation was at odds with Baracco's normal MO—that put him back on the Corsican's track. And that of the missing Brognola.

"The powerboat and the chopper were decoys," he told Gudrun back at the hotel. "They couldn't be used again, and there was no sign of any others. You can't make a 350-mile flight across the ocean in three ultralights. And yet the final destination was Albania. How was your ex planning to get his clients there?"

"You tell me."

"Same as he always did," Bolan said. "By road—through Trieste and Yugoslavia, using a series of old trucks and jalopies that nobody would look at twice. That's the way I figure it."

"Yes, but there are no vehicles in Venice. It's not—"

"Okay, okay," the Executioner cut in. "But he was stuck with Venice because that's where his clients were escaping from. So what's he going to do once they make contact? Transfer them to the mainland, where he *can* pick up one of his old wrecks, ASAP. Right? And what's the quickest—the only—way of making that crossing when half the army and all of the police force are looking for you?"

Gudrun frowned and shook her head. "It would be too slow and too risky by boat," she said, her red hair swinging from side to side like a tawny bell. "So it has to be the causeway, straight across by road or rail."

"Got it. So the police are going to have to earn their bread with a little more legwork."

The police weren't keen. They'd been working since dawn, some of them all night. Honor was saved and three Red Brigades thugs were dead. They weren't concerned about locating a supposed Corsican whom none of them had seen—and what charge could you bring against a man who'd tried to help escaping prisoners . . . and failed?

As well, they weren't sure of the Executioner's exact status. It was the federal agent from Washington who'd had the letters of introduction. Now if *he* was to ask them for further help . . .

Bolan raised the point that it was Brognola who was missing.

Sighing, one of the police chiefs, his eloquent hands spread wide, said, "Perhaps. But there is no actual *proof* that he has been abducted, is there?"

"He was here and now he isn't. He's not in his hotel or anywhere else I can find him. The man I'm after was here and now he isn't, either. What other interpretation can you put on those facts? In addition to the broken windshield and the blood on the deck."

"Perhaps your friend fell and cut himself? A quick check of the hospitals—"

"Already done," Bolan interrupted. "Zero."

"In that case, perhaps later. Because you must realize there are an enormous number of routine things to take care of in a city this size before..."

It was only after the Executioner called his friend, the *commendatore* in Turin, that he got some action. And even then it was dusk before anything positive came in.

Questions had been asked. The nearest a vehicle could get to the old city was the big Fiat garage at the inner end of the causeway, on the north side of the Grand Canal. From there one had to take a boat...and then walk. There was no record at the garage of any elderly vehicles coming or going at the relevant times—and no one had seen anyone sick, drunk or injured being helped or loaded into any specialized vehicle, such as an ambulance.

It was the same story at the railroad station. Until a redcap, apparently more observant, recalled the three hampers consigned to Mestre and realized that only one had gone on the specified train. The other two, empty, were still in the baggage check.

A replica gondola, floating free near the Scalzi Bridge, clinched it.

"It's clear as a bell," Bolan told Gudrun after the gondola was discovered. "He made it back to the narrow canal while I was still on the roof, surprised Brognola and then hid him in the curtained pavilion where his clients had been concealed. All he had to do then was pole the gondola on up to the Grand Canal, cross to the railroad station and somehow feed Brognola into that hamper. We'll find it was loaded into one of his derelicts at Mestre."

Bolan was right. They collected the Alfa Romeo roadster from the Fiat garage and drove back across the causeway to Mestre. Baggage handlers there remembered loading a heavy hamper arriving on the train from Venice onto an old flatbed truck, which had taken the A.4 pike for Udine and Trieste.

"He's on the way back to his own base," Gudrun told the warrior as they left the bright lights of the city behind them and headed eastward into the night.

"And that is?"

"Not too far from Udine. Twenty miles from the junk-yard where you escaped from him."

Gudrun shifted down to pass a convoy of trucks. There was still plenty of boot left in the veteran speedster. She swung back into the inside lane as Bolan said, "Tell me about Baracco and what you think he aims to do."

"You have to know two things about him," Gudrun replied, "apart from the fact he's a monomaniac. One, he may be crazy but he's a very dangerous man. Two, he won't allow possible witnesses against him to stay alive."

"And where does that leave my friend?"

"Six feet under if you're not careful." Gudrun's voice was somber. "And quick with it. I know Bart, and I know the way his mind works. He's going to lean on your friend—and he can lean very heavily—until he's found out what he wants to know. After that I wouldn't rate Mr. Brognola's chances very high."

"What will he want to know?"

"Everything about the two of you. Who you work for, what evidence you have, who else you may have confided in. He'll want to know just how many people he has to eliminate before he's in the clear again. Once he knows those things he'll kill Brognola."

"He might not find out anything. Brognola's tough."

"He won't be tough enough to hold out against Bart. Not when the son of a bitch is mad, and he'll be as sore as hell. That's two operations you and your buddy screwed up, directly or indirectly—the only two he ever lost out on. His business depends on a one hundred percent success markup. I tell you there's nothing he won't do to get even."

"Okay," Bolan said. "Show me the place, and I'll go in and get Brognola out. You want to get even with him, don't you?"

"It's not that easy. You can't just go there. All the approaches are under surveillance. There are sensors and trip wires and things even I don't know about. Also the forest around there is very dense."

"So?"

"So I think it would be better if we stopped here and you rented a car. I think it would be better if we split up and approached separately. I think the smart way to play it would be for me to go ahead and get the lay of the land. After that I can come back to you and report, so we can work out a rescue plan together."

"No way." Bolan shook his head. "I couldn't allow you to do anything alone. Your ex-boyfriend is as mad as hell, so now he'll be doubly dangerous. You told me that yourself. Forget it."

"You don't understand," Gudrun said passionately. "This man has destroyed my image of myself. He's...well, you know what he's done to me. I do what I do because I want to, not just because of your friend. I have to do it for myself, to regain my self-respect. So it's not a case of whether or not you permit me to take part. I'm going on to his place anyway. All that has to be decided is whether you come with me or wait until I check back on the situation there."

"I'm still not happy."

"That's just too bad." The woman pulled the Alfa Romeo to the side of the road. Beyond a stretch of marshland, the square tower of Torcello's Church of Santa Fosca rose floodlit above the dark lagoon. "Look," she said, "I know the trails in this forest like the back of my hand. I know the crazy folly where he lives so well that I can move secretly and watch and listen where it would be impossible for two. I can avoid the trips and traps from memory where it would waste time pointing them out to you. Your friend is in great danger. Don't you think it will be quicker, safer in the long run, if I go ahead as I suggested? Then once I come back to you with the intel, we can decide the best way to attack."

"I still don't like it. You'll be in great danger yourself."

"Nobody will even see me," Gudrun promised. "Even if they did... Well, he knows this car, but he knows nothing of my connection with you, because I never showed my face in Venice. He'd simply think I'd come back to bawl him out over this Mafia bitch. Don't you see?"

Bolan sighed. "Well, okay," he said reluctantly, "but you don't have to come back to me. Remember the little baton radio my friend used in Venice? I have a couple here, tuned to the same frequency." He reached over into the back of the roadster and pulled out the airline bag. "Take one with you and keep in touch. Call me the moment you know the score and *I'll* come to *you*. You can show me a place on the map not too far away where I can wait."

She switched on the light below the dashboard, unfolded the map and traced a route with one finger. Then she leaned across him and opened the passenger door. "Paoluzzi in the village there will rent you a car. Don't expect me to call much before midnight.''

Bolan unleathered the Beretta from his shoulder holster and held it out to her. "Take it," he offered. "I have the AutoMag, and you can't go in there defenseless.''

She nodded and took the gun. The Alfa Romeo shot away with a crackle of exhaust. He watched the twin taillights dwindle and then vanish around a corner at the entrance to the village. He started to walk.

Behind him and to his right, the illuminated domes, towers and classical facades of the city lay like a honey-colored mirage above the black desert of the sea. Bolan remembered how the men of this same village had dismantled their houses, loaded the stones into barges and sailed across the lagoon to build Venice, a town that could be defended on all sides, when they tired of eternal raids by Visigoths and other barbarians from the mainland.

After fourteen hundred years of civilization, he reflected grimly—thinking of Baracco, of the Red Brigades, of the Middle East terrorists and of the Mob—the barbarians were still there.

The only vehicle Bolan could rent from Paoluzzi's waterfront garage was almost as beat-up as one of the Corsican's—an aging Toyota Land Cruiser that looked as though it had been abandoned in the middle of the Paris-Dakar rally and only recovered after ten years of Sahara sandstorms. But the engine sounded relatively healthy and the tires were new. He filled the gas tank, handed over far too many dollars as a deposit and began to follow the route Gudrun had indicated on the map.

He drove slowly. The total distance was less than ninety miles, and it was a long time until midnight. The Land Cruiser rumbled past the marshes flanking the Piave estuary, where rich industrialists from Treviso, Mestre and Portogruaro would be gathering at dawn for the duck shooting, crossed the river via the bridge at San Dona and headed for the Tagliamento at Latisana. The Executioner, too, would be shooting at first light, though the game—he fervently hoped—would be rarer and more important than the ducks downed in the mist over the marshes.

Bolan ate at a canalside truck stop near Ceggia. In the yellow sodium light flooding the parking lot, he could see fishing boats, wicker fish traps and long skeins of net behind the semis and their trailers. By the canal gates, three sailing barges waited for the dawn wind that would run them down to Venice.

Five miles up the Tagliamento valley, Bolan stopped again, ran the Toyota into a disused gravel pit and snatched a couple hours of badly needed sleep. But the sky in the east was lightening, and it was after five o'clock before the transceiver lying beside him on the seat bleeped for the first time.

HAL BROGNOLA BLINKED himself awake. It took some time for his mind to clear, and the blurred images revolving slowly in front of his eyes meant nothing to him at first.

Then, piece by piece, the jigsaw assembled itself: the empty gondola drifting backward until it bumped against the powerboat at the entrance to the canal; the sound of distant shots; the helicopters circling and then sinking down over the stairway where the Executioner had followed Baracco and his fugitives; the unexpected appearance of the Corsican himself on the Grand Canal quayside; his leap onto the cruiser with a blackjack in his hand, and then... nothing.

The Fed jerked fully awake. Baracco was standing in front of him, squat, powerful hands resting on his hips. "So," he grated, "the number two snooper is back in command of his senses. So much the better. Baracco will be able to find out the truth that much quicker. And then he will be free to deal with at least one of the interfering bastards who have *dared* to thwart his plans."

His lips curled back from his teeth, and his eyes flashed venomously as he spit out the last words. Brognola involuntarily flinched from the fury in his voice.

Or at least he tried to. Movement, however, was impossible. He was sitting in a stoutly built rustic chair, wrists wired to the arms, knees and ankles to the front legs. The wide baggage strap that passed over his chest and behind the chair back was so tightly buckled that he found it hard to breathe.

"I guess it's useless asking who you are, what you have to do with this Bolan, who the two of you work for, and why you are interfering in my life with your goddamn snooping?" Baracco asked in a quieter tone.

"Quite useless."

"As I thought. I can tell a professional when I see one. It would save me a lot of time—and you a lot of pain—if you were able to do the same. For I aim to get that information, and I don't give a damn how I do it. Also, I am pushed for time, so my methods will necessarily have to be ... crude."

"You talk like a heavy in a World War II movie," Brognola said. "Supposing I was to come across with this intel. What happens to me then?"

"I shall kill you. You must pay the price of the knowledge you and your friend have gained by your spying. Both of you know too much for the safety of my organization."

"If I'm going to die anyway, why should I talk first?"

"To save yourself great suffering before you die."

"Well, you might have *me*, but you don't have my friend."

"His time will come. I shall have him soon."

"I doubt it," Brognola needled. "He's smarter than you."

"He wasn't all that smart in Prague," the Corsican sneered. "Come now, answer my questions."

"I have nothing to say."

"Very well. We shall see." Baracco sighed heavily and left.

Alone now, Brognola saw the room clearly for the first time. It was a strange place. There was one more chair—the twin of the one he was bound to—a rolltop desk littered with newspaper clippings, a huge refectory table...and that was all. Through a window above the bare, dusty boards of the floor, the Fed could see the wall of another wing of the building, turreted, spired and battlemented with hewn stone like a castle in a fairy tale.

Except that, unlike the fairy-tale mountains that humped themselves above flower-strewn fields in storybooks, the peaks, spurs and bluffs beyond this stronghold were composed of towering stacks of scrap iron.

Brognola switched his attention back indoors. His bonds had been tied by an expert. He couldn't reach them with his fingers or detect the least sign of resilience when he flexed his muscles against them. And there was nothing nearby that could be of any help. The remains of a delicatessen meal lay in waxed cartons on the big table, but there was nothing in sight that could be used as a tool.

Footsteps echoed in a flagstone passageway outside the door. The Corsican was coming back.

He carried a small piece of machinery in a cast-iron housing, two lengths of high-tension cable, a six-inch cranked handle and a half-dozen bulldog clips. "A magneto," he said proudly, laying the housing on the table with a heavy thump. "Twenty-four-volt Bosch from an old sandtipper out there. The Foreign Legion in North Africa used to say there was nothing like them for persuading folks to volunteer information! And it's nice that we can provide one, as it were, from stock. I always knew there were many uses for a wrecking yard."

He laid the rest of the equipment down by the magneto and walked to Brognola's chair. "Now, friend, we will see how sweetly Baracco can make you sing." He reached forward and seized the American's shirt, ripping it open from neck to waist in a single savage gesture.

BROGNOLA WAS UNCONSCIOUS, slumped forward against the retaining strap with his head hanging, when the clatter of the helicopter's rotors broke the silence in the big room. Leaving the cables still clipped in position on the unconscious man's seared flesh, Baracco ran out to a stairway that spiraled to the ground inside a Gothic turret.

His retreat looked even more surreal from outside. It had originally been built as a hunting lodge for a Milan tycoon furious over the loss of the Massif de Mercantour hunting grounds when that part of Italy was ceded to France after a plebiscite in the 1870s. Gudrun had called it a folly, and that was what it was: a Gothic extravagance, the battlements and ramparts pretentiously concealing what was in fact a relatively small house. It had always looked curiously unreal in its forest hollow, but surrounded by a turbulent sea of scrap iron, as it now was, the place became at once a creation of the wildest fantasy.

Over a groundswell of bedsteads, iron railings, cooking utensils, disused ovens and lengths of railroad track, great crests of heavier wreckage swept toward the building in a rusted and remorseless tide—a flood that culminated in a tidal wave of smashed car bodies, dented boilers and the skeletons of traction engines that had once, in their day, hauled entire circuses around the country.

Dwarfed by this metal deluge, Baracco stood waiting.

The chopper sank down from the sky over the mountains that rose near the Austrian border, skimmed the surf of green treetops that washed against the foothills and lowered itself neatly to the ground in an open space between one of the mounds of scrap and the outer wall of the folly.

If he had been conscious, Brognola would have recognized it as the twin-rotor machine that had provided one of the diversions during the assault on Murano that same morning. But there were no decoy mafiosi with shotguns in the cabin now. The hatch slid back and a single figure dropped to the ground. Brown boots laced to the knee strode purposefully across to the porch where Baracco was waiting. The curves of a supple body moved enticingly beneath a formfitting leather flying suit. Then the flight helmet was removed to reveal the face of Mariella, the blonde from the tavern in Prague.

Baracco kissed her and took her to the room where Brognola was being held prisoner. She glanced cursorily at the inert figure, then wrinkled her nose at the odor of seared flesh. "Has he come up with anything yet?"

"Nothing we hadn't guessed already," the Corsican growled. "He's tougher than he looks."

"You mean he's said nothing at all?" Mariella demanded.

"Oh, he's *talked* all right. They all talk when the current is flowing. Pain and Pentothol make a persuasive mixture." Baracco waved a hand at a hypodermic syringe lying on the table. "So we know for sure he works for some American security service. We know where his office is, and we know he has the President's ear. Big deal. But we *don't* know any more about this Bolan—what's his angle, how far he has got, what he aims to do. What I do know is that I'm going to kill the son of a bitch. Give me another half hour with this creep and I'll find out..." He picked up an electric soldering iron from the table and rammed it viciously into a wall socket.

"My people know about Bolan," the woman said. "I've been checking. You can leave him to them. There's already a contract out. He's caused the Families quite enough trouble already. As far as this man here is concerned, you don't have time to take it any farther. You'll have to get rid of him, fast. My principals want action. We have clients waiting to be moved in three different European countries already."

"All right, sweetie, all right." Baracco was at once contrite. "Why the hell should I waste my time and yours trying to discover why a do-gooder should want to pass himself off as a murderer anyway?" He pulled the smoking soldering iron from the wall.

"How will you do it?"

"I have a plan. Obviously his death must be arranged so the authorities believe no other person was involved. I know the ideal place—in the valley less than a mile from here."

"Good. Do we do it now?"

Baracco shook his head. "It'll be dark very soon, and it'll take time. I'll need your help. We'll take him down there and fix it as soon as it's light. Meanwhile we can work out final arrangements to move your three clients.''

"Tell me about the plan."

There was a wide, open hearth at one end of the room. The chimney was joined on the floor above by a flue from a smaller fireplace in an empty, unused bedroom. Baracco had never found out, but conversations in the lower room could be heard clearly by someone crouching by the chimneypiece in the upper when no fires were burning. Gudrun, Bolan's transceiver in one hand, was crouched there now.

24

"As you would expect," the voice coming from the transceiver in Mack Bolan's hand reported, "the scheme is quite diabolical. It seems there's an old railroad viaduct that crosses the head of a valley near Bart's place. It was built toward the end of the last century to carry some single-track branch line toward the mountains. But the Austrians cut the track while advancing on Caporetto in World War I, Mussolini tore up the rails to make munitions in the thirties and your people dropped bombs nearby during the German retreat in 1944."

"But the bridge itself is still standing?"

"In a very bad condition," Gudrun confirmed. "It was damaged by blast and shrapnel, wind and frost have eaten away most of the mortar, and it's practically standing on dry-stone pillars now. It could come crashing down at any moment."

"You're beginning to make me feel uneasy."

"The old railbed exists as a rough, weed-grown trail. You can still get a car down it, at least as far as the bridge, but there the track is blocked with barbed wire and the viaduct is closed even to pedestrian traffic. It's too dangerous to use."

"And this diabolical plan?"

"They're going to put your friend in the cab of an old truck. He'll be lightly drugged so that he won't be wise to what's going on, but he won't be bound or gagged. Then they aim to shove the truck out over the viaduct and—"

"Down will come baby, Brognola and all?"

"That's it. The structure is so shaky that a motorcycle could start it crumbling away. A heavy truck will collapse the whole thing—it won't stand the weight."

"I don't get it," Bolan said. "Why not just shoot him?"

"They want it to look like an accident, with nobody else involved. It's far enough away not to be connected with Bart's place. The truck they're using is the one Bart used when he snatched you from the carabinieri. There were a dozen cops brutally murdered in that operation. The investigators will assume your friend was the killer. The tire tracks will match, and there's other evidence."

"They'll think he freed me once I'd been snatched back from the police, that he was on his way back to Austria on some minor route and he figured on taking a shortcut and came to grief on the way. Is that roughly the scenario?"

"That's what I heard," Gudrun said.

"Okay," the warrior continued crisply. "The facts. How are they going to do it? You said *shove* the truck out over the bridge?"

"Not literally. The wire barriers can easily be moved. And the approach trail is on a downgrade that continues halfway out across the viaduct. They aim to tie a rope to the rear of the truck, give it a push to start it rolling down the slope, then winch it out gradually as it crawls across the bridge. When the weight collapses the bridge and the truck falls, they'll cut the rope... and hurry down to the valley bottom to unfasten the other end."

"Got it," the Executioner said. "The killer killed, making his getaway. It's not the best plan, it won't stand up to expert examination, but it'll get them off the hook at least until State starts making official inquiries. By then they'll be long gone. They don't ever have to use this place again, particularly if the Mafia is buying in."

"What do you want me to do?" Gudrun asked. "Come and join you?"

"No. Stick around there. Hang on until I contact you. I can't be explicit, because I'm going to have to play this one strictly by ear. But keep listening, okay? Meanwhile I need more facts. What time is the 'accident' scheduled for? How far am I from this viaduct, and how do I get there? Because whatever else goes down, Brognola isn't going to die."

There was an icy determination in the Executioner's voice, a steely resolve that masked a cold fury held in check. It was something Gudrun hadn't heard before. "I'll give you a six-figure map coordinate," she said. "Where are you now?"

"Between Nimis and Tarcento, less than ten miles from the Yugoslav border. According to your briefing, I shouldn't have more than a twenty-minute drive."

"That's right. It's cutting it fine, because they're starting as soon as it's light, but they do have preparations to make. You should be there in time if you take the right roads. Do you have the map there?"

"Right in front of me."

"Okay," Gudrun said. "Now here's what you do." She ran over a complex set of directions, and Bolan in his turn roughed out a contingency plan for her to follow. Then he said, "Tell me one thing. You keep saying 'they.' But you told me Baracco was strictly a lone wolf unless he was actually operating an escape. So where does the hired help come from here?"

"It's anything but that." There was a note of rancor in the reply. "It's the woman I told you about, the mobster's daughter from Prague. My...successor." Gudrun laughed bitterly. "She seems to be mistress in more senses than one. She gives the orders, she makes the decisions, she works everything out. She's certainly the boss where Bart's concerned. Yet she keeps on talking about 'my principals' and asking questions, questions, questions, as though she were worried about the credit-rating of his damned network."

"It all adds up to what we thought."

"You'd almost think the cow was trying to buy her way into his business, the way she bought into his bed."

"Yeah," the Executioner replied, "you would, wouldn't you?"

EARLY RISERS WERE FISHING on the banks of the Tagliamento River as Bolan started the Land Cruiser and the sky above the mountains turned orange, green then finally blue.

There were willows on both sides of the river and mulberry trees in the fields across the road. Bolan remembered a line he had read once about this part of Italy—"heavy with autumn quiet, and wet from the fall rains." Well, if, like the man said, the rains came, they were certainly coming again! Within ten minutes a cloudbank blowing up fast from the south blotted out the clear sky and heavy drops began splattering against the Toyota's windshield.

By the time the vehicle turned up the sunken road where the stream from Baracco's valley ran into the Tagliamento, the rain was lancing down from a slate-gray canopy to bounce knee-high off the pavement. Bolan saw the brown sail of a barge negotiating a canal behind a line of trees, a low red farmhouse with a big barn, and then he was in the chestnut forest and the valley began twisting up into the foothills northeast of Udine.

As soon as the viaduct came into view, he stopped the off-roader and took a pair of binoculars from the airline bag.

The old bridge, still more than a mile away, spanned a scrub-covered cleft between two belts of forest: seven tall, narrow arches with a revetment at each end and six slender pillars in between. Even from this distance Bolan could see clearly that the small blocks of yellow sandstone had been seriously damaged by erosion.

There were two small observation platforms built out over the third and fifth arches—refuges for linesmen when a train passed—but otherwise the single-track road was guarded only by a solitary iron rail above the shallow parapet.

It was no big surprise, Bolan thought, eyeing the flimsy structure through the binoculars, that they had been forced to bar the approaches.

He drove on and found to his consternation that he had probably made an error when reading the large-scale map of the area. For instead of climbing to the rim of the valley as he had expected, the lane plunged suddenly down and followed the stream along its floor.

A network of dirt roads and forest trails crisscrossed the landscape here, and he had clearly confused two of them in his haste. And so now—although he would arrive at the precise map coordinate that Gudrun had specified—he would be below the viaduct instead of above it.

Agitatedly he traced his path back on the map until he located the point where he had missed the correct route. To regain it, he would have to go back seven or eight kilometers—more than four miles. Could he afford the time?

Once more he focused the glasses on the bridge. It was nearer now. At the higher end he could see something—the

cab of an ancient truck above a clump of bushes, the roof
of a sedan shining in the rain, figures moving.

He couldn't go back. No way. The macabre stage for
Brognola's murder was already set. Not one moment could
be lost; the only thing to do was to go on....

The valley road was screened by trees. There was nobody
actually on the viaduct yet or visible along the approach. It
was just possible that he could run the Land Cruiser up to
the arches without being spotted. Anyway, he would have to
try.

Overhanging branches and the steepness of the banks
prevented him from seeing the ground beyond the lip of the
valley and would presumably stop those up there from
seeing him until he was within fifty yards of the bridge. But
the slope on which the great piles had been built was gen-
tler, the trees had been cut down and the scrub was no more
than waist-high. For a short distance on both sides of the
viaduct the road—and anything on it—would be visible to
anyone above. If they happened to be watching.

Or listening.

The ancient Toyota wasn't the quietest of vehicles. The
road was evidently not often used, for there was a line of
grass running down its center. A laboring engine at this time
of the morning would surely be the one thing guaranteed to
attract the attention of Baracco and his Mafia mistress.

Bolan cut the engine and coasted the vehicle to a halt beneath the last of the overhanging trees. He unleathered Big
Thunder, grabbed the bag and ran for the bridge, keeping
as close to the bank as he could.

The road ran beneath the third archway. He stopped
there, panting, relieved for a moment not to have the rain
lashing his face, and gazed upward. According to Gudrun,

it was the top of the fourth arch, above the stream, that was in the most dangerous condition.

Bolan reckoned the height of the viaduct there had to be around a 150 feet—a multiple facade soaring skyward on slender piles that tapered slightly toward the top. Now that he was immediately below, he could see how precariously those pillars supported the old railbed. The stonework was cracked and fissured in dozens of places, and there were great gaps at the top of the central arch where chunks of masonry had fallen away. Even the vital keystone seemed to be among the jumble of blocks around which the stream frothed.

He peered around the edge of the pillar and looked up the bank, making out the top of the truck's cab. The slope hid the rest of the vehicle and the people working on it. Any minute now, though, that cab might start moving over the bridge. And that would mean Brognola would be moving too, moving to certain death when the bridge collapsed beneath the vehicle.

There had been no cries of alarm, no panicked shouts from above. So far, so good. He had made it to this point undetected. But what now? Somewhere up there Gudrun would be waiting with the Beretta to help him; he had told her to hide along the approach road and contact him when he appeared. But she was expecting him to appear from *above*. And time was running out: he dared not wait to call her on the radio and explain. Not anymore. He had to get up there and stop that truck.

Fine. And, yeah, he might be concealed now, but once he emerged from behind the pillar and launched a rescue operation scrambling up the bank, he would rise into view after the first few yards—a target Baracco couldn't miss.

From where he was, deep in the valley, there was only one way to make the top of the viaduct: he would have to scale the weathered face of the pillar itself.

It was an idea born of desperation, but there was a slim chance it might work. In any case, it was his only chance.

And Hal Brognola's.

He could begin the climb on the inner side of the pillar, unseen by the killers above. And when he reached the curvature of the arch and had to move around to the outside, he could at least profit from the fact that the pillar tapered and would thus be leaning very slightly away from him—perhaps no more than two or three degrees, but that was a hell of a sight easier to deal with than a perpendicular face.

To balance that was the disadvantage that he would be in full sight of anyone who cared to look that way during the final part of the climb. And he would have to cope with the rain. Bolan shrugged. There was no point weighing pro and cons. By one of those inexplicable twists of fortune that favor the brave, he had asked Brognola to include four mountain climber's pitons along with the gear in the bag. He stuffed these into his pocket, slid a small, heavy-headed hammer into the waistband of his pants, pushed off the safety on the holstered AutoMag and approached the face of the pillar.

Mack Bolan had carried out a great many dangerous maneuvers in his life as a combatant, and a good many ill-advised ones, too. But the most ill-advised and most dangerous of all was that wild climb in the rain up the crumbling facade of the viaduct near Baracco's retreat in Italy.

For the first twenty or thirty feet the sandstone blocks were fairly large and the interstices between them correspondingly wide. Climbing was simply a matter of wedging in the toes, reaching up to locate a handhold, taking the body's weight on the fingers as a foot scrabbled for a higher toehold—and then repeating the process. But as soon as the blocks grew smaller and the cracks narrower, the trouble began. Rain was gusting across the valley in horizontal drifts, plastering Bolan's hair to his head, weighing down his clothing and rendering slippery the polished surface of the stones. It was also turning the crumbs of old mortar and eroded flakes of sandstone in the gaps into a greasy paste in which fingers and toes skidded more easily than grasped. Under such conditions, climbing up an almost vertical face without a rope was a nightmare.

Every inch became a test of willpower, coaxing the agonized muscles and overtaxed sinews to hang in for just that second longer while the exploring foot found a temporary resting place that wouldn't flake away, the groping fingers discovered a crevice that was secure, that wouldn't crumble into nothing the instant any weight was put on it.

When the Executioner was sixty-five or seventy feet from the ground, the face he was climbing began to curl outward over his head: he had reached the curvature of the arch. Now he'd have to move to the outside of the pillar.

Gritting his teeth, he started to edge around the right angle. At one point he was splayed out with his left hand and foot on the inner surface of the pillar, his right clamped around the corner, to the outer. The problem now was to swing the left hand and foot outward and past that edge, without dislodging the right while doing it.

The warrior knew better than to look down. Fleetingly he remembered his hazardous dash across the girder on the construction site in Venice. He was higher up now—perhaps not much higher, but the drop seemed greater. And just as fatal. He had no wish to cast his eyes over a perspective of wet stone plummeting to the road and the stream far be-low. But he did have to look up.

The pillar, rising from the bank, wasn't as high as the two supporting the central arch, but there was still more than thirty feet of smooth, damp stonework to traverse before he made the parapet. His glance raked the whole wide expanse of the bridge, the low clouds scudding across the sky above. As they streamed out of sight behind the parapet, it appeared that the clouds were stationary and the bridge moved...leaning over toward him, forcing him back, back.

Suddenly the niche supporting his left toe crumbled away. His foot shot into space. He plunged downward.

The shock of the fall tore his left hand away from its hold and his right foot from around the corner. For a breathtaking moment his body dropped to the full extent of his right arm and he hung giddily over the void supported only by the four fingers of that hand. The air was torn from his lungs in a frantic gasp. From below—seconds later, it seemed—he heard the patter of rubble on the road.

He fought for purchase, pressing himself as close to the wet stone as he could to minimize the strain on those fingers. At last his foot found a ledge, the ledge held firm, and then his fingers groped for and found a crack level and solid enough to hold him.

Beads of sweat mingled with the rain streaming down his face, but for the moment the panic was over. With laboring breath he resumed the climb.

The next crisis came when he was no more than ten feet from the top. Perhaps it was because he remembered his near-fall when he'd left the girder, perhaps because he recalled the French and Italian belief that disasters always come in threes—but suddenly he could go no farther. The rain increased in fury, half blinding him; the rising wind plucked at his sodden pants; his muscles finally refused to drag his weight against the pull of gravity anymore.

Spreadeagled between heaven and earth, the Executioner pressed his face to the cold stone. His breath gasped hoarsely in the extremity of his exhaustion. There were points beyond which even his iron will was unable to drive him. He was, after all, no superman—just a highly trained specialist in excellent shape. But even for such individuals there are limits. And for Bolan the limit had been reached: if he was to continue he would have to use the pitons and risk the attention the noise of the hammering would draw.

Warily, leaning as hard as he could against the slight incline of the pillar, he withdrew one from his pocket, shoved it into a crevice where his fingers could also retain a hold and freed his other hand to hammer it in. Raising his right foot, he stepped up and rested his weight on the steel peg. He was about to hammer in the next one when he heard from somewhere above a rhythmic squeaking he couldn't at first identify. Turning his head slowly to the right, he squinted along the line of the viaduct toward the top of the bank and the abandoned railbed leading down to it.

From this height, for the first time, he could see Baracco and Mariella. They were crouched by a winch in the middle of the trail, paying out a hawser hooked to an ancient Wartburg truck. And the truck was rolling slowly down the grade toward the viaduct. The squeaking was coming from one of its wheels.

Bolan's mind raced. They hadn't heard him hammer in the first piton; they would surely hear the second, especially since he was now high enough to be visible. But the higher he rose, the tougher target he would present. He was exposed, but from the winch it would be an extremely fine-

angled shot, and the stone parapet would obscure the sightline.

If the gunners moved out wide, of course, they wouldn't
be able to miss. But this was something they couldn't do:
they had to remain operating the winch until the truck
gained the unsafe central portion of the bridge. If they left
the rope and let it run free, the truck might simply come to
rest against the parapet ... or even go over the edge before
it reached the weakened section. And this would at once
provoke a suspicion that the man at the wheel hadn't been
in control of his senses at the moment of the accident.

The chosen scenario, on the other hand, was based on the
assumption that the victim was driving normally when the
viaduct collapsed beneath him. A wrecked truck beneath a
structure that was still intact didn't fit the picture at all.

For Bolan the equation was simple: until he made the old
track and was in a direct line of fire, the higher he climbed
and the quicker he was, the safer he would be.

Relatively.

The sounds of hammering registered over the thrashing of
wind and rain as Bolan stepped onto the second piton. He
heard a shout from the winch, followed by the bark of a
heavy-caliber pistol. But he paid no attention. The squeaking was perilously close. The ancient truck was rolling slowly
out over the first arch. He found a crevice and started on the
third piton.

Another shot cracked out. And another. Something that
sounded like a large insect hummed through the air behind
Bolan's head. Seconds later a shower of sandstone chips
lashed his forehead as a slug flattened itself against a block
near his right hand. Instinctively he shrank back, and the
hammer slipped from his grasp and fell.

Bolan swore. Was the peg wedged in firmly enough to take his weight? He wrenched the four-pound AutoMag from its holster and tapped the piton with the butt. Two more near misses sent fragments of weathered stone flying from the parapet above him. He reversed the gun and blasted two thunderous shots toward the winch. Baracco and the woman ducked behind the winch.

And it was then that the warrior's luck held good. The remaining few feet of stonework were so degraded that there was no need to use the last peg. He swarmed up the fissured wall until at last his lacerated fingers grasped the parapet itself. He heaved himself up painfully for the last time to subside facedown on the old railbed beyond the lip.

The truck, between the second and third arches, was just drawing level with him. Through the grimed window of the cab, he could see the lolling head of Hal Brognola drooped over the wheel. Bolan levered himself to his feet, knees trembling. He launched himself toward the door of the cab, prepared to wrench it open and dive for the hand brake.

At that instant the guns by the winch opened fire again. Bolan was hit in midleap and flung to the ground. The Wartburg rolled on over the third arch.

Then two things happened. In the cab, Brognola jerked abruptly upright and blinked his eyes. In back of the truck, a heap of old sacks was thrust aside and Gudrun appeared. She vaulted over the tailgate and dashed for the cab before the astonished pair by the winch recovered enough to fire at her.

Snatching open the door, she jumped on the running board, leaned in over the awakened Brognola and hauled frantically on the hand brake between the seats. Shuddering, the Wartburg ground to a halt with its front wheels only inches from the section over the central arch. The gravel ballast that had once supported the track was long gone, but on the muddy, weed-grown surface of the viaduct a network of small cracks now appeared, raying outward like the filaments of a spiderweb.

"Quick!" Gudrun shouted. "For your life's sake, man, drop out the far side and lie underneath. *Move!*"

Brognola was tougher than he looked. He had suffered a lot of pain, but he wasn't physically damaged, which explained why the drug effects were wearing off quicker than Baracco had anticipated. And although the clouds veiling his mind hadn't entirely dispersed, he was alert enough to react to the note of command in Gudrun's voice. He shot into action by reflex.

As she dropped back to the road on her side of the truck, the big Fed threw open the other door and fell out onto the ground. Together they crawled beneath the front wheels, where the angle of the grade protected them from bullets whistling their way from behind the winch.

"What the hell's going on?" Brognola demanded, the aftereffects of the narcotic still blurring his words. "Where am I? Who are you? What are we doing here?"

In three crisp sentences Gudrun told him. "But it's your friend I'm concerned about," she finished. "He was hit just before I pushed you out of the cab. Right now he's lying between the offside rear wheel and a kind of platform built out from this viaduct like the flying bridge of a ship."

"Mack? Where? I'll go get him." The urgency of his old friend's predicament galvanized Brognola. He wormed his way to the rear of the truck, scuttled swiftly out to grab the Executioner's ankles, then dragged him back into shelter as a fusillade of bullets clanged into the ancient vehicle above their heads.

"Is he hurt bad?" Gudrun asked anxiously.

It was Bolan himself who replied. "I'm all right. I was knocked over by the impact because I was in midair when I was hit. But it's not even a flesh wound. Just a crease on top of the shoulder. It's hardly bleeding. But I thought I ought to play possum in case they decided to have a second try." He looked up from under the rear axle, wincing as he took his weight on his elbows. "If only I'd been able to make that climb with the Heckler & Koch on my back," he said, aiming the AutoMag at the killers farther up the slope. Gudrun chugged out a burst from the Beretta.

"You take who you want," she muttered. "I'm gunning for that Czech bitch!" The two guns fired simultaneously. Mariella and the Corsican ducked hastily out of sight behind an old Steyr sedan that was facing back up the grade a few yards behind the winch.

"If we could keep them pinned down there while Hal restarts the engine and backs off the bridge..." Bolan began. He stopped talking and looked upward. Rain was falling on his head.

Baracco had loosed off a volley from behind the sedan and a stray bullet, penetrating the wooden back of the Wartburg's cab, had smashed into the hand brake, knocking it off its ratchet and allowing the truck to resume its interrupted descent. Slowly, inexorably, their cover withdrew, leaving the three of them exposed on the rain-swept viaduct. The truck rolled onto the cracked center section, continued across it...and then suddenly disappeared.

As soon as it received the full weight of the Wartburg, the arch disintegrated. The entire center, along with the truck, dropped from sight, plummeting downward with a roar like that of the trains the viaduct had once carried on their way. From below, the shattering reverberation of the impact was followed by a cannonade of sandstone blocks and small stones from the raw edge of the chasm. A cloud of choking yellow dust mushroomed up over the gap and blanketed them from sight.

Through the swirling fog they heard Baracco shouting, "No, no! Don't shoot now! We'll get them alive and drop them over onto the wreckage."

"All right, Bart," Mariella called. "But how do we—"

"It's perfect," the Corsican interrupted. "It works in fine with my original plan. Two extra bodies will make the ambush of the riot truck more believable. They'll think Bolan—or Cernic—was on his way back to Austria with the driver!"

His voice sank to a murmur, and they could distinguish no more words. When the dust had cleared enough for them to make out the winch they could see him standing by the blonde and pointing up the hill toward his property. Mariella nodded. She climbed into the sedan and Baracco started to run back up the grade.

Bolan was frowning. "There's a helicopter up at his place," Brognola told him. "They'll be able to take us from two sides at once."

"Especially if we stay blocked here," the Executioner said tightly. "And look."

He pointed at the Steyr. Crouched in the driver's seat, Mariella was reversing the vehicle cautiously toward the bridge. She steered around the winch, following the long snake of the hawser that had snapped when the Wartburg had fallen. The rear wheels of the Steyr ran out over the first archway.

Bolan hesitated. He was conventional enough to hate killing a woman—even if she intended to kill him. Gudrun had no such scruples; she emptied the Beretta's magazine. The sedan's rear window starred. Bolan compromised and fired low. A tire rolled off a wheel rim and gasoline sprayed from the drilled tank below the spare, but the old sedan continued to advance.

When the vehicle was over the second arch, less than twelve yards away, Mariella stopped and ducked out of sight behind the padded bench seat. Clearly her orders were to block them there, as Bolan had thought, until Baracco arrived with the chopper.

The rain redoubled in force. Beneath them, they sensed the viaduct tremble in a surge of wind. Then, with no warning, it happened again. Safe enough while the structure was whole, rigid and anchored at each end, the second arch had lost its stability once the viaduct was breached.

Beneath the car the old railbed appeared to warp. They watched, horrified, as the parapet on one side dipped sickeningly, canting the surface at a crazy angle. The heavy sedan started sliding toward the edge as huge cracks zigzagged across the width of the bridge. They could see Mariella frantically fighting to reach the door on the upper side and open it.

Then, as thunderous as an artillery barrage, road, parapet, refuge, car and guardrails slumped into nothingness, vanishing in a cloud of dust as dense as the first.

In the distance they heard the whine of a turbojet and then the clatter of rotors. In a few minutes Baracco would be back gunning for them in the helicopter. And though the Corsican's confederate had vanished, they were in a worse position than ever... vulnerable as ducks in a fairground shooting galley, marooned on a single isolated pillar of the ruined viaduct.

25

Gudrun's hair was plastered across her cheek. When the dust had cleared somewhat, she asked with a quaver in her voice, "Is there any... I mean, after all you climbed up... would there be any chance of us climbing down?"

It was Brognola who peered over the edge into the dizzying depths of the valley. The single pile on which they were marooned, now that it lacked anchorage at both ends, was swaying like a reed in the wind. Every few seconds they could hear another shower of stones break loose and plunge down to add to the two rockfalls strewn across the road, the stream and the floor of the defile.

He shook his head. "One man climbing up a rigid viaduct was crazy enough. But for three of us climbing down with the pillar rocking like this... We might just as well jump over."

"When Bart comes back, do you think he...?"

This time it was the Executioner who answered her. "Once he sees his lady friend's gone—and with her his Mafia link—there'll be no point in his carrying on this plan to take us alive. Like you said, Gudrun, this man's at his most dangerous when he's mad. And he'll be mad as hell now. Remember, too, that he doesn't like to leave witnesses."

Brognola was about to speak again when Bolan held up his hand. The rotor whine coming from the direction of

Baracco's place changed in pitch. Seconds later the chopper skimmed the trees farther up the valley and soared over to circle the pillar.

They saw the stocky, powerful shape of Baracco slide back the Plexiglas hatch. He leveled the mini-Uzi machine pistol with one hand as he coaxed the chopper nearer and lower with the other.

Bolan pushed Gudrun and the Fed to the ground and flung himself across them as the rasping stutter of the gun drowned the noise of the rotors. Fragments of rock spurted up from the road and drew blood from the big man's cheek as the line of 9 mm death ripped past perilously close to his head.

The helicopter turned and prepared for another run. But this time Mack Bolan was ready. Suddenly he, too, was angry—angry at the continuous runaround all over Europe, angry at the waste of time and energy on what should have been a simple mission, angry at his own failure to wrap it up in Venice. He stood upright on the wrecked pillar, seventy-five inches of rugged determination fueled by an ice-cold fighter's brain, a dark angel of death with nothing but a nearly foot-long stainless-steel avenger between him and oblivion.

Sighting the tall shape half veiled by the driving rain, Baracco's lips drew back from his teeth in a snarl. At last he was going to even the score with the meddlesome bastard who had gotten far too close to him these past few days. And his uncooperative U.S. government friend. And the little bitch who must have given away the secret of his base. The pillar was less than one hundred yards away. Baracco squeezed death from the magazine.

The "effective" range of the mini-Uzi was said to be 150 yards. In fact, like all quick-fire autoloaders, the gun's rate

of climb was such that its "accurate" range was closer to
fifty yards. And at that distance the .44 AutoMag, whose
240-grain boattails were capable of drilling through the solid
metal of an automobile engine, was at least as lethal.

As Baracco hosed death from the chopper's doorway,
holes in the Plexiglas surrounded his head. Bolan fell, the
soft tissue of his left calf cored by one of the Uzi's bullets.
But by this time the helicopter was too far beyond the pillar
for the Corsican's gun to vector in on the fallen warrior. He
lifted the chopper over the lip of the valley, spun it around
and swooped back toward the pillar.

Brognola had taken the reloaded Beretta from Gudrun
and was firing at the forward rotor. Bolan lay on his back
on the muddy track, his knees drawn up, sighting between
them along Big Thunder's barrel, the skullbusting cannon
held two-fisted at the full stretch of his arms.

Baracco's features twisted into an evil grin. For a moment he let go of the chopper's controls, bringing both
hands up to steady the stubby machine pistol, the target,
forty yards distant, dead center in the sights.

A shadow crossed the Plexiglas. Incredibly a second helicopter, smaller than the Corsican's, dropped down through
the low cloud front. For a fraction of a second, his finger
tensed to blow the Executioner away, Baracco's concentration wavered and he glanced upward in astonishment.

In that timeless instant Big Thunder bellowed. Once,
twice, three times Bolan caressed the curved lever that
blasted a terminal sentence the Corsican's way. The heavy
slugs pierced his forehead and right hand and smashed
through his chest.

The Uzi emptied its magazine. Hurled backward by the
impacts, Baracco sprawled across the helicopter's controls,
leaving a relief map of blood and brain tissue spattered over

the Plexiglas roof. The chopper sideslipped, lurched momentarily upward and then flew straight into the viaduct on the far side of the gap where the central arch had been.

A burst of fire, so bright that it flickered scarlet on the underside of the clouds, erupted at the point of contact. The undamaged half of the viaduct exploded outward and then fell to the valley floor to form a blazing funeral pyre with the fiery wreckage of the helicopter.

Gudrun screamed. She was on her knees in the mud, drenched hair clinging to her skull, her wet cheeks streaked with mascara. "I'm...I'm sorry," she sobbed. "I know he tried to kill us, but he was...he used to be... I was very fond of him once."

"It'll pass," Brognola soothed, putting an arm around her shaking shoulders. "It'll pass. It's over and done with. You have to think of the future now." He gestured skyward.

The second helicopter was hovering twenty feet above the ruined pillar. A rope ladder dangled from the open hatch to the weathered parapet. A familiar voice hollered over a bullhorn that couldn't disguise the fruity accents of county Cork.

"Goin' up now, ladies and gentlemen! Goin' up! Networks, settlement of accounts, information. Top floor rescue service. Goin' up now, please!"

"Tufik! What the hell are *you* doing here?"

He had to wait for an answer. Each increasing gust of wind was making the pillar shudder. Hassan, the mustached, sideburned bodyguard who was piloting the chopper, had only just closed the transparent hatch after Bolan had been assisted up the ladder when another fountain of dust rose hundreds of feet into the air and the solitary column from which they had been rescued shivered into fragments on the valley floor.

"But how did you know what was going on?" Bolan asked again as Gudrun applied an emergency dressing to his wounded calf.

She looked up and smiled. "I'm afraid that was me," she admitted. "You had lent me the transceiver, remember? I know a little about them. Bart used to..." Her voice faltered, then she continued. "He taught me how to use them. I switched the frequency, called up a friend and asked her to pass on a message. I thought I ought to call up my employer and explain why I was late for work!"

Bulging over his wheelchair, Tufik allowed himself a fat chuckle. "A fine enterprisin' spirit, Mr. Bolan, don't you agree? As positive an approach as your own, I'd say...or the one I'm employin' here meself at-all. But seein' as how it's well short of four o'clock, you can at least profit from the cheap-rate daytime tariff, you."

"Daytime tariff?" the Executioner echoed. "Cheap rate?"

"To be sure, to be sure. For the Vandervell Emergency Escape Service. I'm after startin' a network, you know, a European network to be used for gettin' the boys out of scrapes an' all. Do you not think that's a grand idea?"

"Tufik, you're too much."

"Considerin' the distance involved, the rates are very reasonable."

"Send me the bill."

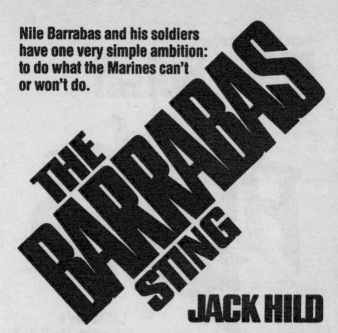

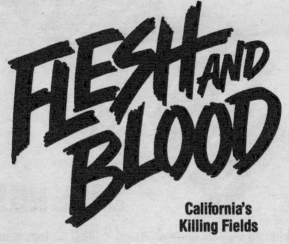

Take
4 explosive books
plus a
mystery bonus
FREE

TAKE 'EM NOW

FOLDING SUNGLASSES
FROM GOLD EAGLE

Mean up your act with these tough, street-smart shades. Practical, too, because they fold 3 times into a handy, zip-up polyurethane pouch that fits neatly into your pocket. Rugged metal frame. Scratch-resistant acrylic lenses. Best of all, they can be yours for only $6.99.

MAIL YOUR ORDER TODAY.

Send your name, address, and zip code, along with a check or money order for just $6.99 + .75¢ for postage and handling (for a total of $7.74) payable to Gold Eagle Reader Service. (New York and Iowa residents please add applicable sales tax.)

Remove from pouch...

unfold once...

unfold twice...

and they're ready to wear.

GOLD EAGLE

Gold Eagle Reader Service
901 Fuhrmann Blvd.
P.O. Box 1396
Buffalo, N.Y. 14240-1396

GES-1A

Offer not available in Canada.